Power and confide

He had a hard edge, ~~and cut~~ with knifelike precision through every bad element that ever rode a New York subway. Yet he had the face of a gentle warrior. Sienna's breath caught. She felt a stir of sexual chemistry.

He was as lonely and grief-stricken as she was. Her heart twisted. Who had hurt this man? She wanted to go to him, comfort him and ease his sorrow. Sienna smiled.

A crooked, charming smile touched his full mouth. Twin dimples appeared on those taut cheeks, making him appear younger and boyish. She felt all her own pain slowly evaporate. Gods, he was handsome. An odd connection flared between them. Sienna locked her gaze to his, desperately needing someone who understood.

Then her nostrils flared as she caught his scent. Hatred boiled to the surface. Not a man. Draicon.

The enemy.

BONNIE VANAK

fell in love with romance novels during childhood. After years of newspaper reporting, Bonnie became a writer for a major international charity, which has taken her to destitute countries to write about issues affecting the poor. When the emotional strain of her job demanded a diversion, she turned to writing romance novels. Bonnie lives in Florida with her husband and two dogs, and happily writes books amid an ever-growing population of dust bunnies. She loves to hear from readers. Visit her website, www.bonnievanak.com, or email her at bonnievanak@aol.com.

THE COVERT WOLF

BONNIE VANAK

HARLEQUIN®

entertain, enrich, inspire™

Recycling programs
for this product may
not exist in your area.

ISBN-13: 978-0-373-88551-0

THE COVERT WOLF

Dear Reader,

In 1943, my uncle Ed was drafted to fight in World War II. Once, while his unit remained safely outside, Ed sat inside a burned-out building, working on a bomb that he held between his legs. He was just a kid, praying the entire time that he wouldn't blow himself up.

The courage of Edmond Fischer, and many other servicemen and women, inspired me to write *The Covert Wolf*—the first in a new series about a top-secret group of U.S. Navy SEALS who are also paranormals.

Matthew Parker is a Draicon werewolf and a navy SEAL who is tormented by the death of his best friend in Afghanistan by pyrokinetic demons. Matt is determined to find a magick orb the demons want to use to destroy the world. He teams up with Sienna McClare, one of the few who can identify the missing Orb. Working together, Matt and Sienna discover the inner strength to accept their true natures, and the quiet courage it takes to do the right thing—no matter how scared you are.

Happy reading!

Bonnie Vanak

In memory of my father-in-law, Frank Senior.
We love you, and miss you.

Prologue

Afghanistan, Helmand province

The clay desert was hard-packed, mirror-flat and easy to scan. But the foothills, ah, the damn rugged outcroppings of rock and earth that began the river valley, that's where they would hide.

Where I would hide, if I were targeting a kill, thought Lieutenant Matthew "Dakota" Parker as he scanned the dangerous terrain.

With its engine still running, their Hummer was parked on the isolated roadway as Matt and his partner checked out a suspicious trace of spectral magick he had glimpsed on a small berm. As a Draicon, his senses were sharper in wolf form, but damn, it was hard to drive, as Adam joked, when your paws didn't touch the pedals. They didn't train you for that in BUD/S, the intense twenty-six-week program that weeded out those not tough enough to become a U.S. Navy SEAL.

But a shape-shifting rat could see that spark of trace magick. It glowed black.

Demon-black, empty and soulless.

Or as his teammate Ryder Thompson always said, "Empty as the bottom of my damn wallet after leave."

Matt smiled as he thought of Ryder, aka "Renegade," a fellow Draicon wolf whose specialty was languages. Like Matt and Adam, Ryder was a member of SEAL Team 21's elite Phoenix Force. Eight men, all great guys. All SEALs, part of Naval Special Warfare. Like Delta Force, they were so secret the Department of Defense never admitted they existed.

Except their human counterparts had no idea what they truly were....

The Phoenix Force was a special counterterrorist ghost squad, but the terrorists they fought had fangs and claws. Every member was a paranorm. Only a few high-ranking officials knew their special abilities, including Keegan Byrne, a four-star admiral who was a Primary Mage. Byrne could wipe a person's memory clean with the snap of his lean fingers.

Standing on the berm, Matt kept his Heckler & Koch MP-5 submachine gun trained on the jagged outcropping of rock, his gaze and his senses sharpened as he watched Adam. Chief Petty Officer Adam "Wildcat" Barstow was his best friend and swim buddy. The black jaguar's sharp claws dug into the pebbled sand as he pressed his nose close to the ground.

Adam turned, shifted back into human form and used magick to clothe himself. The SEAL was dressed like Matt— lightweight desert battle dress uniform, boots, gloves and vest weighted with survival gear, plus seven magazines and hand grenades. A cammie helmet covered his ash-brown hair. Adam frowned as he flexed his fingers.

"Damn sand. Gets in my paws. All clear."

Matt scanned the sand, bothered by a niggling instinct. He knew what he'd seen. "Spectral traces of demon magick don't just vanish. Not even with this wind."

"There's nothing out here, Dakota. No lions, tigers or bears. We'd have seen them," Wildcat pointed out.

They were returning to camp after searching for a local warlord rumored to be hiding in the hills. The warlord had a fondness for roadside bombs targeting NATO troops. The marines accompanying them had already searched this area. Matt and Adam were a half mile behind the marines when Matt had spotted the black trace of dark magick.

He didn't like it. Something reeked about this op. And the commanding officer back at base had specifically requested their presence.

No paranorms out here, not even a desert jinn. The desert was empty of magick. Yet the niggling suspicion wouldn't quit. Matt rubbed the back of his sweating neck. He didn't like how vulnerable and exposed the gun turret made Adam.

"Let me take the gun. You've been on top long enough," he urged.

A distant look came into Adam's eyes. For a moment, he saw an odd flash of grief. Then the jaguar gave the ghost of a smile. "Not a chance, Dakota. You always wanna be on top."

"Gets me no complaints from the ladies," he cracked.

The wind blew over the rocky sand, stirring the dust. His unease grew. Anything could be hiding in those hills. Insurgents, suicide bombers.

Or worse.

Gooseflesh erupted on his bare forearms. Matt glanced at Adam, newly mated to a beautiful black-haired jaguar shifter. They were trying to have a baby, he remembered.

"Spooky out here. Wildcat, you drive," Matt urged.

Adam shot him an amused look. "You need the big gun to hide behind, Dakota? Why? You scared? Wuss."

He laughed, glad to see the melancholy gone from his friend's face. They climbed back into the Hummer. Adam stood in the gun turret, his upper body outside as he manned the .50-caliber machine gun, continuing his sweep of the sands. Matt disliked the armored-up Hummer. It added too much weight and the damn thing had a rep for the doors jamming during an attack, trapping whoever was inside.

They drove onward.

"Hold on. Traffic ahead." Matt's instincts sharpened as he spotted a man standing by a hill beside the road, waving to them. "Check him out."

"Huh. Not a hell-raiser," Adam said, using the squad's code word for enemy paranorms. "And doesn't carry the stench of Taliban. Just a human friendly."

The gray-bearded, elderly man pointed to his leg. Blood stained his tattered trousers. He was wounded. Needed medical assistance. His expression looked strained. Terrified.

"Help me," he mouthed.

Matt stopped the Hummer. "I'm getting out. Can't catch his scent."

"Stay there." Adam's voice was sharp with concern. "I got this."

The elderly man opened his jacket, showing rows and rows of dynamite. With a look of stark terror, he thumbed a switch.

"Get down!" Matt yelled to Wildcat.

The bomb exploded laterally, but the heavy armored vehicle held. Matt swore as he jimmied the door.

Jammed.

"Yo, Dakota. I'm a little stuck here."

From the force of the blast, metal compressed against Adam as he stood in the turret. His legs were pinned.

"Hold on."

Matt tried pulling him down, but Wildcat was too tightly wedged. Using his werewolf strength, he managed to pry back a piece of damaged frame from Adam's legs but, as he did, suspicion raced through him. No ordinary blast could cause such precise damage. It had to be…

He looked out the window, saw a pulse of black spectral magick. "Whiskey, Tango, Foxtrot," he yelled.

Ten insurgents carrying AK-47s appeared on the sand. Only these had pointed ears and pale skin, instead of leathery, tanned skin. Darksider Fae. They began spraying the vehicle with small-arms fire.

They'd been set up.

Adam fired back, the machine gun rattling like thunder. The enemy dropped dead, then their bodies began to smoke. The Fae vanished in an explosion of dust.

Darksider Fae were hard to detect because they could impersonate anything, such as a certain arrogant C.O. back at base. They were rogue Fae, their leash held by a bigger master. But who? Matt whipped his head back and forth, searching the sands. The human grandfather was bait, forced to kill himself.

Adam's voice crackled over his headpiece. "Damn it, Dakota, I've been hit."

"How bad?" His heart raced as he forced himself to calm.

"A little bit. Bleeding like an SOB."

Jaguars didn't heal as quickly as Draicon werewolves. Matt cranked around, saw blood dampening Adam's pants leg.

"Have to shift, only way out."

Magick shimmered in the air as Adam shifted, and the energy from the change peeled back the metal, freeing him. The large, black jaguar leaped off the Hummer and landed on the sand.

"I'm coming, buddy," Matt signaled, and grabbed his Medipack.

His skin crawled as he saw the blood matting the jaguar's

midsection. Matt couldn't think, couldn't breathe. Gutshot. Fatal wound.

His training kicked in. The camp was only an hour's drive away, but he had to save him by keeping the bleeding under control until Wildcat received medical attention.

The jaguar turned its head and, for a moment, sorrow filled its gaze.

Something hot and evil stirred the air.

Matt jimmied the door again. He tried shotgun side, but it was also stuck. The wind stirred the pebbled sand, spiraling it into miniature sandstorms. His heart leaped into his throat as the sandstorm blew closer. The big cat charged the sandstorm.

Damn it! The storm dissipated into four distinct, gray shapes.

Pyrokinetic demons.

Panic squeezed his throat. With a sickening twist of his stomach, Matt saw the pyros assume form. Two went for the jaguar. Two more spun toward the Hummer, flames pouring from their gray talons, from their opened mouths.

Wildcat was wounded and fur gave little protection against fire.

He grabbed the fire extinguisher from the back, kicked the passenger door with every ounce of werewolf strength. It swung open. He had just scrambled out the other side when he heard Adam's scream.

Matt hit the sand, rounding the Hummer. With a deafening yell, he hit the extinguisher's switch. The device emptied, spraying a demon, who squealed and died.

He lifted his H&K MP-5, firing away to shoot the other bastards when the flames hit his legs. The flame-retardant material began to slowly peel away beneath the five-hundred-degree heat. Matt ducked back, gasping. Felt like someone flicked a lighter inside his bones. The pain was acid-hot, but he had to get to Adam. His buddy was hurt.

Snarling, he pushed on, firing his weapon. The demons were retreating, falling back over the slope, their powers sapped. One turned and aimed a blast of dying flame straight at Matt's chest. He screamed in agony, but kept firing until the demons faded into the wind.

Matt struggled to stay conscious as an excruciating pain fogged his mind. He had to save his buddy.

It was the last thing on his mind as he fell to the uncaring earth.

Chapter 1

Lieutenant Matthew Parker wanted to ram his fist into a wall when he thought about how demons, aided by Fae, had killed his best friend, Adam "Wildcat" Barstow. Instead, he rubbed the heel of his hand against the subway's plastic seat.

Never had he felt so alone, trapped in this conveyance filled with humans who would never know about Wildcat. Never pay respect to Adam for serving his country with devotion.

There'd be no military parade, no funeral with a flag-draped coffin. No newscasters with solemn faces talking of Adam's courage and skill. There wasn't even a body to bring home. Adam had been burned to ashes, his remains scattered. Matt wanted to scream at the passengers, shouting Adam's name until his throat went hoarse. No one would mourn Wildcat other than his grieving family, who thought he had died in a car crash. All memories of Adam's existence had been purged from any human or paranormal who knew him.

Matt felt his neck muscles grow tight as a blizzard of smells and sounds assaulted his senses. He tried shutting them out as he'd been taught in training, but he was drained, his defenses lowered. The creaking of the subway car as it sped on the metal tracks toward Times Square, away from Brooklyn and Adam's weeping mate, grated on his ears like spikes. Desperate for a connection, he looked around for someone to pay attention to him. Just one paranorm like himself, who would acknowledge his existence.

He rode a subway filled with human robots. No one looked up, even gave him a curious glance. He was invisible.

Someone, just look at me. I feel so alone. Doesn't anyone care?

And then a sweet fragrance caught his attention. A scent of meadows and mountains, cool, crisp air and forest. It refreshed his weary spirit. Matt's nostrils flared. A very female fragrance. Draicon werewolf, just like him.

His pulse pounded with awareness and a sudden sharp bolt of desire. Then he caught a tendril of fear threaded through her scent. Protective instincts sharpened with knifelike awareness.

She was scared. Who was she?

He scanned the crowded train.

Two seats away on the opposite side, a woman sat with her head bent. Long, straight brown hair, parted down the middle, spilled past her shoulders and curtained her face. She wore the uniform of corporate America—black woolen pencil skirt with matching jacket, white, starched blouse and sleek, expensive black high heels and leather briefcase.

She slipped off the heel of one shoe and absently let it rock back and forth against her heel. She was scared, but hiding it well.

He admired the curve of her calf, the arch of her foot. Matt unclenched his fists.

Look at me.

A subtle but strong command. Matt pushed a little more, using his powers of mind control. *Look at me. Please.*

The woman glanced up. Sexual awareness shot through him like a bullet. Her nose was small, her mouth wide but soft and sweet-looking. In her eyes he saw a reflection of his own haunting misery, so deep it shattered him. Tears filled her mossy green eyes.

Who had hurt her?

Nothing pushed his buttons faster than seeing a vulnerable Draicon female, alone, without pack to protect her. He wanted to comfort her, and beat the living crap out of whoever made her cry. His teammates teased him about his shining-knight complex. "Because it always gets you laid," Wildcat had insisted.

Once after a mission overseas where Matt had rescued a pretty kidnapping victim, Wildcat brought a white horse onto the base, along with an empty suit of armor. "Your new uniform," he'd teased.

Thinking about Adam, his throat tightened again. *I miss you, buddy.*

Matt concentrated on the woman. With her creamy skin, delicate features, combined with a strong, stubborn chin, she looked slightly exotic and fey. He could nearly taste the sweetness of her mouth, with its full and lush lower lip. He felt another stir of sharp chemistry, a pure male response to a lovely female.

But striking as she was, it was the grief that called to him.

He longed to wipe away her tears with the edge of a thumb, coax a smile to that down-turned mouth. Matt focused all his efforts.

Please, he thought desperately. *Look at me.*

* * *

Sienna McClare was Fae, accustomed to open air and field. Not this boxy subway car.

The oily smell of fear clogged her nostrils, leached from her pores. The train with its human cargo felt like a coffin. The scent of humans mingled with something darker and more sinister. She was trapped. No way out of this speeding deathtrap. Panic surged, bright and sharp.

Breathe. Just breathe.

She inhaled deeply and thought of deep green forests and quiet glades. Tall pines waving in the wind, the chatter of birds and scolding of squirrels, a deer cropping grass. A wolf watching a deer, waiting. Prey. Images of fangs flashing, tearing, wet sounds...

No!

She fought the panic freezing her blood. Draicon werewolves were vicious killers. Merciless as her father—the man who'd raped her Fae mother and then killed her when his pack attacked her mother's Fae colony after his pack returned for Sienna.

Air blew through the vents, but it wasn't enough to banish the smell of humans. They belonged to someone. She did not. Not in this city with its neon lights and busy streets.

Or anywhere.

Sienna hated glamouring herself as a Draicon werewolf, but it was necessary if she were to find the Orb of Light. Someone had stolen the Orb from her colony, the Los Lobos Fae. A Draicon who'd been seen in the area previously was suspected. Sienna had eagerly seized the chance to help when Chloe, leader of the Fae colony, had approached her and promised that once she found the Orb and returned it to them, she'd receive a hero's welcome back into her colony. No longer would she be an Outcast. The Fae would not pretend she was invisible. They'd cast her out when she was older and able to survive on her own, because she was a hybrid. The bastard child of a sweet-faced Fae and a Draicon killer. Her mother's people had raised her with love and affection, making her feel accepted, and then, eight months ago when she turned twenty-one and was considered an adult, they'd kicked her out.

If she found the Orb, Sienna could return to the only home she'd known. *I just want things to go back to the way they were.*

In two hours, she'd meet with a U.S. Navy SEAL assigned to help her find the Orb. Chloe had been vague about details. Sienna didn't care if it meant working with the devil himself. She'd do it.

Sensing someone staring, she glanced up and focused on a man across the aisle. He was heavily muscled, wore a black leather jacket, black jeans and boots. Dark, wavy hair wreathed a solemn, handsome face with brutal cheekbones, a square chin. Eyes as blue as the ocean studied her.

Power and confidence radiated from him. He had a hard edge, as if he could cut with knifelike precision through every bad element that ever rode a N.Y. subway. Yet he had the face of a gentle warrior. Sienna's breath caught. She felt a stir of sexual chemistry.

He was as lonely and grief-stricken as she was. Her heart twisted. Who had hurt this man? She wanted to go to him, comfort him and ease his sorrow. Sienna smiled.

A crooked, charming smile touched his full mouth. Twin dimples appeared on those taut cheeks, making him appear younger and boyish. She felt all her own pain slowly evaporate. Gods, he was handsome.

An odd connection flared between them. Sienna locked her gaze to his, desperately needing someone who understood.

Then her nostrils flared as she caught his scent. Hatred boiled to the surface. Not a man. Draicon.

The enemy.

* * *

Matt willed the woman across the aisle to connect with him. He assumed a nonthreatening posture, his arms open, palms spread.

Come on, sweetheart. Smile at me. You're not alone. We're the only Draicon in this steel cage.

Hope surged as a small but vital connection flared between them. He leaned forward, his heart beating fast. Their gazes caught and met. The woman pushed at her mink-brown hair, and gave a small, shy smile.

He let his own smile widen, let her see the pull of sexual awareness between them. Interest flared in her gaze, and she tilted her head.

Then suddenly her smile wobbled. She made a moue of disgust. Slipping her shoe back on, she shook her head.

"Draicon dog."

The word was a low mutter, but his sensitive hearing caught it as if it were shouted. Stunned, he sank back into his seat. She called him one of the most filthy insults among their kind.

Ice slid over his heart, made his spine rigid. Matt felt his smile crack like brittle glass.

Then he gave her a long, cool look and turned away. Ignoring her, as she'd ignored him.

Reeling in his control, he resisted the urge to punch the wall again. Matt folded his arms, stretching the shoulders of his battered leather jacket. He dragged in a deep, calming breath.

And smelled something dark and foul.

His gaze landed on a man in a suit. Italian, expensive. But the wearer had cold, dead eyes. He stared at the Draicon female as if she were steak. Matt inhaled again, catching the scent of shaved metal and putrid sickness. He briefly touched the man's mind and reeled back from the dark images there.

Not good.

The subway stopped at the Canal Street station. The Draicon female gave one last disgusted look at Matt and slipped out of the car.

The human suit followed, his expression hungry.

Matt leaped up as the doors began to close. Werewolf strength easily held them open and he bounded onto the platform.

The woman was in danger. And he couldn't ignore a threatened female, no matter how badly she'd treated him.

Both had vanished into a tunnel leading to another platform, but he caught their scents. Matt tracked them, increasing his pace. Worry stabbed him. The tunnel was well lit, but he'd seen that man's expression, smelled his lust.

The business suit intended to rape her.

Not on my watch.

Wolf snarled to the surface. *Down, boy.* He resisted shifting into his animal side. A wolf stalking through the subways would attract attention. He could handle this as a human. The Sig Sauer holstered at his side was an old friend, but his hands were weapons, as well. He could kick that guy's ass for daring to even think about hurting a woman.

Heels click-clacked ahead of him, the sharp tap of the woman's shoes and the brisk sounds of the suit. Matt hugged the wall, every sense screaming awareness.

There.

Before a short set of stairs, the suit had pinned the woman against the wall. No one else was around. Black briefcase lying on the cement, opened, papers spilled out. The suit flashed a dark smile, his fingers splayed along the female's throat. Light glinted off the polished metal of the knife he held against her throat. A thin trickle of blood dripped onto her pristine white collar.

Matt suppressed a low growl and remained still, gauging

the best move. He didn't want one more drop of blood spilled. Except from that bastard.

Even as he started forward, his footsteps silent, the woman glanced at him. She rolled her eyes. At the very same time, the attacker turned his head.

Matt sprang forward, but the woman punched her would-be molester in his soft stomach, sending him reeling. Cursing, he raced forward.

The suit recovered, his face tomato-red. He came at her, the wicked blade raised.

She snarled and flung out her hands, raising her shoe. Her pointed shoe. The tip landed straight in the man's groin.

Wincing, Matt watched as the suit let out a high-pitched, unholy scream. He cupped his groin, the knife tumbling to the floor with a clatter.

The woman kicked him again. This time the man yowled like a cat. The Draicon female studied him with a look of satisfaction.

Matt squatted down besides the attacker, squeezed a nerve on his shoulder. The suit fell unconscious as the Draicon female retrieved a cell phone from her briefcase. She thumbed in 911 and spat out instructions, then hung up.

Blood dripped from the small wound, staining the white collar of her shirt.

"You can leave now," she told Matt in a rigid voice.

The dismissal was curt and brisk. Matt stared in disbelief.

"I know you're not deaf, because I saw your reaction when I called you a dog. So, are you going to leave? I've got this."

He gritted his teeth. "I was trying to help."

She rolled those lovely eyes again. "Thanks for the help, hero."

"He cut you." His tone was curt, hiding the concern.

She wiped the droplets off her neck. "It's just a flesh wound."

At his hard stare, she shook her head and bent over, show-ing the delectable curve of her bottom as she gathered papers into her briefcase. "Not a *Monty Python* fan. 'Course not. Draicon hotshots like you prefer *Lassie*. Although I doubt you have half the strength of Lassie."

"Stop it."

Glancing up, her eyes widened at his sharp tone. He clenched his fists as she snapped the briefcase shut.

"You can defend yourself. I get it. You don't want help. I don't need an instruction manual. But the Lassie dig—" Matt struggled with his rising temper "—has to go. I don't know who knocked the brick off your pretty little shoulder, sweet-heart, but it wasn't me. So ditch the dog references, got it?"

He heaved in a controlling breath. "I'm not your enemy."

Eyes wide and green as soft moss held his gaze for a mo-ment. The previous misery had returned, making her look vulnerable and young.

"That's what you think," she said softly.

With a sharp turn of her polished heels, she slipped up the stairs and vanished from sight.

Matt rubbed his aching neck. This had been the ultimate bitch of a morning.

Couldn't wait to see what the afternoon would bring. Lieu-tenant Commander Dale "Curt" Curtis, commanding officer of SEAL Team 21, had scheduled a top-secret briefing about the pyrokinetic demons who'd targeted Matt and Adam. His C.O. had told Matt to prepare for a new assignment.

With a new partner.

Even though he dreaded the idea of a new partner, Matt welcomed the chance to kick demon ass. If a new partner meant finding the leak, so be it.

As for the lovely, contemptuous Draicon… An ominous foreboding filled him.

He had a bad feeling he would see her again.

Very soon.

Chapter 2

The upscale hotel in Times Square boasted a grand view of the bustling streets and the colorful theater marquees. Sienna tapped her foot as she waited in the crowded lobby bar. Odd place for a meeting.

She ran a finger down the glass of water, catching a drop of condensation. Sienna brought it to her mouth, slowly licked it off. She sensed someone staring, and turned.

Son of a jackal...

Leather Jacket Draicon focused on her with a laser blue stare. Those eyes tracked every move her finger made, his gaze smoldering, his mouth compressed.

Had he followed her? And why? Her heart pounded hard at the idea. She studied the werewolf.

Heat surged through her, curling the tips of her toes in their not-so-sensible heels. He resembled a fallen angel with a face sculpted by an artisan's chisel and cold blue eyes that could cut steel. Limbs sprawled out before him in a position of utter confidence, he looked dangerous.

He shifted position, the move opening his jacket and revealing a pistol strapped to his side. Sienna felt blood drain from her face.

Armed all this time.

Not a man, or a Draicon, to mess with.

As if he read her mind, he lifted the mug of beer in a mock salute and drank deeply. Fascinated, she watched the muscles in his throat work. He set down the glass, his gaze never leaving her as he backhanded his mouth.

"Woof," he murmured.

Then he stood, dropping a few bills on the table, and left. Crimson flooded her cheeks. *I deserved that.*

"Oh, I love your Jimmy Choos!"

Startled, she turned. A buxom blonde in a print dress stood before her table. At her side was a severe-looking businessman, a hint of silver in his short-cropped dark hair. He carried an expensive leather briefcase and wore a gray suit with a crisp red tie. The blonde was gorgeous. She carried a large designer purse on her arm and was staring at Sienna's footwear.

Rather, her legs.

"Such fabulous shoes," she gushed. "They display your legs nicely. You have great legs."

"Samantha's a connoisseur of fine footwear," the man said. He gave her a small smile. "I apologize for taking up your time."

The woman simpered, and squeezed Sienna's hand. "Have a lovely day, darling!"

As they walked off, Sienna glanced down at her palm. In it was a card key in a white envelope that had instructions printed across it.

Her contacts. In disguise, most likely.

As her heart raced with trepidation, she put the card in her purse. This was worse than she'd been told if they couldn't even meet in the open. Maybe she should back off. It wasn't too late.

And then what? Go home in defeat? Live alone for the rest of her life, wondering what the black hole in her mind hid?

Finding the Orb meant more than acceptance back into her Fae colony. It meant recovering her lost memories. Everything in her early childhood was a panicked blur. Flashes of a forest, quiet waters and the terror of being shoved into a dark hollow, screams of terror raging around her, a hot crimson igniting the night sky... The snarls of a wolf, teeth bared as it tore into throats, blood splashing and flowing like water...then darkness.

A distant memory tugged, too deeply buried to surface. Every time she tried searching for her past, she met with a closed door. Who was she? Which side ruled her?

Fae or Draicon?

Draicon, no way in hell.

Sienna paid her bill, leaving a generous tip. As instructed, she took the elevator down, then lingered in the lobby for ten minutes, made certain no one was following her, then went upstairs.

The room had a connecting door. She opened it and entered a lavish suite.

The woman named Samantha was inside, sweeping the walls with a device that resembled the metal wand employed by airport security staff. She finished and turned with a cheerful grin. "Nothing. Clean. Not even a bedbug."

Mischief danced in her brown eyes. "Need to check you, Miss McClare. A total pat-down. Don't worry, I'm a professional when it comes to frisking women."

She didn't like the idea of this woman checking her over. It made her nervous. "Why the search? And the covert activity?"

"Can't take any chances," Samantha said.

"I can assure you, I'm not hiding anything." Sienna clasped her hands, willed a smile. If this woman searched her, she'd get too nervous. Drop the glamour. The glamour fed her confidence, enabled her to look cool and professional.

Samantha gave her body an admiring glance. "Ah, not quite. There is definitely something about you."

"Any excuse to flirt, huh, Shay?"

That deep, drawling voice, smooth as the burn of whiskey sliding down a parched throat. Sienna's heart went still as Leather Jacket Draicon ambled with lethal grace through the connecting door, joined by the same dark-haired man who'd accompanied Samantha in the lobby bar.

The Draicon halted and stared. Ice glittered in his sharp blue gaze as he closed the door.

"You? Hell on wheels, this has to be a damn joke. Who are you?" he snapped.

The dark-haired man gestured to the Draicon. "Sienna Mc-Clare, meet Lieutenant Matthew Parker, U.S. Navy SEAL. Matt, Sienna's Seelie Sidhe Fae from the Los Lobos colony."

Lieutenant Parker looked stunned. "She's a Draicon."

"I'm not."

"Prove it, sweetheart." His voice was low and dangerous. "Because if you're one, and not the Fae we're expecting, you're in a heap of trouble."

All three looked at her. Sienna forced down her nervousness. She released the glamour to show her natural form. Pale, nearly translucent skin replaced the slightly darker tint. Her eyes became larger and more slanted. She pushed back her hair to display her pointed ears.

"There. Satisfied? I'm Fae, not a Draicon werewolf. Now, can I ask, what's going on and who you are?"

The dark-haired man gave a slight smile. "Lieutenant Commander Dale Curtis, commanding officer of SEAL Team 21.

Sorry for the precautions, Miss McClare. It's necessary for security reasons. Lieutenant Parker will be partnering with you on this mission…."

"I'm sorry. I can't work with this man."

"Sit down, Miss McClare."

The order was said in a soft tone, but steel threaded through the commander's voice. Sienna sat, clenching her hands, refusing to look at the Draicon.

"Let's get one thing straight before we start," Lieutenant Commander Curtis said as he joined her. "This arrangement goes against my guts. I wanted my team alone on this. It's too risky. The Fae are insular. Your aunt didn't even want to meet. We had to work out details in a damn telephone conference. Unfortunately, she had a point. And a weapon I can't do anything about. She can control the weather."

Now a grim smile played on his mouth. "Unless I'd like a permanent hailstorm in Little Creek, we have to work together. You know the Orb, and your ability to glamour is powerful. I agreed to this, but no Fae is going to dictate the SEAL I chose. I don't care if my house gets pelted by hail for the next thirty days. You're with Matt. He's a damned fine tracker. He could find an ice cube in a snowstorm."

Sienna's cheeks burned. She gestured to the blonde, who looked amused at the tension.

"I'd rather work with a woman," she told him. "What about her? I don't need a navy SEAL."

Lieutenant Parker laughed. "Shay?"

Stunned, she watched Samantha's body and face shimmer, and change shape. Full, lush lips became firm, the round cheekbones concave…

Replacing Samantha was a man dressed in black jeans and a cutoff black T-shirt. A shock of sandy-brown hair spilled down to his collar. Boyish mischief danced in his hazel eyes as he took a seat opposite her.

"Chief Petty Officer Sam Shaymore at your service, Miss McClare."

Sienna gave him a warm smile. Finally, someone she could relate to. "You're a Fae."

Lieutenant Parker took a chair, swung it around and straddled it. "Shay's a Phantom. A Mage who can shift into any kind of life-form."

"Just one of my talents." Shaymore opened a palm. A current of electricity sizzled there. He closed his fist, and the energy vanished.

Unease raced through her as she studied Shaymore, leaning back in his chair and folding his heavily muscled arms. Mage. They were much higher on the food chain than Seelie Sidhe. Some were endowed with powers that could cut a Fae in half before she could chant a spell.

She slid her chair out from the table and glanced at Lieutenant Commander Curtis. "Are all of you...paranorms?"

Curtis flicked a hand and she found herself sliding back toward the table, as if an invisible, courtly hand had pushed her chair in. "Primary Mage."

Sweet mercy, a Draicon, and two Mages. Three powerful men who made her magick look puny and small. They studied her like an insect pinned on a board. Sienna resisted the urge to bolt. She lifted her chin and forced herself to calm.

"Primary Mages can do advanced telekinesis, throw energy bolts and shift into animal form. Just to let you know." Contempt etched Lieutenant Parker's face. "Or didn't they teach you that in forest school?"

"Lieutenant Parker, are you going to have a problem working with Miss McClare?" Curtis's tone was even, but held an edge of command.

"No, sir."

Words seemed forced, his jaw taut. Chief Petty Officer

Shaymore looked amused. "I can work with her. Be a real pleasure and I can be friendlier than old sour wolf here."

"Screw you, Shay."

"Up yours, Dakota."

Parker gave a mocking grin. "Go grow a set. Steel ones."

"Nothing wrong with mine. That's what all the ladies say."

They were a team, males who shut her out. Sienna gave them a cool look. "All the ladies?" she asked politely. "Or just the ones you disguise yourself as?"

The men turned and stared. A deep laugh rumbled from Lieutenant Parker's throat.

The rich sound was as enticing as warm chocolate on a cold night. Sienna guarded herself against it. This man was a Draicon wolf.

Parker checked his laugh. "You mind changing back? Those ears are distracting, Mr. Spock."

Sienna fought the urge to glamour into a poodle. What was his problem? She assumed her human form and pointedly ignored him.

"I don't care what history you both share. Whatever it was, it ends now. I need both of you sharp, alert and working together as a team." Curtis leaned forward. "This goes beyond any personal differences. Understood?"

"Yes, sir," Parker said as Sienna nodded. When everyone sat at the table, Curtis began.

"We're meeting here because ST21's compound may be compromised...."

"ST21?" she asked.

"SEAL Team 21," Curtis explained, snapping open his briefcase and pulling out a file. He handed a sheaf of papers to Parker, along with credit cards and a thick wad of cash. "Your cover to find the Orb is a couple traveling the country and looking for antiques. Miss McClare will be posing as your wife."

"Sister," the lieutenant said roughly.

"Fine. I'm placing you on official leave, Matt, to cover your absence. Can't take chances."

Sienna held up a hand. "Can you please explain what's going on?"

Silence hung in the air. No one looked at her. She sensed no one wanted to tell her, or work with her. They were a team and she wasn't one of them.

Just as the Fae had, they were shutting her out.

"I don't like this. We don't need to work with a Fae. I can find the Orb on my own." Parker gave her a pointed look. "I don't trust the Fae. It was a Fae bullet that—"

He cut off his words, staring at the wall.

Oh-kay. Wonderful. She'd made enemies just by flashing her ears. Sienna swept them all with a level look. "Are any of you, or anyone in ST21, an expert in Old Sidhe? Can you decipher Fae runes?"

Not waiting for an answer, she continued. "Scribbled on the Orb are ancient Fae runes. The runes reveal the Orb's magick and will only react to someone of Fae blood, or someone who's absorbed a power burst from the Orb. Since no one's touched the Orb in years, except for the Draicon who stole it, you're stuck with me or another Fae of your choice. Unless you want to check out every crystal ball from here to California."

"No Draicon stole the Orb," Parker said, glaring at her.

Curtis's expression became stony. "I agreed to have you on this assignment, Miss McClare, against my will. Lieutenant Parker's identity has been exposed. His life is in danger. No one must know Matt is a Draicon. No paranorms, no humans, not even the POTUS."

At her confused expression, he added, "President of the United States. Is that clear, Miss McClare?"

She nodded, feeling sweat bead on her forehead.

"You know how powerful the Orb is," Curtis continued.

"It serves as an amplifier to enhance a person's natural power, both dark and light, which is why it's dangerous," she interrupted. "And it reveals the truth about whatever one desires. For example, if you want to know the true identity of a Fae you suspect is using glamour, you consult the Orb."

Curtis glanced at Matt, emotion shadowing his gaze. "The person who stole the Orb used it to sell intel about Lieutenant Parker and his teammate. They were ambushed by pyrokinetic demons. The demons burned Lieutenant Parker's partner and nearly killed Matt."

Sienna choked back a horrified gasp. The Orb was being used for evil? She had hoped it was merely lost. Now the stakes were much bigger. Pity filled her as she looked at Lieutenant Parker, his expression tight with pain and grief.

"How do you know the Orb is to blame?"

"We have sources. And we have a leak, which is why we're meeting in secret." Curtis turned to the lieutenant. "Shay's providing backup on this op. He'll brief you."

Once again, they'd shut her out, as if closing a door. Shaymore opened the briefcase that had been cloaked as a large Coach purse, and pulled out a fat envelope.

Bile rose in her throat as she studied the photographs he displayed on the table. They were horrifying in their simple, stark details. Bodies, unrecognizable and charred, lay scattered on the sands. Their hands curled into claws, stretching out to the sky.

"One of our paranorm assets discovered they'd torched an entire village after attacking you, Dakota. A community of friendlies."

Sienna swallowed past her gorge. "Why?" she whispered.

Parker leaned across the table, his gaze searing hers. "Because that's what they do, Miss McClare. These demons feed off fire and terror. It infuses them with energy and power."

Sienna had a nagging suspicion she'd seen this kind of nasty work before. But she couldn't place it.

"They've been kept in check before because the bolt holes barring entry into our dimension were secured. About two months ago, a group of Darksider rogue Fae opened a bolt hole in an abandoned building in Nevada scheduled for demolition. Using explosives they'd stolen from Libya, they managed to free four pyrokinetic demons before our people sealed the breach. The pyro demons then torched a nearby apartment building, killing twenty-six people."

She felt sick to her stomach. Her own kind had helped do this?

Shaymore dug out a photograph from the purse. "This is a pyrokinetic demon."

Sienna stared at the mottled gray skin, the angry red slash of a mouth, the tapered, long fingers ending in sharp talons. "How could they move among the humans if they look like this?"

"Glamour." Shaymore rubbed his eyes, as if weary. "The Darksider Fae gave the demons their ability to glamour in return for a higher position in the netherworld. The glamour only holds for a few minutes—"

"Long enough," Parker cut in. "But if they get the Orb, they'll be able to hold it longer."

The possibilities were horrifying. Bile, hot and acid, rose in her throat.

The Draicon looked tight and deadly as a honed blade. "A Darksider Fae bought intel about me and my buddy from the slime who stole the Orb. Then he glamoured himself as our C.O. and ordered us on a mission. The demons waited until the marines in our convoy passed. The jarheads weren't the target. We were. The Fae set us up."

A low growl rumbled from his throat. "Because of that, my

best friend died in agony. If I find the Fae who did this, they won't need a demon to get to hell. I'll send them there myself."

His rage was luminous, raising the room temperature and warming her cheeks. Every instinct urged her to get up, get out and away from this dangerous Draicon. Sienna's eyes widened as he dragged his fingertips across the wood table, scoring it with claws that suddenly emerged.

"Whoa, L.T.," Shaymore said. "I don't have the money to cover damages for this room."

"Easy, Dakota," the lieutenant commander murmured. "The Fae who impersonated the major general was caught. He's been taken care of. We've established new security measures around all key personnel."

Sympathy filled her. She knew how it felt to be helpless and enraged. Sienna watched the Draicon rein in his control. Sweat popped out on his forehead, but his claws retreated.

"This mission is crucial, Miss McClare," Curtis told her. "If the pyro demons get the Orb, they'll discover the identity of every member of the Phoenix Force, and our associated powers. And use it to kill my men, who are the last defense against them."

"Not going to happen," Parker grated out. "I'll do whatever it takes. I'm not going to let innocent civilians be torched like my buddy was."

A horrific image came to mind. Streets lined with bodies, burned and twisted. Mothers, fathers, children. Not a tiny village on the edge of a desert, but a city filled with living people. Turned to a charred wasteland where the silent screams of the victims still floated in the air...

Nausea rolled in her stomach. She could no longer hold it at bay.

"Will you please excuse me?"

Somehow she made it down the hallway, into the bathroom, running the water to cover the sounds of her retching.

It was worse than she'd been led to believe. With shaking hands, she twisted the tap, splashing water on her face. She took several deep breaths, dried off.

Voices raised in anger. In the corridor she paused outside the living room, out of eyesight.

"You can't even mention his name." Parker sounded anguished.

"You know the rules, Dakota. He's gone."

"Damn it, I know the rules. He was my buddy. He fought bravely for his country. We can't even speak of him. Everyone who knew him had their memories of him as a SEAL erased." Parker hissed out a breath. "Adam deserves better. He deserves to be remembered."

"And he will."

She peeked around the corner. Curtis emerged from the kitchen, clutching three amber bottles. He handed one to each man. They raised the bottles, clinked.

"To Adam," Curtis said.

"To Wildcat," echoed Shaymore. "A damn fine warrior."

"To Chief Petty Officer Adam Barstow, the bravest soldier I've ever known. The best buddy I ever had. May the spirits guide you to the Other Side as you live on forever in our memories."

The men drank. Parker tipped his back and took a long pull, his throat muscles working. He wiped his mouth with the back of one hand, set down the drink. Glass cracked beneath the pressure of his squeezed fist.

"Matt," the lieutenant commander said gently.

"It should have been me. I sensed there was something off…."

He twisted and turned, his nostrils flaring. "Spying on us?"

Sienna walked into the room, her heart pounding. Anger and grief etched Parker's face. She knew all about grief, how it ate you up inside. And to not even be permitted to remember a lost one…

"His name was Chief Petty Officer Adam Barstow." A statement, not a question.

"You weren't supposed to hear that."

Fear skidded along her spine as she saw Parker's cold expression. This Draicon wasn't only a deadly wolf who ripped prey apart, but a trained navy SEAL as dangerous as the weapons he wielded. More than six feet of muscle and deadly force regarded her with cold blue eyes. She eyed the pistol holstered to his hip.

The lieutenant's jaw tightened. "His name isn't to be mentioned outside his team."

She kept her voice low and gentle. "Are you going to shoot me? At least grant me the courtesy of saying his name. He was a man who died for his country. Everyone deserves to be remembered after they die. What makes him so different that his name is top secret?"

"Because it is," Parker said, but she caught the flash of deep grief shadowing his face.

Both the lieutenant commander and Shaymore stood. "Thank you, Miss McClare, for your condolences." Curtis gave Parker a meaningful look. "Matt, I'll leave this to your discretion. Knock on the door when you're finished."

The connecting door closed behind the men. Do what? Kiss her? Or kill her? Wild thoughts surged through her. Sienna studied Matthew Parker's full, firm mouth, set now in a grim line. "What's going on?"

The lieutenant ran a hand through his thick, dark hair. "I'm going to wipe your memory of what you overheard. It's easier if there's no one else in the room."

Her jaw unhinged. "What? Why?"

Grief shadowed his expression. "It's a condition of being a SEAL on ST21. If we die, any memories of us as SEALs are erased. Our families are allowed to remember us, but there's no recollection of us being SEALs. You weren't supposed to know about Adam."

As he reached into his pocket and withdrew what looked like a cell phone, panic surged.

"You can't!"

Sienna's stomach pitched and rolled. Pushing back from his chair, Parker approached her, power shimmering in the air. His broad shoulders blocked out the overhead light. She tensed and held out a hand.

"You're not going to let me remember anything about your unit after we're done?" She tried to keep her voice from trembling.

"It's all right. It won't hurt. The NeuroBlaster targets specific memory centers. You won't feel a thing." Parker's voice was low and soothing.

Deep inside, a door was locked and she'd tried pushing it open for a long, long time. Sienna suspected it was a long-buried memory.

"Please don't do this," she whispered.

"I must."

But it could wipe out the memory she desperately longed to surface. Sienna shrank back as he approached. Magick shimmered around him, pushing at the air. He looked regretful as he pressed buttons on the NeuroBlaster.

"If you're going to erase my memories when this is over, why now erase the memory of the SEAL who died? When knowing what the demons did to him may help us pinpoint who stole the Orb? I need all the information I can get. This doesn't concern only him, Lieutenant. You're gambling with the lives of countless innocent civilians."

It was a long shot, but she had to gamble. Sienna clasped her hands together. Parker lowered his hand.

He seemed to struggle with a decision. Finally he pocketed the device. "I'm not letting you out of my sight, though. Get it? That's the condition. We stick together."

She released a quivering breath. "Thank you."

"Don't thank me. After this is over, I must take your memories. Deal?"

She'd deal with after much later. For now, she had a respite. Her mouth wobbled in a tremulous smile. "Deal."

She held out her hand in a formal gesture of thanks. Parker took it, his palm swallowing hers. A shiver raced through her as he stroked her hand with a thumb. Current sizzled between them, a flare of something deep and significant. The scent of pine forest, leather and pure male invaded her senses. He was overwhelming from a distance, but this close…her hand trembled in his.

Retreating back into formality, she pulled her hand away. He frowned, his gaze whipping around the room.

"I smell something…dark." Parker's nostrils flared. He pounded on the wall and the men came into the room.

"Shay, did you do a full scan of the suite for bugs?" Parker demanded.

"Clean." The Mage rapped his knuckles on the table.

"You didn't scan her."

All three men stared at her. Her blood pressure dropped. Sienna couldn't move. Parker took the cylindrical scanner and swept it over her body. It gave a sharp, tinny beep and lit up red as it hovered over her shirt collar.

"Hellfire," Shaymore muttered.

Something was crawling on her neck on furry, tiny legs.

"Stay absolutely still," Parker said softly, setting down the wand.

"Hitchhiker demon worm. Careful," the lieutenant commander warned.

She wanted to bolt, but forced herself to stay still. Sienna reached up to pluck it off.

"Don't." Parker crept toward her, his gaze intent on the creature. "Your move will trigger its defenses."

"Get it off me," she whispered.

"Easy now. Close your eyes and mouth. It accesses your body through your orifices."

She felt it approach her cheek, linger near her mouth, then move downward over her neck. Sweat broke out on her forehead. Her heart pounded like thunder in the silent room.

Then suddenly the crawling sensation was gone. Something pressed against her chest like two hands doing compressions.

Sienna looked down. Latched to her blouse was a worm the size of her palm. It opened its mouth to reveal rows of pointed teeth. Yellow foam dripped from the yawning jaws.

Matt tackled her hard, toppling her to the floor. The move threw the creature off her body. He seized the worm, which released a high-pitched squeal. A hard yank and the SEAL twisted off its head. Gray goo splattered.

Breathing hard, more scared than she wanted to admit, she sat up. He squatted beside her, patting her down, his brow furrowed. The lieutenant used the wand again and frowned.

"Need to do a physical check." Then he gave an apologetic glance. "I'm sorry, but I have to make sure nothing else is on your clothing. May I?"

At her nod, he slid his hands over her body, gentle but thorough. Heat flushed her at the intimate examination. A lock of hair fell over his forehead and she felt a sudden compulsion to brush it back, feel the soft silk between her fingers.

The lieutenant ran his fingers lightly over her breasts, his jaw tight, his gaze impartial. A man with a touch like that would be amazing in bed.... Sienna put her hands to her burning cheeks.

"You okay?"

She gave a breathless laugh. "Fine. Considering a worm almost ate into my Donna Karan suit. My only good suit."

A small smile touched his mouth, erasing his weary look, and it made him appear younger and more approachable.

"Did you have any contact with anyone today, other than us? Anything unusual? Demon hitcher worms are transmitted through touch."

"This is New York. I probably bumped into hundreds of people."

"Must have been recent. They can't survive more than a few hours, which is why they're rarely used by demons." His expression tightened. "Blood. The subway, the suit who followed you. He cut you. You had blood on your collar."

Sienna thought about it. "The man on the subway. He cut me with a knife. I changed shirts after I got to my hotel. How could he have infected me with the worm?"

"The worm was on the knife. They begin as microscopic organisms, hiding on hard surfaces and then blend with whatever clothing a victim wears so they can hide." Matt touched her healed wound. "He wasn't trying to molest you. He was planting the worm. You've been followed and targeted, and traced. You okay?"

The deep tone of his rough voice slid over her raging nerves, soothing them in an odd way. She didn't trust Draicon wolves. Yet it was Lieutenant Parker whom she turned to now, laying her palm into his outstretched hand. He pulled her to her feet, his action decisive, his gaze alert.

Sexual awareness flared between them. For a long moment his gaze locked on to hers, the blueness of his eyes smoldering with heat. He looked at her not as an annoying Fae, but as a female. A very desirable female. Just as quickly, he released her hand. He turned with a menacing scowl toward the chief petty officer.

"What the hell were you thinking? No, wait, you weren't.

Because you're always about trying to get into a female's pants. You didn't sweep her for bugs, and look what happened."

Low and deep, his voice proved more dangerous than if he'd shouted. Shaymore's expression went flat. He stiffened.

"I'm sorry, sir. I got distracted."

Matt got in his face. "You're a fine operator, Shay, but you let a pretty face get to you and you're not only burning yourself, you're burning us. Think next time."

Lieutenant Commander Curtis looked concerned. "Are you all right, Miss McClare?"

She nodded. So formal, his concern was courteous, not the simmering emotion she'd sensed from Lieutenant Parker. Matthew. Matt. She said his name to herself silently.

Pairing with this sexy, lethal Draicon could prove dangerous. Those steely blue eyes promised heat, and could peel back all her defenses, leaving her bare and exposed.

Sienna shuddered. Yet she needed Lieutenant Parker's help if she were to recover the Orb of Light.

Chapter 3

Sienna was serious, but spunky, Matt thought as reluctant admiration filled him for the Fae who rode silently beside him. Her gaze was focused on the smokestacks, traffic and lead-gray sky that blurred past them.

Her long, dark hair spilled over slender shoulders. They'd burned her clothing and Matt had bought her new clothes, just in case they missed any stray hitchhiker worms.

But the crisp new jeans hugged her body and the mulberry sweater was too tight. He tried to keep his focus on the road, but hell, he was male. Couldn't resist a peek at those long legs. She stood around five foot seven, petite for a Seelie Fae, with generous female curves. As formal and brisk as his examination had been, it had been torture. A man could cup her breasts in his palms, feel her soft and silky body beneath him, those long legs tangling with his as he...

Swearing under his breath, he concentrated on the highway. His C.O. had fully briefed him on Sienna McClare while the Fae showered and changed. He knew everything, from her shoe size to her job as a clerk in a convenience store to recent purchases she'd made of classical music CDs. Everything except why she'd been living alone outside her Fae colony, when the Fae were traditionally forest dwellers and social creatures. That had been a gap in her file.

He'd told Sienna as much as he could about their destination. Thanks to intel from their vampire buddy and his extensive network of spies, they'd gotten a bead on a witch in northern New Jersey. She'd asked local covens for protection spells against pyro demons because she'd used info from the Orb to "set up a Draicon werewolf and a jaguar overseas." Now she was running scared.

Be afraid, he thought grimly, remembering how Adam died. *Because if you helped kill my buddy, I don't know if I can control myself.*

For the first time he realized he might. Maybe that was why his C.O. sicced the pretty Fae on him. Curt knew Matt would hold it together around a female. Always had in the past.

There's a first time for everything.

"Can I drive?"

"Not on this freeway."

Sienna blew a breath on the window and rubbed her index finger over it. "What are the plans once we reach the witch's house?"

"I'll question her. You hang back, keep an eye out."

"Question her? You won't hurt her, shift and scare her? Show a little fang and terrorize her into talking?"

"Why would I do that?"

"I'm sure you've done it before. That's what Draicon do best."

Matt gritted his teeth. She was pretty, but infuriatingly stubborn. "Sweetheart, someone sold you a bad bill of goods about my people. We may have a bad rep among some para-norms…"

"But underneath you're all sweetness and good? Nice dog-gies who like car rides and sticking your heads out the windows to catch the wind? I heard you were all snarl and growl."

His fingers tightened on the steering wheel as he resisted the impulse to do exactly as she'd suggested.

"I'm a U.S. Navy SEAL. My team and mission come first. Just as your Fae colony comes first for you."

Silence draped the air for a moment. "I have no colony anymore. No family."

Words spoken so quietly, he wouldn't have heard them if not for being Draicon. Matt changed lanes and sped up. Odd, how they had that in common. His family had been close, hell, his own brother-in-law supported him joining the teams. It was Étienne who suggested Matt's abilities would come in useful for the newly formed Phoenix Force.

But in the ten years he'd been a SEAL, his family had become more distant. They'd started nagging about quitting, settling down into pack life, finding a mate and starting a family. The bonds he shared with his teammates were thick and strong as steel cable. He couldn't leave the teams. Not with dark forces becoming more clever, and endangering more and more civilians.

His team was his pack now. With a small pang, Matt realized he forgot how to be fully Draicon. He wouldn't know a real relationship if it kissed him. He was a ladies' man, but one-night stands were the norm. Relationship, hell, he couldn't commit. Not when he got called out on an hour's notice, or worse, never came back at all.

Like Adam.

Matt remembered Tatiana's sobs. He couldn't do that to a mate. He didn't want one, didn't want to fall into the trap of settling down and falling in love. Because falling in love meant giving up what mattered most to him, being a SEAL.

"Can we start over?" Her voice was soft, a rub of velvet against his frayed nerves. "If we're going to work together, we should try to get along. I'm sorry for the dog references."

"And I'll try not to make any Mr. Spock jokes."

Sienna gave a small, sweet laugh, the sound stirring his jaded self. "Are all your assignments like this?"

"No. We either go in as a pair—" he swallowed hard, thinking of Adam "—or as a team. I'm used to covert action, get in, get out and get gone. This is a little different for me. For one, I've never worked with a female before, let alone a Seelie Sidhe who can glamour as a Draicon."

Not that I'd trust one. Never.

"My glamour isn't limited to Draicon. It just happens to be the form easiest to me."

"Why?"

She shrugged, pushed at a lock of hair, showing her pointed ears.

"Those have to go. They're too obvious. Glamour yourself into a Draicon. We're getting closer to our target."

Sienna shot him an annoyed look. "Aye, aye, captain."

"It's lieutenant."

She made a sound and then muttered, "Fine. You want Draicon?"

Matt nearly lost control of the car as she shifted. A gray-and-white timber wolf sat on the seat. She grinned, showing sharp canines.

Startled, he jerked the wheel to the left, turning into the other lane. A driver he cut off blew the horn. Matt straightened out the car and glared at Sienna.

Sienna the wolf put a large paw on the window button, rolling it down. She stuck her head out the window, tongue lolling.

She had a sense of humor, after all. He slowed down, and as he thumbed the window up, she jerked her head inside.

"I'd let you drive, but I don't think your paws would touch the pedals."

With a low whine, she shifted into her human form. "You'll really let me drive?"

"Naw." He considered. "You probably drive like an old lady."

Magick shimmered in the air again. This time, she took the form of a NASCAR driver.

Matt laughed. Sienna resumed the form of a Draicon female, an impish smile on her mouth. Her very red, very wet mouth. A kissable mouth.

Concentrate. "Back on the subway, tell me, what were you doing on Canal Street?"

"I was following a lead in Chinatown." She pushed at the long fall of her silky hair. "I've been working on my own, disguised as a Draicon, trying to find the Orb. A Draicon in Brooklyn told me a shop owner was selling something like that in Chinatown."

"Did you find anything out?"

She shook her head with a small sigh. "It was a dead end. The shop had closed and the owner passed away. He was probably yanking on my chain."

"Or worse. Intending to wrap that chain around your neck." He aimed her a stern look. "No more going solo."

When she opened her mouth, a line furrowing between her brows as if to protest, Matt added, "Or I'll take those memories I left intact."

Her mouth closed.

Minutes later, they drove down a narrow lane flanked by oak and maple trees. Matt turned into a street lined with two-story elegant homes, each house boasting about half an acre of property. Sienna blinked.

"Guess spell casting is a lucrative business these days."

He didn't reply. His gaze was focused on the patrol car blocking the street. Yellow crime scene tape was strung across the lawn of a brick home. Dread churned in his stomach.

"That's her house?" But even as their gazes met, he sensed she knew.

Making a U-turn, he drove out of the neighborhood, down the lane and turned down an adjacent street. Matt parked and shut off the engine.

"I'm going inside to check things out. You stay here."

"You said I was supposed to stick by your side. And how do you plan to get in? Shift into your wolf shape? That might raise a few brows. Or get someone to call animal control. I'll go with you and glamour us so we blend in with the background. The cops will never know you're here."

He gritted his teeth. Didn't like it. He needed his team, not this sassy, pretty Fae who didn't even know what a pyro demon could do to bare flesh.

They were stuck together. And she was a Fae who could glamour.

"Fine. But follow my orders," he grated out.

They cut through a well-manicured lawn, Sienna keeping up the cloak of glamour to hide their presence. Uniformed police and detectives in worn jackets milled in the driveway. A maple tree, resplendent in fall crimson, stood guard next to a pole where an American flag fluttered in the slight breeze. With its black shutters, crisp brick and trimmed bushes, the house looked no different from its upscale neighbors'.

Except for the blood splatters on the green grass.

The magick shimmered for a minute as Sienna gasped. Matt shook his head. "Don't fall apart on me now."

She shot him a cool look. "I don't fall apart."

"Good girl. Keep up the glamour or they'll see us."

As they neared the house, Matt led her to the deserted side of the house, sheltered by a tall hedge.

"I'm going inside. Stay here."

"Let me help. I can glean some information while you're inside."

Matt clasped her shoulders, feeling delicate bones and soft skin. She was courageous and tough, as he'd seen on the subway, but this was different. Eyes green as a forest gazed at him. The same sharp, sexual energy jumped between them like an electrical wire. He became fully aware of her slight stature, how broad and big he was compared to her. Beneath the tight sweater, her breasts were full and lush. A man could cup them in his palms, stroking his thumbs slowly over the nipples until she became flushed and aroused. Draw her close until the jagged need became consuming.

Trying to ignore her delicious scent, he roped in the tight control that enabled him to endure hours of physical pain during Hell Week. He focused on the mission. She was female, and his primal instincts were to keep her safe. No matter how many would-be human molesters she could take out with her knee.

"No. It's too risky. This wasn't my choice, but I agreed to this assignment. I had my doubts about working with you."

"Because I'm a civilian?" Those mossy green eyes regarded him with frank amusement. "No prob."

Suddenly Matt faced a tall, gangly G.I. in a mesh-covered helmet, vintage cammies and worn army boots. There was a distinct smile on the G.I.'s face as he stood straight and tall and then hefted a squeaky-clean rifle.

"Hey, there, Lieutenant Dan. Is this better?" she drawled.

Saying nothing, he gave her a pointed look. She sighed and resumed her normal form. "That wasn't good enough for you?"

"If you're going to conjure Tom Hanks, then *Saving Pri-*

vate Ryan would have proved a better argument," he said mildly.

Her pert nose wrinkled. "I don't like war movies."

"My point exactly."

Sienna made an irritated sound. "What is it, Lieutenant? You don't like females? Or civilians? Or your tighty whities are a little too tight?"

More sass. He folded his arms, waited for her to get it. He had endless patience. Once, he'd disguised himself as a wolf and spent three nights lying in a hollow log in an attempt to catch a rogue shape-shifter. Sienna tilted her head, the long fall of her mink-brown hair spilling to one side. The move gave her an exotic, sexy look. "Oh, wait. Maybe it's because I'm Fae."

"Score. That's not changing. Neither is the civilian or—" he gave her legs an appreciative glance "—the female part. And you have no experience in covert ops. So I'm calling the shots."

"Bit of a control freak, aren't we?"

Checking his sidearm, he ignored that comment. If he were more of a control freak, maybe Adam wouldn't have died.

"Wait." She caught his hand. Matt stared at the slender fingers covering his. The intoxicating scent of warm female made his senses whirl. Too long since he'd felt a woman's soft touch. Too long since he'd had a woman in his bed.

"When you go inside, I'll stay outside, pretend to be a curious bystander, see what I can overhear."

"No."

Sienna dropped his hand and sighed. "Listen, we don't like each other, but we have to work together. With all these police around, who would hurt me?"

He fought the urge to send her back to the car. His Draicon senses screamed danger. But she was right.

"You sense anything off, you come and get me. Deal?"

She knuckle-bumped him, green eyes huge in her solemn face. "Deal."

"FYI, I don't wear tighty whities."

"Oh, you're a boxer wolf? What do you wear?"

Matt dipped his head close to her shell-like ear. A few strands of silky hair lifted with his warm breath as he gently blew.

"Nothing," he whispered.

The spice of her female scent sharpened. Matt grinned and touched her mouth, parted in a small *O*. "Stay alert."

Cops lingered in the back, dusting the sliding door that led into the kitchen. Black fingerprint powder smeared the sparkling glass. He waited a moment to ensure Sienna's glamour hiding him would hold, then slipped through the opened door.

Except for a few blood splatters on the floor that had been marked off, the kitchen was neat and clean, with polished oak cabinets, a shiny black granite countertop and dish towels with apple motifs hanging from the stainless-steel stove. Dark, malevolent magick shimmered in the air. The stench of sulfur and rotting flesh mingled with the coppery scent of blood. Matt clamped a hand over his mouth as he headed into the adjoining dining room.

A young woman sat at a long maple table, sobbing. "I didn't do it. I swear, I loved my mother. It was El Diablo. El Diablo!"

The devil?

The front door opened. The police hustled the woman outside. Matt searched with all his senses. Nothing here, no warding spells, no candles, as if someone had erased evidence a witch lived here.

He started searching the bedrooms, opening drawers quietly, checking every corner. Upstairs in a small rose-colored bedroom, he ground to a halt, catching the scent of fear.

It rose over him in a wave, crashing into his senses and

making his eyes water. Matt rubbed the heel of one palm into his chest, trying to ease the crushing weight.

Stronger by the closet. He opened the door and peered inside. A miasma of terror screamed into his mind.

Methodically, he searched the closet. Sorting through layers of clothing awash with the smell of mothballs and cedar, he lifted boxes and set them aside.

A hidden recess in the closet revealed a locked file box shielded with a pentagram. He pulled it out and broke the spell locking it with a simple incantation his C.O. had taught all the team.

He combed through the files, his gorge rising as he scanned them. Then he found a business ledger. His instincts were right. No Draicon had stolen the Orb.

Yet another reason not to trust any Fae. He pocketed the ledger and replaced the files.

As he went into the room, he caught sight of himself in the dressing table mirror. His form shimmered.

The glamour was fading. Fast.

He had to sneak out. Racing over options, he started for the bedroom door and heard pounding footsteps. Matt withdrew his Sig Sauer 9 mm pistol, cupping it with one hand. Sienna burst into the room and ground to a halt, staring at the gun's barrel.

He sheathed the weapon as she gulped down a breath, eyes huge in her face. "We've got to leave, right now. I was talking with one of the cops when one of them suddenly... It was horrible. His form, it just...I don't know..."

"Wobbled?"

She nodded. "Like when you throw a stone in water."

He glanced at the window. "Where?"

"Downstairs. But I think he knew I could see through him. He may be another Fae. Or something else. The daughter, they were leading her out, she was screaming that a demon tortured her mother for information, and went too far, then set the daughter up to make it look like—"

"It's okay," he soothed. "You did good. Where's the rest of the police?"

"They're all outside, since they're done wrapping up the crime scene."

"Good. Let's go."

The stench of sulfur grew stronger. Matt herded Sienna out of the room, grinding to a halt. He slid an arm around her waist and yanked her against him, away from the specter blocking the way at the hallway's end.

The specter shimmered, losing the glamour of a police uniform.

They were screwed.

"Draicon. You have something I need," the demon hissed. Then it smiled and held up a hand, tipped with long, gray talons.

Flames burned at the tip of each finger. Matt's throat went drier than sand.

No way out past the pyrokinetic demon.

He and Sienna were going to fry.

Pulling his sidearm free, Matt screwed on the long barreled silencer, knowing gunfire would bring the cops running. He fired at the creature, hoping to slow it. But as the bullets whizzed at the demon, flames burst from its fingers.

The steel and silver-tinged bullets melted in midair. Sienna gasped. Damn it, the new ammo was specially designed to withstand the demons' defenses. No dice.

They needed CO_2. "You don't happen to have a fire extinguisher handy in your bag of Fae tricks?" Matt unscrewed the silencer, and pocketed it with his service pistol. He pulled Sienna behind him.

"There's a bathroom behind us. Let's go, we need water, have to have water."

"Water doesn't kill them. Only puts out the fire and you need a lot of it. CO_2 smothers their oxygen, keeps them from breathing."

The ragged sound of her panting filled his ears. Panic radiated from her as Sienna stared at the demon. He could feel her pulse pounding, smell her fear. Knew the demon scented it, as well. They dined on terror.

"He's going to burn us. We have to get out of here."

"Stay calm," he urged, backing her away from the demon.

Flames burst out of the demon's fingers in a hiss, scorching the walls. A framed photo of the witch and her daughter began to burn. Then the demon turned and sprayed fire down the stairs, cutting off their exit.

Sienna whimpered, turning pale as milk. Matt gripped her hand. "I'm not going to let anything happen to you. You need to stay calm and don't panic. We'll get out of this."

Smoke began filling the hallway. She coughed, and laughed. "We will? Okay, super *lupus,* guess it's time for a weenie roast. Except I doubt you like having your weenie roasted."

Putting up a brave front. Knew all about that. Had done it a time or two. His admiration kicked up a notch.

"Depends on who's doing the roasting. Definitely not him."

Matt turned, searching the hallway. At the end sat a cherry-wood bookcase with leather-bound volumes. No good, but the covering...

The Indian weave table runner.

"Create a distraction. Talk to it. Feed its ego. Demons love having their ego stroked."

"As long as you don't ask me to stroke anything else," she muttered.

"If something happens to me, get into that back bedroom and escape out the window. Drive as fast as you can to a place where you feel safe, and call that number on the card you got earlier."

She coughed, nodded. "Nothing's going to happen to you," she whispered.

Sienna faced the demon as Matt backed up to the bookcase. "Hey, Officer Hot Stuff. That was some glamour you pulled. Never guessed you were a demon. Fooled the cops, too."

Matt removed the runner, folded it behind his back.

The demon smirked. "You're a pretty one. You'll look even nicer when I melt your face."

Sienna blanched.

"Enough. You found the witch's ledger, Draicon? Give it to me and the girl lives. Perhaps."

"These?" Matt pulled the book from his back jeans pocket. He ripped out a few pages, tossed them into the flames licking the walls. "Go get them."

Screaming, the demon dove for the papers burning out of control. Matt pushed her to the side and whispered, "Get ready. On my word, conjure a fire extinguisher in my hands and run into the east side back bedroom."

The demon raised its hands toward Matt, its slit of a mouth yawning open, showing daggerlike teeth. Timing was everything. If Sienna dropped the illusion, his ass would be cooked.

"Now."

Sienna invoked the image of a fire extinguisher. "Take this, hot stuff," she yelled, pointing the apparition at him.

Screaming, the demon drew back, its hands dropping. As it looked behind for a way out, Matt tackled it in a full body slam. He jammed an arm at the demon's throat and stuffed the blanket into its flat nostrils and oval mouth, cutting off its oxygen supply. The demon's body heat burned through the arm of his leather jacket, cooking his skin. The metal of his sidearm began to warm like a skillet over an open flame. An eerie scream choked out of the pyro demon. The heat intensified, but Matt continued to smother the cloth, now singeing beneath the flames creeping out of its mouth.

The pyro demon tried to draw in a breath, found only woven cloth. It gasped and its reddish-yellow eyes fluttered.

Unconscious for now.

He gave a hard twist, breaking the creature's neck. Permanently cutting off all oxygen.

Smoke clogged his lungs, heat painfully burning through his leather jacket. Wincing at the pain of his burned hands, Matt crawled the length of the smoky hallway to the back bedroom. He tried to draw air into his lungs, and coughed. Then someone yanked him into the room.

He kicked the door shut with a booted foot, buying them time. Sienna was already yanking off the bedspread, stuffing it beneath the door to block the smoke.

A distant screech of sirens sounded. By the time the fire department arrived, it would be too late. And how the hell would they explain anything?

Two stories down, but they could make it. Smoke curled into the room from the door frame. Coughing, Sienna clamped a hand over her mouth.

Matt ran to the window. Ignoring the pain in his burned hands, he jerked it upward. The wood frame splintered beneath the force.

"I've heard Fae can fly. Now's a good time to find out. Me first. I'll cushion you, but if I don't, hit the ground in a roll, Sienna."

He jumped, aiming for a thick bayberry shrub. Branches scraped his face, but the bush protected his bones from breaking. He rolled out, held out his arms.

"Jump."

Sienna fell, rather than jumped. He caught her, wincing as her weight made contact with his burns. Matt set her down, whistling through his teeth, the agony in his arm graying his vision. Swaying, his eyes watering and lungs burning with smoke, he fought to remain on his feet. Sienna's soot-covered face looked anxiously at him.

"Better get that NASCAR illusion ready, sweetheart. Because this time, I think I will let you drive."

Chapter 4

The white house with the bright red shutters was quaint and small and in a quiet neighborhood near downtown Forrest Plains. Perfect place to hide and recover.

Heart pounding like a war drum, Sienna found the key beneath a statue of a grinning gnome. As she replaced the gnome, it politely lifted its hat. She blinked.

"The owner has an odd sense of humor," Matt rasped.

He was shaking badly now. Sienna slid an arm around his waist, helping him inside. She locked the door behind them.

The living room had a large, faded olive sofa, and two green recliners. A basket of dried wildflowers sat in the hearth of a stone fireplace. Silver-framed photos adorned the cream walls. It looked like an average, middle-class house.

The only difference was a painting hanging over the fireplace. A large, gray wolf, head held aloft and proud, standing in a forest.

Her stomach pitched and rolled. Great. Portrait of ole grandpa. A wolf.

"It smells like a den in here," she muttered.

"Belongs to a buddy. Draicon. He took his family to visit relatives. Told me I could use it any occasion I wanted. The occasion calls for it."

Instinct warred within her, her Fae side shrieking in fear at the wolf scent, her Draicon side welcoming the cozy and welcoming house. She told her Fae side to shut up and deal. They needed a place to lie low. And he was badly hurt. Worry raced through her.

Matt limped over to the sofa, coughing violently. Sienna ran into the kitchen, pulled open an oak cabinet. She filled a glass with water and brought it to him. He gulped it down, then wheezed.

"Thanks. It's not a beer, but it'll do." He winked at her.

"You need a hospital, Lieutenant Parker."

"Unless you can conjure up the illusion of a medic, no chance in hell. Too dangerous. I'll heal. Give me a few minutes. I'm a fast healer." He leaned back and closed his eyes. Long, dark lashes feathered his sooty cheeks.

The anger she'd harbored against all Draicon melted a little. He was wolf, but courageous and steady. Not like the Draicon who'd abused her mother.

Sienna sat beside him. "Let's get the jacket off. Then I'll see about conjuring up a steak. You're low on energy, and from what I know about your kind, protein will suffice."

He opened one eye. "That or sex." Matt gave a rueful glance downward. "Though I doubt that part of me will cooperate right now."

Heat flooded her cheeks. She helped him sit up, and gently tugged the jacket off his uninjured arm. Sienna sucked in a breath. "I can cut it off you."

"Just do it."

A harsh whistling noise hissed through his teeth as she pulled the other arm free. Sienna winced at the red burn on his muscular forearm and his burned palms and fingers. He surveyed the injuries and shrugged. "Not too bad. Considering that pyro demons can melt steel and reduce bones to ash."

Fire strong enough to burn bone. They'd be dead, if not for Matt's quick thinking.

"Thank you for saving me," she said quietly.

He looked at her steadily with those deep blue eyes. "No problem. Your glamour helped us out of a tight spot. You're not bad for a Fae."

As she bristled, he added with a teasing smile, "And you're much prettier than the ones I've run up against."

The whiteness of his teeth contrasted with his dirty face. Sienna felt a tug of unwanted attraction. He was a cool operator, and the sheer sexiness of that smile melted her.

She found a medical kit in the main bathroom and washed his injuries, treating them with a cooling cream. His jaw turned to stone as he endured her ministrations. It had to hurt, but he was stoic.

Hard muscles of his arm quivered beneath her fingers as she spread on the cream. Mingling with the stench of ash and soot was the delicious scent of his cologne, and something richer and purely male.

Her Draicon half reacted, making her soft and aching. Sienna bit her lip. Fae, she was Fae. Not Draicon.

When she'd bandaged the wounds, he turned. "Thanks."

Tension hovered in the air as he gazed at her, his expression steady and warm.

Sienna stared at his jaw, the bristle shadowing his lean cheeks. So different from her, so very male.

So very Draicon.

A small, but persistent connection flared between them. He rested a bandaged hand over hers. She shivered, imagining him undressing her, those big hands gliding over her body, coaxing and teasing....

Sienna gently pulled free and went over to the fireplace hearth, curious about this wolf and his chosen profession. "So, you're a soldier. It must give you a big advantage over the others, to be a wolf with strength and healing abilities. Was it easier for you to become a navy SEAL?"

"I went through the same training, except every paranorm who strives to become a SEAL has extra tests to pass after we become SEALs. Makes the playing field even with humans who complete BUD/S, Basic Underwater Demolition/ SEALs. Most civilians think SEALs are all firepower and muscles." Matt gave a crooked grin. "They don't realize half the battle is up here."

As he tapped his forehead, she gave him a puzzled look. "Your mind?"

"Physical strength is important, but mental strength is equally important in defeating the bad guys."

"So how would you learn to defeat a paranormal bad guy? It's not the same as defeating a terrorist."

"Same basic techniques. Study the enemy. Get to know him as intimately as you know yourself. What drives him?" Matt's gaze went distant. "Although in our case, we can't see the enemy until it's too late. If we had, maybe Adam..."

He fell silent. Sienna felt a tug of sympathy. Not wanting to grieve him further, she changed the subject. "Back at the hotel, Chief Petty Officer Shaymore called you Dakota."

"All the guys on my team have nicknames. I like John Wayne movies. Even the worst one of his, *Dakota,* so they slapped that on me."

His teammates shared close bonds. Sienna wistfully longed for the same. Her few Fae friends had been distant and aloof, not playful and friendly. "I've never had a nickname."

"Maybe I should give you one." He cocked his head, considered. "Pixie. You're small and feisty like one."

"I am not," she protested.

"But you are cute."

"Oh." A furious blush chased across her face.

"Very cute." His grin faded, replaced by an intent look. All alone here, with this big Draicon wolf, the chemistry between them hot and intense.

Sienna drew in a deep breath, willing her arousal to lessen. "What did you find at the witch's house?"

Matt's expression became guarded. "Spells for warding off pyro demons. And bank receipts, a business ledger and a Craigslist ad. Evidence."

As she sucked in a breath, he added, "Don't worry. I let them burn on purpose. All the info's up here."

He tapped his head again. "The ad was cryptic, selling secrets revealed by a crystal ball. The witch recorded the transaction in the ledger, making a note of the seller's name and place of business for future reference. She paid two hundred thousand dollars for the intel about myself and Adam from the Orb's holder. She sold it to a Darksider Fae for three hundred and fifty thousand dollars, a nice little profit for herself. Only she didn't realize who the real client was until it was too late, when the pyro demons decided to cut out the middleman."

Cold dread crept up her spine at the SEAL's hard expression. "Who was the seller?"

Eyes the color of an icy ocean swept over her. "His name is Tim McMahon. He's Fae. Seelie Sidhe."

Words sank into her like steel claws, shredding her insides. "It can't be… The thief was a Draicon."

"No, Sienna. He's Fae. One of your own." His words sent a chill through her. "From your own colony, Los Lobos."

He stretched out on the sofa and fell fast asleep. Never had

Sienna seen anyone crash that fast. He'd muttered something about taking a combat nap and bam!

Sienna brought in their bags, showered and changed into fresh jeans, a cable-knit turquoise sweater and sneakers. Her suede boots were ruined. She sighed and set them aside. A month's pay from the little convenience shop where she'd worked and they were good only for the garbage can.

The kitchen was bare of food. Her stomach rumbled. Sienna rubbed her arms. She was low on energy herself. Unlike Draicon, Fae didn't need beef. They could survive on sprouts and berries. They were creatures of the forest, protectors of innocents.

Betrayers and dealers of dangerous secrets to pyrokinetic demons.

Her palms gripped the granite countertop. Tim. She knew him. He was quiet, introspective and hovered on the fringes of the society. He'd left the colony the same time the Orb went missing. Why hadn't Chloe suspected him? It made no sense.

Because Chloe wouldn't dare suspect one of her own pureblooded Fae would commit such treason, Sienna realized. Instead, she blamed a Draicon who'd been seen in wolf form near the sacred ground.

All her beliefs and convictions about her people crashed like a house of cards smashed by an uncaring hand. Emotion rose in her throat. Not Draicon but Fae had been the real enemy all along.

She had to regain herself. Everything in her world was collapsing. Sienna lifted her head and stared at her watery reflection in the microwave.

"I am Seelie Sidhe of the Los Lobos colony, guardians of the Orb of Light. I am pure and honorable, a protector of nature and innocents. I will never defy the land, nor bring shame to my people. I embrace all living things good and natural, and walk with honor."

But the pledge sounded hollow to her ears. Walk with honor? Tim had not. One of her own kind!

Exhausted, confused, she needed to eat, regain her composure. Which was she?

Draicon or Fae?

Was either species truly honorable?

Lieutenant Matthew Parker certainly was. His actions dictated it. Tim may have recited the oath along with every other colony member, but it had been a lie.

Matt lived the oath of honor with every step he took.

And yet he was Draicon, like the man who'd fathered her, and then killed her mother.

Could she ever trust a Draicon?

Sounds of the shower began. Matt was so quiet, she hadn't heard him wake up. An image, unbidden and erotic, filled her mind. He was soaping himself, running the bar along those smooth, taut muscles, water beading off his sun-darkened skin. His head flung back, eyes closed, growling with pleasure as she fell to her knees, removed the soap from his hands and began lathering him much lower...

No longer cold, Sienna gulped down a breath.

As a distraction, she paced the kitchen. It was pretty, homey and welcoming. Layered through the air was a scent of love and deep affection that pulled at her In deep yearning. It was the type of cozy house she'd always envisioned for herself.

"Hey."

Dressed in jeans and barefoot, he stood in the doorway, hair slicked back, droplets beading the thick waves. The bandages were gone from his now-healed wounds. A long-sleeved flannel shirt hung open, showing a muscled abdomen strong enough to break bricks. Dark hair feathered his chest, arrowing down his stomach and vanishing into the waistband of the jeans.

Arousal filled her as she thought about following that line much lower. Her body loosened with want and yearning. Sienna felt warm and open.

His pupils darkened as he swept his gaze over her. Matt's nostrils flared. He'd scented her desire.

She licked her lips. "There's no meat here. Um, I mean, nothing here to eat…and I'm hungry."

"Me, too," he said, his voice hoarse as he stared at her wet mouth.

He pushed back at his damp hair. "Let me get dressed, and we'll go out for a quick bite. I saw a sandwich shop around the corner."

When they reached the restaurant, she ordered a hamburger with cheese and an order of fries. Matt paid for their purchases and brought them over to a quiet table by the window, facing the door.

He always had his back to the wall, facing whoever walked inside. Tension tightened his body, but not from the hot encounter with the pyro demon.

Nope, this tension was purely sexual from something equally smoking hot. He watched with avid hunger as Sienna poured ketchup over a fry and delicately licked it off with her small, pink tongue. Thinking about what delights that tongue could deliver…

Desire heated his blood until all he could think about was how much he wanted this woman in his bed. How much he wanted to bury himself deep inside her, driving into her until she clung to him and screamed, and all the animosity between them became animal passion.

Big mistake. He lowered his gaze and dove into his hamburger.

They had the dining area to themselves. Still, he kept a guarded eye on the street. Small houses dotted the lane, some with bicycles scattered over the driveways. It was a solid family area, known among his kind as a safe zone. Draicon lived here among humans.

His gaze shot back to Sienna, who was devouring her burger with zest.

"I thought Fae were vegans."

She stifled a burp with her hand and gave an apologetic look. Damn, she was so cute, so charming.

So Fae.

Matt took another bite, grimly concentrating on his other, more appeasable hunger.

"I'm starved. I guess everything caught up to me."

"I didn't know Fae ate meat. I thought all they liked were sprouts. Except the ones who have an appetite for killing."

Guilt shadowed her expression. She bent her head, studying the red basket containing her fries. "I doubt it." Sienna glanced around. "We can talk openly here, right?"

Matt nodded.

"I want to know something." Her fingers curled around the basket's edge. "Tell me, how did Adam die?"

His stomach tightened. Out of all the questions he'd anticipated, it wasn't this. As appealing as the hamburger had been, it turned to cardboard in his stomach.

"Please. I need to know."

"Why?"

Direct, commanding, curt. She raised her chin.

"Maybe that will help me understand why you hate my people."

Fair enough. Though he doubted it would change anything. They were too opposite. Too different in their worlds.

Matt closed his eyes, seeing the sand swirl around him, feeling it sting his face. Smelling the heat and the arid air, the sharp tang of metal. He told the story, each word slicing open wounds that were still fresh. When he got to the part where Adam died, he struggled to speak.

"The pyrokinetic demons caught up with Adam outside. I heard him…"

Scream.

Moisture filled Sienna's eyes. She slid a hand over the table, but Matt pulled back. He couldn't let her touch him. Couldn't break apart.

"You tried to help. You were amazingly brave in facing the demons. You did the best you could," she said gently.

"It wasn't enough."

The image came back to him, searing pain from the burns, shoving down the oily panic clogging his throat as he lapsed into unconsciousness.

"When I regained consciousness, I didn't dare radio back for help. The Darksider Fae could be imitating any one of the troops. Shay was on standby. Called him and made him give me the code of our squad. He came and fetched me, did a glamour so it looked like I was fine. Our C.O.—you met him, Lieutenant Commander Curtis—made sure I had private quarters to recover. Then he did a cleanse of everyone who'd come into contact with Adam. No one remembered him, or that he'd ever come to Afghanistan."

"Oh, Matt," she said softly. "That must have been horrible."

Here was the one person he could talk to about Adam. Sienna, a stranger, who silently forged the connection he'd needed back on the subway. The safety clicked off his hard-won control. Words burst out of him like machine-gun fire.

"It was as if he'd never existed. He was my swim buddy. We went through BUD/S together—we were teammates, best friends. I was closer to him than my own family. I was there at his mating ceremony. And I couldn't even be there at his damn funeral because I had to pretend I never knew him. Because no one is supposed to know about the Phoenix Force. So when we die, all memories die with us."

A stray tear escaped, sliding down Sienna's perfect cheek. Seeing her cry for Adam made him no longer feel alone in his grief, but also made him protective. Made him want to cup her face in his hands and kiss away her tears. He hated seeing her cry. Matt lifted a hand, then dropped it. Gods, he felt so damned confused lately.

"What about his body?"

"We made a promise in the team. No man gets left behind. Shay returned for Adam, but couldn't find anything. The pyro demons had reduced him to ash, and his ashes had been taken by the wind. There was nothing left of him to return to Tatiana, his widow. Nothing."

After wiping her eyes with a napkin, Sienna covered his hand with her own. "I'm sorry, Matt, for what the Darksider Fae did to you. To Adam."

First-name basis. No more Lieutenant Parker. And she'd said Adam's name again. He struggled against the urge to kiss her senseless in thanks and took a long pull of his water.

Backhanding his mouth, he shook his head. "I should have saved my buddy. We were tight. Always watched each other's backs."

She stroked his wrist, her thumb making little circles. Always calm and cool, his rare outburst was alarming. It was Sienna, her soft, sweet smile and genuine air of concern. She dug beneath his defenses, past the emotional berm he'd erected since Adam's death.

"Too crowded in here," he muttered, glancing around. "Let's get back. I'll arrange for transport, airline tickets."

"To New Mexico?"

Matt nodded. "Home of your friend Tim. I'll do some initial recon…"

As she gave him a questioning look, he sighed. "Reconnaissance. Scout out the shop and the lay of the land for a couple of days. And then move in. If the pyro demons know he has the Orb, those guys aren't patient. I need to retrieve it before they do."

Back at the house, Sienna watched Matt type on his laptop. Since returning, he'd been quiet and aloof. When he snapped the computer shut, she waved a hand.

"Hello? Remember me? The one who's working with you?"

He gave her a long, cool look. "Not anymore. The stakes have changed. I know who has the Orb, and how to get it back. I'm sending you home."

A quivering began in her belly. Sienna took a controlling breath. "Not so fast. I understand you're angry at my people."

Matt remained silent.

"But I didn't steal the Orb. We're a team in this, got it? Those were the terms. We both get the Orb and I show my people it's safe once more."

A bitter laugh escaped him. "Safe for how long? Your people did a helluva job guarding it. It's because of them Adam's dead."

Sienna's throat tightened. She felt his anger, his pain and frustration. But she had to convince him to let her stay. If he forced her return, he'd wipe her memories....

Her precious memories.

Worse, the name of her people would be forever smeared with disgrace. Now more than ever, it was crucial she finish this task and restore their honor.

Sienna took his palm and unfolded it, studying the rough calluses and strong fingers. "The Fae believe that when someone dies and their ashes are scattered to the four winds, it doesn't mean that person is lost. He then becomes part of the earth and part of every living thing. That's what became of

Adam. He lives on in every breath of wind, in the laughter of every child."

Silence draped the air. His shoulders relaxed, losing the tightly wound tension that knotted them. He lifted his face, his eyes very blue.

"All Fae are not evil," she said gently. "Even the Unseelie, the Dark Fae, have their good side. The Darksider Fae are rogue, but they are few and live outside the boundaries and clan system of Fae. We Seelie Sidhe Fae are secluded and insular, but compassionate. We respect all living beings."

His gaze sharpened. "A compassionate people. Then what put the chip on your shoulder about me, Sienna? About werewolves?"

Dropping his hand, she studied the tips of her faded sneakers. Fae preferred bare feet, touching the earth to maintain contact. She never had.

"Hey." A firm hand cradled her chin, lifting it upward. His palm was warm and strong. "Tell me. What did we do to you?"

The gentleness of his touch made her toes curl inside the sneakers. Sienna took a deep breath for courage. Maybe if he knew, he'd cut her a break and let her stay.

"I'm not pure-blooded Sidhe. I'm only a half-breed. Half Fae and half Draicon."

At his startled look, she yanked away and grated out the damned truth. "Mothered by a Fae from the Los Lobos colony, and fathered by a Draicon who raped her...and then killed her when his pack came back to try to claim me."

Panic squeezed her heart as flashes of the past emerged, like a rapid slideshow. "*Probably* killed her when he raided the Fae colony to get me."

"Sweet gods. How old were you?" His voice was gentle, contrasting with the hard edges of his expression.

"I think around five, maybe four. I don't remember that much."

"No wonder you dislike Draicon."

Dislike was a lukewarm term. For years she'd hated them. It was a relief to finally talk about what happened. Among her people, it had been an ugly secret no one ever discussed. "It's so much easier to hate than try to understand. It's fueled me for so long that it's hard to let go."

"Hate does that to you. It feeds you power to seek justice." Matt's expression tightened. "You were just a little thing. I'd kill the bast…the Draicon who did that to your mother. Did she ever say who it was?"

"I don't remember much. I've tried." Hands curled tight, she watched her knuckles whiten. "Aunt Chloe rescued me during the attack. The Fae beat back the Draicon pack. I think…they killed my father. I don't know! I want to know, but I can't remember." Misery knotted her throat. "I have snatches of dreams, of images. Chloe told me when the time was right, I'd learn the truth. About what, and who, I really am. But I know what I am. The daughter of a vicious killer." Her voice dropped to a bare whisper. "So what does that make me?"

Compassion flared in his gaze. "You're Sienna McClare. What your parents were isn't important. It's what you make of yourself that counts."

"That's why the Orb is so important to me. If I find it and bring it back, my people will accept me back into their colony."

At his incredulous look, she sighed. "They turned me out on my twenty-first birthday, because I'm a hybrid and don't belong. I do belong, and once I prove my loyalty to their side, I will."

"Is that what you truly want?" he asked quietly.

"More than anything. I need my people. They're all I've ever known. With them I'll feel..."

Connected.

"Wolves aren't so bad, either," he murmured. Matt stroked a thumb along her jawline. "Draicon. No Fae could pull off that effective a glamour with scent, as well. I knew there was something sweet about your scent."

A half smile touched her mouth. "That's my Fae half."

His gaze locked on her lips. "So sweet," he murmured.

He'd put his life before her own. Gotten burned, cushioned her fall, kept her safe. For so long, she'd functioned on her own, accustomed to fending for herself. Not one single Fae had risked his life for her.

She thought about how much she wanted to draw close. Feel that tensile strength holding her close, the slight abrasion of his day whiskers against her soft cheek

As he leaned down to kiss her, Sienna closed her eyes.

She sighed on a breath as his mouth met hers. It was a sweet kiss, his lips warm and soft. He was gentle, his mouth reverent as if he held back, waiting for her. All the other kisses from the few Fae males had been cold, lacking in passion and tenderness. Sienna wanted more. When she parted her lips and licked his mouth, he deepened the kiss. He tasted like the most exquisite wine, of moonlit nights and dazzling starlight. The kiss melted her bones and spoke of sheer need, a painful longing finally met.

Her senses spun as he slid his arms about her waist. It was breathtaking and dizzying, searing her with wicked heat. Sienna clung to him, feeling the thick muscles of his wide shoulders, the sheer solidness of the man.

She was hot, her clothing constricting her, needing to get bare, feel his skin warm and smooth against hers...needing more, needing his mouth against her body. Needing him to lay her on a soft, wide bed and take her as a man takes a woman.

Sweet mercy.

Alarmed, she pulled back, breathing hard. Surrendering to desire for him meant surrendering all hope of belonging to her colony. She couldn't align herself with any wolf.

Not even an honorable navy SEAL who'd risked his life for her.

"Stop it. Leave me alone." She pulled out of his arms.

"Sienna, talk to me."

Shaking her head, she retreated into the bathroom. Sienna closed the door and leaned against it. Gods, what had she done? It should have been just a kiss.

But it felt like so much more.

Chapter 5

The city of Santa Fe was pretty and artsy and normally Sienna would have enjoyed seeing the sights. But not now.

Sienna paced the lobby of the elegant downtown hotel as Matt dealt with the front desk. Wide sofas with a taupe and sienna Indian print were scattered around the luxurious lobby. A distressed wood round table held a welcoming pitcher of fruit punch and crystal glasses. It was very upscale and luxurious.

Something about this city, despite its charming, artistic flair, screamed danger. Beneath the exciting energy and charm, she sensed an undertone of unusual darkness. She couldn't tell if it was real, or her imagination.

Somehow, she was losing the Fae ability to sort truth from fiction. And if she lost that ability, what was next?

The more time she spent with Matt, the less Fae she became. The flare of attraction between them proved too much. Too confusing. Too upsetting. Once she was inside her room, she'd change back to her Fae form.

Sienna clenched her hands as Matt turned, swinging his heavy duffel bag over one shoulder and lifting her suitcase as if it weighed no more than a lunch box.

"The key to my room, please."

He gave her a cool look. "We're sharing."

Dumbfounded, she gaped at him.

"I'll take the sofa. I've slept in much worse." He began climbing the stairs.

She scurried after him. "I can't stay with you."

"I warned you, no going solo. You're sticking with me at all times."

Gritting her teeth, she waited until they ascended to the second floor. As he set the bags down and inserted the room key into the lock, she grabbed his arm. Smooth muscles rippled beneath warm skin. Matt raised an eyebrow.

"I can't stay with you. I need my own room. Besides, aren't we supposed to be brother and sister?"

His mouth was a grim slash. "After what happened in Forrest Plains, no way, pixie. I registered us as a couple staying together. I've agreed to let you stay on this op and I've been charged with your care and protection. What I protect, I don't ever desert. Got it?"

The door swung open. He gave her a gentle but firm push inside.

"My care? Says who? I don't report to the navy."

"You do now. Did from the moment you agreed to this assignment. As senior officer, I'm pulling rank, Miss McClare."

A huge bed dominated the room, boasting a hand-woven Indian print bedspread. Fine art prints of southwestern landscaping hung on the terra-cotta walls. In the corner sat a small, distressed wood writing desk. The guest suite was expansive, comfortable and stylish.

Her anxious gaze swept the interior, looking for any place, even a balcony, to find solitude.

Nothing. Except the bathroom.

Panic constricted her throat. Sienna struggled for control. As he tossed the luggage onto a bench and unzipped his duffel, she darted into the bathroom and locked the door.

Gripping the sink, she stared at her reflection. Breath wheezed in and out of her lungs.

I am Fae. I am Seelie Sidhe.

With every ounce of power she possessed, Sienna concentrated, willing away the Draicon glamour to resume her natural Fae form.

The air shimmered for a moment. Nothing. *I have to do this. I must. I am Seelie Sidhe.*

Sienna directed a blast of pure power at the mirror image. The glass wavered for a moment, and then cracked in half. Stricken, she stared at the shattered image of herself.

Draicon still.

"Sienna. You okay?"

Blinking hard, she willed the image to change. Nothing. *Please,* she thought desperately. *I am Fae.*

A fist pounded on the door. "Sienna, answer me now, or I'm coming in there. On the count of five."

Finally, the image wobbled. Pale skin replaced sun-darkened skin, her eyes grew larger and greener, and the telltale pointed ears returned.

She unlocked the door just as he kicked. Matt tumbled inside, but recovered in a graceful roll. He stood, jamming a hand through his thick hair.

"What's going on?"

Sienna fingered her ears with a relieved sigh. "Nothing. Can't a girl have her privacy to put on her face?"

She swept past him with a regal sniff. A very Fae sniff.

As they made their way toward downtown Santa Fe and the busy city square, Sienna paused to window-shop. The flowered print dress flowing down to her ankles resembled vintage hippie. So did the way she'd coiffed her hair, pinning it up and jamming a flower in the locks. Sandals adorned her feet.

Even glamoured as a Draicon, she looked Fae, Matt realized.

They spent two days in Santa Fe, touring the sights downtown and scouting out the area to defray suspicion. Each night he spent squeezing his six-foot-plus body onto a sofa the size of a tin can, letting her have the king-size bed. What kept him more awake was the delicious scent wending through the air. Lilacs, forest and sweet female. Last night Sienna had fallen into a deep sleep, one hand curled beneath her pink cheek, the other splayed on the pillow. It would have taken so little to crawl into bed with her, coax her awake with a slow kiss, watch desire flush her skin as she opened her slender arms to yield to him....

He'd cursed and rolled over instead.

This morning, after a hot breakfast of omelets and buttered toast, they shopped once more. They resumed touring downtown, casually making their way toward Tim the Fae's store. Matt hated this. The big, bad navy SEAL side of him wanted her out of this op. Having Sienna with him made her a target.

The Draicon wolf hated it, as well. The primal wolf in him wanted to haul her pretty ass over one shoulder, march her back to the hotel room and lock her inside, making sure she was safe.

Out in the open, he kept his guard up, watching for anything suspicious.

The distance yawned between them deep as a canyon. Matt stuffed his hands into his jeans pockets, pulled up the collar of his faded denim jacket and tipped the cowboy hat farther down. The hat provided cover, hid his face. He missed his leather, missed his comfortable clothing, missed his buddies and their tight camaraderie.

Here, with this Fae who seemed as far away as Europe, he felt out of place. Cold ice settled over him. But he couldn't stop thinking about that kiss.

It had rocked his world, sent him hurling back on his heels. Judging from the sweetness of her response, the way her tongue swept over his, how she'd leaned into him willingly…

Matt scuffed a boot heel into the sidewalk, viciously wishing this mission were over. Sienna McClare was ripe for the taking. Women fell into his bed. He could find one now, relieve his sexual frustration, if not for his promise to never leave Sienna alone.

Matt didn't want to leave her alone. Not for reasons he'd given her, either.

Since meeting her, his libido had gone curiously cold, except in her presence. He felt aware, awake. Alive, for the first time since Adam's death.

She twisted his guts into a knot. Matt watched her press her nose against the cold glass, a longing expression on her face. She looked like a child left out in the cold and it kicked him hard. Knew what that was like, when everyone around you seemed like a stranger and no one understood.

He'd experienced that after Adam's death, when his parents came to visit at the base. Instead of comforting him, they'd made him feel even more alone.

"What's got your attention, starshine?"

She glanced at him. "Starshine? Why'd you call me that?"

Her voice, aah, it was soft and sultry, rubbing against his taut body like a stroke of silk. Matt wanted to play it cool and fast. He found himself staring in rapt fascination at her wet, pink mouth. The truth nearly tumbled from his lips.

Because you're like starshine, distant and glittering and lovely, but unreachable. Yet I see you and I feel at home. As if no matter where I go, all I have to do is look into the sky and know I'm not alone.

What a wuss-ass thing to say. *Gods, am I turning into an emotional wreck? I sound like a lovestruck pup.* He cleared his throat.

"Beats me. I should call you Tink for Tinker Bell. Flying away to Neverland?"

The eager, hopeful expression faded. Hurt stamped her face. He felt like kicking himself.

Sienna rubbed at the glass. "I'm not military, certainly not one of your teammates, Lieutenant. But I'm not vacuous or whatever image you have of fictional fairies. No matter what you think of my people, that's not me. So cut it out with the insulting nicknames."

This was all going cockeyed. "I will if you stop calling me Lieutenant and call me Matt."

"Yet you pulled rank on me."

He rubbed the back of his neck. "Just to get you in line. I was exhausted and needed rest and not an argument. Rank means little to a SEAL. We're not like regular military. We respect our leaders because of their experience and abilities, not the bars and stars they wear."

Sienna blew a breath on the glass, drew a star. "I like that. The Fae lifestyle has a strict structure, and the leader has absolute authority. At times I question why, and wonder what it would be like to live outside those confines."

He cocked his head. "Seems like you were so busy trying to cheerlead the Fae, and brand yourself as one, and now you've changed your mind?"

Expecting a protest, a hot defense, he was surprised to hear her tiny, regretful sigh. "I don't know… It's something I thought about for a while after they forced me to leave. But they're the only family I've ever had. There are so many confusing things lately. Can we walk?"

He did not move. Instead, he gestured to the window. "What were you looking at?"

She gave a wistful sigh, the sound tugging at his heart. "It's nothing."

"Tell me."

A small shrug. "Just the boots. Red suede. They're so pretty. I saved for a pair, and they were ruined at the house by the smoke. It's okay. I'll get another pair, someday. It's not important." She fingered the print dress. "I shouldn't be coveting clothing, anyway. It's not important to the Fae."

"Hey." He placed his hands on her shoulders, feeling delicate bone and muscle beneath the gentle pressure of his fingers. "Forget about what they expect. What is it you want?"

She didn't answer, only licked her soft, pink mouth. Desire raged through him as he tracked each move of her tongue.

Huge green eyes gazed at him. Her skin looked luminous and soft. He wanted to trail his fingers over it, savoring the texture. Need boiled through him as he inhaled her scent, feminine, delectable. One kiss. Once he felt the velvet warmth of her mouth beneath the subtle pressure of his, he'd coax her to open to him. The loud pounding of her heart and the dilation of her eyes encouraged him.

He could kiss her senseless until she yielded. When she returned with him to the hotel, he'd have her make those damn enticing feminine sighs of pleasure as he slowly undressed her, tumbled her into bed and stroked her skin, parting her silky thighs, sliding into her soft, tight wetness, bringing her to one height of pleasure after another....

Control threatened to spill through his fingertips. Matt dropped his hands, knowing if he continued to touch her, he'd lose it. Sienna was like an addicting drug.

"Let's push on," he muttered.

Sienna blinked, as if she'd been under a spell. Forcing himself to slow down and not head directly to the Fae's store, he patiently waited as she shopped, eyeing pictures and sculptures and jewelry.

Near the busy square, they ambled up a deserted-looking street, pausing outside a shop window. The faded turquoise sign featured a dragonfly and read Spirit of the Dragonfly. Fine Jewelry and Collectables.

Matt glanced up and down the street. "No one's around. It's time."

She glamoured him as a jowled, wealthy rancher, stomach oozing over his silver belt buckle.

Amusement filled her eyes. "Yee-haw. Take a look."

As Matt studied himself in the glass, she looked at the window display. "Tim always did make nice things."

A spotlight shone on a violet shawl curled around a small turquoise purse. Sienna touched the window.

"Oh, it's so lovely."

She splayed her palm against the pane. Her mouth parted and her eyes grew smoky with such deep longing it hurt to look at her. Then she gave a small distressed sound, touching something deep inside him. Misery etched her expression. He ached at that look. Suddenly he only wanted her to be happy, show her cheeky, confident grin.

"What is it?"

"That purse, I want it so badly. It's so lovely, so different. I wish…I could afford it."

The small handbag had turquoise beading and multicolored stones set into the fabric. It seemed more a work of art. Sienna opened her wallet and counted the dollar bills inside. She glanced at the price tag in the display window.

The wallet closed with a sharp snick. Huge green eyes seemed to beseech him. "Did you ever want something so badly and know it was as out of your reach as the stars?"

Matt lifted his hand to caress her cheek. He dropped it. "Yes."

"There's something about it, like if I had that purse on my

shoulder, I could show the world that I'm Sienna McClare and I know who I am, and what my purpose is."

She gave a little laugh. "Stupid. As if anything I could buy could accomplish that."

Matt felt a bond of understanding. At times, he coveted things that were impractical but he'd wanted all the same. A home in the country where he could kick off his boots, relax with a sigh and a bottle of beer on the porch. A place to rest, recover and settle down. It warred with his lifestyle of always moving, always on guard, always alert for enemy operatives, human or other.

Such a home meant settling down. And he didn't want to settle down. Couldn't give up the excitement of being a SEAL, the quiet satisfaction of a job well-done, the population kept safe.

Still, he wondered what it would feel like.

The purse wasn't a mere fashion accessory. In the depths of her huge eyes, he saw a yearning for something more, a frivolous symbol of beauty that clashed totally with the strict, austere lifestyle of the Fae.

Having the home in the country was a faded dream, but hell, one little purse for her? If it meant making her smile again, seeing her eyes sparkle, why not?

Matt made an impulsive decision. "Our cover's changed," he murmured. "You're my guide around Santa Fe and I'm a looking for a gift for my girlfriend."

Lines furrowed her brow. "Why?"

"Just go with it."

Waves of uncertainty radiated from her. He needed her confident to deal with Tim. "Listen," he said urgently. "I know this is tough. He's going to see you and be defensive. I need you sharp, alert and using every ounce of charm you have. He can't suspect anything because if he does, he'll bolt and clam up and we'll never learn anything. I have faith in you, Sienna. Are you with me in this?"

Sienna raised her face, her mouth set in a determined line. "I can do it."

The little silver bell tinkled merrily as the shop door opened. No one was inside, except a tall, lanky man who glanced up from behind the glass counter. He scowled when he spotted Sienna.

"What are you doing here?"

Her initial expression conveyed her hurt before she covered it with a bright smile. It lit her face and made her eyes sparkle like jewels. Damn, she was a good operator. For a wild moment, Matt wished she'd smile for him that way. The image flickered past like a shooting star…she was sitting on the front porch, book spilling from her lap as she greeted him coming up the steps, laughing and holding out her arms in eager anticipation.…

"Nice to see you, Tim. I'm on a business trip. Mr. Sawyer is looking for an expensive gift for his girlfriend. She likes turquoise." She spread her hands, looking innocent. "I remembered how much you enjoy crafting beautiful things from turquoise. So I brought him here."

Sienna's glamour cloaking him wouldn't last long. Had to make this quick. He didn't like the Fae's body language. Big sale or not, he didn't want them here. Draicon senses attuned, he scented the sour stench of fear.

"Miss Sienna, thanks. I won't require your help any longer. Why don't you look around, see any interesting baubles in the back?"

Soon as she vanished into the other room, Tim relaxed. He started to pull out a tray of turquoise bracelets.

Matt lowered his voice conspiratorially. "I want to surprise her. The gift's actually for Miss Sienna, she's been such a great tour guide."

Tim glanced around nervously. "I have just the thing for her." He came from behind the counter to the purse in the window display. "I crafted this handbag myself. It's hand-stitched and features local stones and gems."

Odd. Just what Sienna wanted. Matt stared at the handbag, wondering if it were woven with Fae magick. Perhaps it called to her because of such magick.

"How much?"

"Five hundred and sixty dollars. With tax."

He shook his head.

Tim's smile dropped. He twisted his hands. "I can make a deal. I can let you have it for an even four hundred dollars, cash only, though."

"Too much."

Clearly nervous, Tim began to sweat.

"Look, I really need a sale today. Business is down. How about one hundred and fifty dollars?"

Something was off. He wanted to get rid of this purse and he wanted Sienna to have it. Matt opened it, half expecting a bomb inside. He began to search it.

The Fae rubbed his thin hands, the sound of the dry palms searing Matt's nerves. He wanted to grab the guy by the throat and pin him against the wall like an insect.

Make him confess why he'd betrayed his people. Why he'd done it. The memory of the image of Adam's scream cut through him like shrapnel. The urge for revenge became a pounding need.

Matt finished checking out the bag. His expression never changed as he snapped the purse shut and handed it to the Fae. "Gift wrap it."

As Tim rang up the purchase, Matt handed him a wad of cash. Their fingers touched briefly.

A violent rage filled him. This Fae, who'd rejected everything his people valued, was responsible for information that killed Adam. Matt struggled not to raise a fist and send it crashing into his long nose.

Tim's hands shook as he gift wrapped the purse and shoved it into a turquoise shopping bag. The Fae looked like a frightened rabbit facing a salivating wolf.

Not far from the truth, Matt thought grimly.

Sweat beaded the Fae's pasty face as he glanced around. "You have your gift. Now, please leave. I need to close shop."

Unsheathing the knife on his ankle and flashing the cool steel might make this bastard talk. Make him say Adam's name, over and over, until it spilled like a litany from his mouth.

Matt bit the inside of his cheek. Not with Sienna here. There were other ways.

Very briefly, he touched the Fae's thoughts.

A screaming haze of red and black colors blazed at him. Matt cut off the connection like slamming a door shut, his heart racing as if he'd run a three-minute mile. Holy hell, what was going on with Tim?

The Fae was terrified.

Then Tim glanced down at the hand Matt braced on the glass counter. He gave a frightened squeak as he looked at Matt's face.

The glamour faded. No one was around. Sienna was still in the back.

"It's you. Oh, gods, it's you, I'm sorry… I didn't mean it…."

Babbling wouldn't help him now. His temper popped. Matt vaulted over the counter and grabbed the Fae by the throat. "Tell me why you did it, you son of a bitch! The witch sold the intel to pyrokinetic demons who tortured and killed my best friend. Did you see that when you looked into the Orb and saw our faces? Blew our covers?"

Blood drained from Tim's face. "I didn't know. I never

would have done it. I needed the money. The witch told me she'd been dumped by a navy SEAL she thought was a paranorm, maybe a shifter. He and his good friend had laughed about it. She just wanted revenge. I consulted with the Orb and found out what you both were. I figured, you're SEALs, you can take care of yourselves. I didn't know." Tim's eyes bulged out. "Please, you've got to believe me. And you've got to leave now, before it's too late."

His thumbs dug in a little harder. "Too late for what? Where's the Orb? Don't tell me you gave it to those bastards or I'll—"

"No! I hid it. They won't get near it, I promise. It's safe now. Now it's safe." Tears streamed down the Fae's face. "Please, let me go. I only wanted to protect it. There are things you don't understand, forces at work...."

"Tell me."

Pedestrians neared the window and then headed for the door. Matt released the Fae, who gasped and rubbed his throat. He called for Sienna.

"Sienna, let's go. We're done here." He gave the Fae an even look as he took the shopping bag. "For now. I'll be back."

Soon as they exited the shop, Tim slammed the door behind them. A shade rattled. On the shade was printed the words Shop Closed.

As the tourists left with disappointed looks, Sienna frowned. "There's something here." She pointed to the words on the shade.

"Can you make it out?"

Her brow wrinkled in concentration. "It's Old Sidhe. It says..."

"Don't say it aloud," he murmured. Matt glanced up and down the street. A heavy malevolence hung in the air, though the sun burned bright in the cerulean sky. Yet he felt that something was off.

They were being watched, and standing here made them targets. Matt touched the glass. "Shop closed," he said loudly. "Damn it, you'd think this was one of them foreign countries where they take siestas all afternoon. Can you read the fine print saying when he'll open again? Left my glasses back at the room with Sue Ellen. Maybe we can come back earlier than the jeweler said he'd meet us. When did he say he'd meet us again?"

Sienna playfully pulled the rim of his hat down. "Midnight, Jim Bob. Our appointment's for midnight, after he gets that lovely gold ring finished. Let's return to the hotel so you both can tour the cathedral before dinner."

But she trembled slightly, like a leaf caught in the wind. He wanted to slide a protective arm about her waist, kiss away the fear shadowing her eyes. But if he did, he might be tempted to never let go.

Instead, he gave a reassuring wink.

As they exited the street and hit the sidewalk leading to their hotel, Sienna relaxed. The air of thick menace had vanished. Matt heard her small, relieved sigh.

He wanted to hold her hand, something he hadn't done in a long time with a woman. As they went to cross the street, he took her palm. She glanced up with a look of surprise, and then she smiled.

It felt good, having her close. For a long moment, he could imagine they were just another couple out for a day's enjoyment.

A normal couple. Tightness compressed his chest. Yeah, right. With pyro demons and Darksider Fae at their heels. Nothing was normal. Or ever could be, with his life.

Chapter 6

Upstairs in their room, Sienna sat on the bed fumbling with her hair. Pins rained down on the neat spread. She ruffled her long locks and plucked at her dress.

"I hate this," she muttered. "I hate this dress, hate this look. Everything Fae and natural, for what? We live for a code of honor and, seeing Tim, he violated it and took everything I believe and trusted in as a lie."

At her hurt expression, his heart gave a small twist. "You can't judge an entire people on the basis of one bad Fae, especially him."

Moss-green eyes regarded him with sorrow. "Just like I've judged the Draicon? And you've judged my people, as well."

Matt recoiled from the truth, rubbed his chin as if she'd sucker punched him. "Yeah, you're right. It's easy to find blame, see everything in black and white. Guess we're both wrong."

She gave a little sigh. "I don't understand. Tim had everything. He was highly regarded for his craft, he loved nature, he protected the wildlife. And now he's forsaken everything. He can never go back. He belonged. It was his by right and he threw it away. I'd have given everything to have what he took for granted. He left, and everything that is Fae about him is gone. Even the Old Sidhe...I couldn't read it. His scrawling was too obscure, I'm sure that's why I had trouble deciphering it."

He let her talk, let her get it out, knowing she needed to process and deal. When she fell silent, he sat beside her, the bed dipping beneath his weight. "Tell me what you read on the sign."

"'Come back at ten. Tonight.' That's why I said midnight aloud, in case anyone was listening."

"Good thinking," he said quietly. "What else?"

"'Come back when there...are no more objects upon me.'"

"Objects? Translation, please."

She tapped her face. "Eyes."

They had been watched, and Tim knew it. The Fae wanted them back. Wanted to talk when he wasn't being watched. Something else was at stake. Maybe the poor bastard realized he was dancing with the devil and was getting a little too close to the fire.

Literally.

She hugged her knees. "How could he desert his people?"

He touched the edge of her dress, rubbing the cotton fabric between thumb and forefinger.

"Maybe he needed something more. I understand that. Sometimes family can be a bit restrictive."

"But they're your family! Your people... Tim's all alone. I sensed it about him—he had this air of loneliness. A lone wolf. I hate what he did, taking the Orb, but I feel sorry for him. He's miserable."

"He's terrified."

Sienna rested her cheek on her knees. "He's in trouble, and he knows it. And he has no one to turn to. No family. I'd have given anything to have the complete acceptance he had. And he threw it away."

"I know," he said softly. "It hurt when they ostracized you."

The misery on her face tugged a soft spot deep inside. Couldn't help it. He wanted to comfort her.

"It felt like someone shoved me off a cliff. I had a cabin, a job they found for me and a life, but no sense of place or people. No acceptance. Everyone longs for acceptance. You have your team. I think they're more a part of you than your Draicon heritage."

Her insight hit him like a hard punch. She was right. He'd subtly turned his back on his family, his pack, and fully embraced the SEAL lifestyle. Hell, he relied these days more on his sidearm than shifting into wolf. If he didn't have the guys, his unit, what would he do?

How would it feel to lose everything as she had?

"The worst thing in the world is to be alone. Like the last of a species dying from extinction. I have to get the Orb. I have to show my colony that I fit in and belong to them."

"And what about your other half? You're partly Draicon. Don't give up on your wolf side. There's good and bad about both sides."

Sienna said nothing. Her sadness sliced through him. He had to make her smile again, forget about that bastard Tim and what he'd done. That Tim had blithely thrown away his birthright and his rightful acceptance, something she desperately craved.

The shopping bag rustled in his hands as he plucked out the gift box. Matt handed it to her.

"This is for you."

A questioning look in her eyes, she undid the ribbon and lifted the lid. Sienna stared into the box. She lifted out the purse with a gasp. Sienna stroked the beading. A glow lit her face and it seemed to immerse her entire body. She looked up with an expression of utter joy.

"Thank you, oh, thank you! Why did you do it?"

He sat on the bed. "I bought it for you. Because you liked it. And you were so sad. I only wanted to make you smile again."

Damn, he hadn't meant to reveal that. But the shining gratitude in her eyes and the wide smile she gave him was worth it. Long, satiny hair spilled over one slender shoulder. Sienna set the purse down.

"It's a lovely gift. Thank you, Matt. No one has ever bought me anything I ever wanted before." Moisture glistened in her green eyes. "No one has ever done anything so nice for me."

"Ever?" he asked, incredulous.

"No one else cared. You're so different. You notice things. You're not like the others, lost in your own world." Her voice deepened to a husky whisper. "You make me feel so alive."

She leaned forward and he caught the intoxicating scent of her, all female and warm skin. The fragrance made him heady, sent blood rushing to parts much lower. The wolf inside him growled in approval.

Couldn't help it. Matt cupped her face, gently thumbing her cheek, relishing the silky texture. He lowered his head, watching her soft, wide mouth part.

An invitation. Never one to refuse such a tempting offer, he took the plunge.

Her mouth was soft and delicious, tasting of ripe berries. He kept the pressure light, wanting to accustom her to his touch and scent. When her mouth moved against his, he increased the kiss, licking the inside of her mouth, stroking delicately against her seeking tongue.

One kiss wasn't enough. Never enough. Not even dozens of kisses. He wanted his mouth over her sweet skin, the taste of her on his tongue. Watching as her big green eyes grew smoky with passion, her arms stretched out to welcome him.

He wanted to have sex with her. In the bed. On the floor. Bend her over against the desk and take her as a wolf did, again and again, hearing her cry out with pleasure. As her lush breasts pressed against him, need became a wild, clawing thing. Reaching beneath her, he squeezed her bottom and lifted, bringing her closer. Sienna rubbed herself against him, making frustrated sounds. Her hips rose and fell with frantic urgency.

"It's okay, sweetheart. I know what you need," he soothed.

Thrusting a hard thigh between her legs, he rubbed against her, knowing the friction would increase her pleasure. Her skirts draped around her like a flower. Thin silk scraped against his jeans, the sound driving him wild. Matt stopped and she moaned. "More," she begged.

But he let her set the pace. Sienna rocked against him, making little moaning sounds that drove him crazy. Heat from her body inflamed his desire. He wanted to touch her all over, feel her satiny skin beneath his hands. Let her grow used to a man's body, gentling her with his touch.

Seducing her would be easy; she was becoming more aroused. But he didn't want seduction. Not with Sienna. Not loving her and leaving her. Deep inside, he needed something more lasting, more permanent and emotionally fulfilling. Even though nothing about his life was stable.

He wanted a long, slow loving, showing her every exquisite pleasure he could teach her.

He dropped tiny, hot kisses over her throat. Desire drove him now, his muscles locked tight and tensed. Sienna raised her face, her eyes sleepy with desire, passion flushing her face.

Oh, he could give her more. Much more.

Then she unfastened the tiny buttons on her dress and

pulled it down, revealing the white lace of her bra. Making a pleased sound, he cupped her breasts and squeezed lightly. Matt slipped the satin straps off her shoulders. Golden with the light, her skin seemed luminous and begging for him to touch.

Sienna unfastened her bra, letting it fall. He stared at the perfection of her breasts, with their coppery nipples, hard as pearls. From beneath her long, dark lashes, she darted him a shy look.

"You're so beautiful," he said thickly.

Marveling at the silky perfection, he took a nipple between his thumb and forefinger and massaged. Sienna threw her head back on a low moan, her hands braced on his thigh. Couldn't resist. He lowered his head and took her nipple into his mouth. She gasped, the shock of contact making her draw away at first, but as he suckled her, she drew closer, fisting her hands in his hair. Closing his eyes, he flicked his tongue expertly, enjoying her whimpers, the exquisite taste of her. It would take so little to lay her down and spread her thighs open, taste her much lower....

He was a Draicon male, filled with the instinct to claim and conquer. The primitive wolf urged him to mate. As the heady scent of her arousal flooded his nostrils, a low, possessive growl rumbled in his throat. Matt tried to choke it back. Too late.

She went rigid, her heart beating fast. Not with sexual excitement. Fear. He caught the scent threading through her sweet fragrance.

He released her breast with a slow pop, drew back. "Sienna," he murmured. "You okay? Don't be scared, sweetheart. It's only natural."

For a wolf... But not for a Fae.

Sienna licked her mouth, swollen from his possessive kisses. Apprehension clouded her gaze. Scrambling backward, she yanked at her bra and her dress and then sprang off the bed. The bathroom door slammed behind her.

He punched a pillow, hard, sending feathers flying, sexual excitement tightening his body to the point of pain. His cock throbbed, his balls ached.

"Thanks," he muttered to his wolf.

The animal inside him whined in hard disappointment. Next time, he'd use his brain, not his other organ. He wanted her badly, so much his hands shook.

But the hard facts couldn't be denied. She hated Draicon wolves, especially males. And he was a red-blooded, very powerful male Draicon in his sexual prime longing to mate. He represented everything dangerous to Sienna's life.

Matt rubbed the back of his neck. Never had he lost sexual control like this. It was the pretty Fae with the red, wet mouth and the beguiling sensuality simmering just below the surface.

Getting close to Miss Sienna McClare threatened more than loss of his common sense. He was dipping dangerously close to a precipice.

He was starting to care for her. And he could not afford to care for any woman, let anyone into his heart.

Especially not a Fae who denied her Draicon half, and wanted nothing to do with his world.

Dinner was strained, neither of them saying much. Though the beef burrito was excellent and the rice seasoned just right, she ate little. Sienna seemed shaken by the intimacy of what happened. Hell, he was shaken, as well. He'd never felt anything so right, so perfect. Sex for him was a necessity, fulfilling his body's urgent needs.

Not this head-spinning sensation of craving and wanting her so badly he felt like he'd die without having her.

Now as they walked to Tim's shop, he regretted her insistence on accompanying him. His instincts screamed danger. Even though Sienna had tossed up a glamour of an elderly couple enjoying a twilight stroll and window-shopping, it wasn't enough. The need to keep her safe overwhelmed him. And with every step that brought them closer to the store, his senses screamed to send her back to the hotel.

Streetlamps glowed with a soft golden light. Matt tensed as they drew near. The street was empty. Something foul and thick clogged the air, making him want to gag.

Sienna held a hand to her nose. "Sweet mercy, what is that?"

"I don't know." He gently pushed her behind him, every nerve alert. "Stay behind me."

The door to the shop was closed, the shade still drawn, now on both the door and the display window, the lights out. The stench grew stronger. Adrenaline pumped through his body. He turned and looked at Sienna.

"I'm going in. No matter what happens, stay here. If you feel threatened or see anything wrong, call 911."

"This isn't a police matter."

"Do it," he ordered.

"Wait. You're not going in as wolf? Isn't that safer?"

He didn't answer. Matt drew out his weapon. He touched the door's bottom with the toe of his boot.

It creaked open. Awareness shot through him with knife-like precision.

"Be careful," she whispered.

He nodded and pushed the door open wide.

Glass crunched beneath his boot heels. Through a pall of smoke, he saw smashed display cases, their contents emptied onto the floor. Exquisite, expensive jewelry lay in a pile, ripped apart as if by strong hands. The walls were slightly blackened, soot covering them. His wolf shrank back with the odor of acrid smoke, something dark and foul....

Burned flesh.

Matt sidestepped, checked the corner, cupping his pistol. The stench was stronger in back. Through a fog of smoke, he saw something on the floor. A large shape, clawlike fingers curled up, back arched to the sky.

Tim. What was left of him.

He coughed and resisted the urge to retch.

Then the smoke cleared a little and he saw the words scrawled on the floor by the body.

Feau teinl.

Senses screaming with awareness, he quickly searched the store. Not wanting to leave Sienna alone, he exited the shop.

In the dimming light, her eyes were huge.

"Tim?" Her face was pale as moonlight. Matt steeled himself, holstered his pistol and placed his fingers on her trembling, slight shoulders.

"He's dead."

Matt scanned the street. Whoever did it could still linger, watching the store to glimpse new arrivals. Demons couldn't read Old Sidhe, but they wouldn't desert the shop. They were nearby, watching...

Waiting.

A shadowy figure hovered in the doorway of a store across the narrow street. Matt's nostrils flared. He pushed Sienna behind him. "Get back to the hotel. Now. Use that glamour of yours and disguise yourself."

"But you—"

"I'll be fine. Go."

When she'd cleared the street and made it to the parallel side street, she shifted into the form of a teenager with wild pink hair. Good girl, he thought silently.

In the reflection of the store window, he saw his own glamour fade, replaced by a tall man dressed in black jeans, black T-shirt and black leather jacket.

Then he turned toward the shadows. The figure stepped out into a soft pool of light cast by a streetlamp.

A woman with long, red hair and a sultry air about her lithe body. Dressed in a long mink coat, she gave a little smile.

His keen hearing picked up an odd vibration. A distant, but irritating wheeze, like a bellows billowing air into a…

"Fire," he breathed. "Hellfire."

She lifted her hands, and was breathing hard. Not so fast. He was across the street and on her before she could raise her hands to blast him.

But no heat filled her body. She was cold, long since extinguished. Matt pushed an arm beneath her throat, pinning her to the brick wall. The redhead panted, yellow ringing her eyes growing wider.

A minor demon, sent to watch the place and, as a reward, allowed to help torch the owner. She'd extinguished her energy and needed to refuel. Could have already sent out the alarm. Not as powerful.

"Where's your master?"

"Please," she wheezed. "Let me go, I'll tell you. Can't breathe…"

The redhead's lips drew back in a snarl, showing blackened teeth. Her face changed, showing flat holes for nostrils, two glowing pits for eyes and flesh mottled and gray.

Then the features vanished, replaced by the model-good looks.

"I can give you a good time, honey. Real good. You're handsome, sexy. I scented it on the street."

Matt's brain whirled as he thought of a plan. He loosened his grip a little. "Who are you? And why should I trust you won't burn me?"

"My name's Alberta. I won't. Promise. You're too good to waste. Such muscles…much better than that stringy Fae. He was boring. But not any longer. Now he's toast." Her laugh scraped over his nerves like a hot blade.

He seemed to consider. "I've heard your kind is irresistible. Incredible in bed. Very hot."

That laugh again.

"I'll bet you wrapped him around your fingers." Playing the part, coaxing out information by stroking her ego, his stomach clenching in revulsion.

The demon skimmed her hands over his buttocks and squeezed. The urge to retch rose in his throat. He fought it down.

"Nothing like you. I'd like to have you between my legs. He was skinny, fumbling. Too fast. But he was a job."

He nodded at the shop. "That was your work?"

Alberta scowled. "They wouldn't replenish me after I exhausted my powers. But promised I could watch, when they finished with him."

Her hand slipped lower, found his crotch. Warmth spread through his groin as she stroked. Matt's body tightened, his cock growing hard beneath her touch. His mind remained cold and blank.

"You're smart. I could tell that about you. He couldn't resist you."

Red blazed in her eyes as her hands stopped stroking. "Not enough. Stupid Fae, wouldn't tell where it was. We tried, but he was stubborn. Now he'll never tell."

"Talk is cheap," Matt murmured. "Mouths can be used for other things, much more pleasant."

The redhead purred, lightly squeezing his erection. "I need energy. I need you, now. Let's fuck, wolf. You're hard all over. I promise you, you'll never feel anything like my lips on your cock, making you come, again and again. Let me show you."

"What about your master? Won't he return?" Sweat beaded

on his spine, his body turning rigid, his stomach churning with disgust. Had to keep up the ruse.

"Not until later. He saw you earlier." Alberta giggled. "With that little Fae. She's so mousy. He figured you'd be back around midnight. We have time. So let's do it. Right now."

"Not in my lifetime. Or yours."

With a sharp twist, he snapped her neck. The surprised look faded from her face, then her body dissolved into ash.

Gray particles swirled in the air like smoke, floated on the wind and drifted away. It was their way. Leave no evidence behind.

Damn it. Matt jammed a hand through his hair. No more answers than before.

Just more threats.

It wasn't safe here. No place seemed safe. Sienna couldn't stop shaking. She sat on the bed in their hotel room, rubbing her damp hair. Even after a hot shower and scrubbing her skin until it pinked, she could still detect the stench of smoke.

And death.

Tim, poor Tim, the betrayal he'd committed was unforgivable, but to be burned by pyro demons. Yet he hadn't uttered a word, told them the Orb's location. Matt was firm in this.

"Trust me, if the pyro demons found the Orb, I'd be dead by now."

The thought made her skin crawl. No more talk of death. Sienna set the towel down and hugged herself.

The bathroom door opened. Steam drifted out and in the cloud, Matt emerged, a towel slung low on his lean hips. Water beaded in the dark hairs on his powerful chest. His limbs were long and muscled, dusted with dark hair, his feet sturdy. Breath caught in her lungs. Gods, he was magnificent. Remembering the sharp pleasure he'd given her, she felt her body grow hot and tight. She'd wanted him so badly. Until that growl…reminding her of his true origins. And then she'd run, scared. Afraid, not because he was Draicon, but scared of her own response to this sexy wolf.

He ran a hand through his damp hair. "Sorry," he muttered. "Forgot my clothing."

Everything female cried out in disappointment as he retrieved his jeans and shirt, and vanished back into the bathroom.

When he came out, fully dressed, he joined her. Cleaning his weapon, his jaw taut.

"What does *Feau teinl* mean?"

She searched her memory. "It's Old Sidhe. 'Forever gone.'"

Grunting, he slid a magazine into the pistol.

"Who said that?"

"Tim did. It was written…by his body."

"He must have written it as parting words about dying. His soul, flying into the Other Side and leaving this plain. They tortured him for information, didn't they?"

Matt glanced up. "Yes."

"Won't the police investigate and find out?"

"No. I got rid of the body and planted misinformation to keep them from suspecting anything. They'll see a burned store and nothing else."

He carefully set the pistol down on the nightstand, within reach. Then he turned, all seriousness.

"I'm taking you off this mission. I've made a call to my C.O. and he agrees. Fae agreement or not, it's gotten too heated. What they did to Tim…they won't hesitate to do to you. I can take care of it myself."

Her heart dropped to her stomach, then he added, "The conditions still stand. When I recover the Orb, you'll be allowed to show it to your people. That's what you wanted, isn't it?"

To march the Orb in triumph back to her aunt, hear the

wild cheers of the celebrating Fae. Once, it was. The thought of victory soured. It was no longer enough.

She had to push on. Because allowing Matt to go solo, knowing something could happen and she wouldn't be there to help... Sienna swallowed, remembering the burns he'd suffered in the witch's house.

"You need me."

His expression softened. "I need you to be safe more. And I can't guarantee your safety, Sienna. Not if I'm to do my job. Seeing what they did to him...if anything happened to you."

"He was very brave in the end."

Matt nodded.

Imaginary screams echoed in her head, the terror of Tim as the demons had sprayed him with fire, trying to make him surrender the Orb's location. She would tell the Fae of his courage.

After she went running back to the colony, like a coward? And yet, he was right. The stakes were much higher. She could have it all and stay safe, away from creatures that breathed fire and brought pain. The Orb, the acceptance.

Without any of the effort.

Thinking of Tim, she shuddered. A distant memory pricked, teasing like a feather stroked across her mind. The raw stench of burning flesh, the terrified screams...

Fire scared her. Even the friendly, welcoming ones the Fae burned in celebration. She'd always hovered on the fringes, thinking it was her mixed blood.

Maybe it wasn't. Maybe whatever happened when she was very young was tied into her fear.

For a wild moment, she wanted to race back to her cabin in the woods, shut the door and pull the covers over her head. He was giving her the chance.

Then she looked up at his face and the grim set of his jaw.

The thought of facing a pyro demon, smelling her own flesh charring, feeling the hot pain, made her stomach clench. But leaving Matt alone, to bravely search out the Orb and possibly die...

Scared her more. *I can do this,* she told herself.

"You can't get rid of me that easily, Parker. I signed up for this assignment and I'm not the type to back off when things get a little hot. Or a few hundred degrees Fahrenheit, to be more precise. I'm sticking with you. Got it?"

His expression didn't change, but she sensed a subtle shift in him. As if their relationship had crossed an important threshold. "That's Lieutenant Parker to you."

At his teasing tone, Sienna lifted her chin. "Aye, aye, Lassie."

"Hey, quit it with the dog jokes." Then he grew serious again. "Fire terrifies you. I can't promise it won't happen again. Because now the demons will be even more infuriated. They'll see us as their only lead to finding the Orb. Don't make such a quick decision, pixie. I want you to feel free to leave, if you want, because it's not going to be easy. So if you feel the need to pull out, just say the word."

"I have two words. I'm. Staying."

He gave a small smile. "Okay. Get packed. I want to move out ASAP."

Not moving, she waited a moment, wanting to feel him next to her, feel the heat radiating from his big body. Wanting to touch him for reassurance. But if she did, it would lead to other things.

And she couldn't explore those options. Brave SEAL that he was, he was Draicon and very dangerous. Logic dictated that wolves could hurt Fae like her.

Yet in the distant memory that tugged, she caught a shimmering thread of something nasty and terrifying. Whoever had hurt her, threatened her with fire, wasn't wolf.

But something else.

Chapter 7

The Denver airport bustled with travelers. Matt stretched out his long legs, watching the humans mingling with paranorms. A pasty-faced Mage herded his family out of a nearby store and into the throng. The youngest child, barely four, cried out as the crowd cut him off from his family.

The Mage's lips moved and the crowd parted like water. He scurried forward, lifting the child into his arms.

If humans, and paranorms, knew the danger posed by the pyro demons... Matt's guts squeezed like a vise. It was his job to keep them safe, and ignorant.

But not Sienna's.

Head resting against the seat, she watched him with those incredibly green eyes. It was like falling into a refreshing pool. So lovely, the soft curve of her cheek, the full, pink mouth he'd enjoyed tasting. Jeans molded to the curves of her calves and strong thighs. He thought about how smooth those legs would feel as he settled between them, lowering himself atop her....

Matt bit back a groan. Around Sienna, with her sweet scent and curvy body, all he could think about was sex.

He concentrated on the mission instead. They had bought a little time in evading the enemy.

They'd driven from New Mexico to Denver, taking back roads to avoid detection. Sienna had thrown up a very effective glamour for the journey. A grizzled, elderly outdoorsman driving north in a beat-up white van.

So far, it was working.

But for this next stage of the game... His entire body went taut. Why was facing a pyro demon easier than facing his beloved family?

Because a demon just wants to kill you, not marry you off, he thought with sour amusement.

"I know we had to leave New Mexico. But why are we headed to New Orleans?"

Glancing around, he saw no one within earshot. He lowered his voice.

"We need a detour." His expression hardened. "It's about time I had a little talk with my brother-in-law, Étienne, about the Orb."

"How would he know anything about the Orb?"

"Because, pixie, he's the one who last saw its twin, the Astra Orb. And destroyed it."

The flight from Denver was quiet. Matt was grim and silent the entire time. She didn't question him. Caught up in her own internal anxiety, Sienna tried to fend off an ominous feeling.

They were headed straight into the thick of wolf territory.

When they reached New Orleans, he hustled her into a taxi and gave crisp directions. As they sped west on the interstate, he stared out the window in brooding silence. The taxi dropped them off in the French Quarter near Jackson Square. Matt picked up her suitcase and slung his duffel bag over one shoulder. He placed a firm hand on the small of her back, guiding her to a parking lot across the street from the cathedral.

A sleek, black pickup truck pulled up. The driver parked at an angle, jumped down. Tall, with a shock of brown hair, he ambled toward them. Wearing a light jacket, blue jeans, a polo shirt and a wide smile, he looked like an average American.

And then she caught the unmistakable scent of maleness, magick and wolf.

Draicon.

Anxiety churned in her stomach. The man reached Matt, engulfed him in a bear hug. "Hell, Matt, been too damn long. When Cindy found out you were coming here, she was over-joyed." He grinned and pounded him on the back, then lifted the corner of Matt's leather jacket with a questioning look.

"You're carrying." Warmth left his voice. "This isn't a family visit."

"No." He turned, introduced Sienna. "This is my brother-in-law, Étienne Robichaux. Étienne, this is Sienna McClare."

"Miss McClare." Étienne's handshake was brisk, but warmth filled his blue eyes. "Wish I could say it was a plea-sure, but judging from the look of both of you, I doubt you're here for a social call."

Against her will, she liked him. He was honest and direct, and though he seemed friendly, she sensed the same hard edge that threaded through Matt.

"I need to talk with you. I'd have called, but the situation calls for discretion. And you don't have a secure line," Matt told the other Draicon.

As Étienne slung their luggage into the truck bed, Matt caught her questioning look. "Étienne's an ex-SEAL." He helped her into the cab, sliding in next to her. "He encouraged me to join the navy."

"Encouraged him, but never realized he'd abandon his family for the teams." Étienne started the truck and tossed her a conspiratorial wink.

"I didn't abandon anyone," Matt bit out. "You, more than anyone, know what the life is like."

"Which is why I left, and settled down with your sister. I knew my responsibilities to my people."

The slightly accusing note made Matt bristle. "You're the eldest, next to take over. I'm not the oldest in my family. I have plenty of time to find a mate."

"Tell that to your sister. She keeps wondering if her brother will ever give her a niece or a nephew to spoil. Cousins for our kids to play with before they grow too old. Though at this rate—" he winked at Sienna again "—they'll be gray and in rocking chairs by the time Matt becomes a father."

Sandwiched between the two tall men with their tensile strength, she felt petite and frail. They left the city behind and headed down a small road, flanked on both sides by murky water. Gray moss dangled from ghostly trees in the swamp.

Sienna folded her hands in her lap. She sensed Matt's hurt, his inner frustration at Étienne's minor jabs.

"Don't you admire what Matt's doing for his country?"

Étienne gave her a startled look. "'Course I do, *chérie*. I just want what's best for him. And being gone from his family so long, it's not good for him."

"But it's his life. Maybe you should let him make the decision about what's good for him instead of judging him for the choices and the sacrifices he's made."

The Draicon looked over her head and grinned at Matt. "Found yourself a real wildcat of a wolf, huh?"

Sienna clenched her jaw. Wolf. He probably meant it as

a compliment, but it stung her. "I'm not a Draicon. I'm Fae. As for the wildcat…"

The image flashed through her mind, bursting out in a fiery flash. Sienna felt a power surge and surrendered to it.

The change came fast. Bones lengthened and fur covered her skin. Sitting on the seat, she uttered a low, barking grunt at Étienne and raked a hand over the dashboard.

"Holy *merde,*" he yelled.

Étienne slammed on the brakes, and the truck fishtailed. She cried out and Matt yelled, "Watch the road!"

Étienne barked out a rich curse and yanked the wheel toward the spin, expertly controlling the big vehicle. The truck slid close to the embankment, and stopped. Rubber burned her nostrils. For a moment the trio sat, engine running, the truck filled with the sound of their rapid breaths.

Sienna glanced down and froze.

She'd shifted into a black jaguar. Deep gouges scarred the leather dashboard from raking her claws over it. Glamour didn't do that. Glamour was an illusion.

Shivering, she groped for reality, and just as quickly shifted back into her human form, clothing and all.

"Sweet mercy," Matt said mildly. "I never knew you could do that."

Sienna stared at her outstretched hands. "Me, either."

"Damn it, wish one of you would have warned me. Can we stop with the Fae theatrics until we get home?" Étienne backed up onto the road.

"Fae don't shift into jaguars. Not Seelie Sidhe. They can only glamour, not shape-shift into something corporeal." Matt touched the gouges. "These are real."

Too badly shaken, Sienna said nothing. She kept staring at her hands, dread curling down her spine.

"If I didn't know better, I'd say that was another type of magick. But you're Fae so that's impossible," Étienne said.

Oh, the irony of those words. She and Matt exchanged glances.

"Maybe," Matt said softly. "But I'm starting to believe nothing is impossible."

Matt's sister was pretty, with a fall of rich blond hair and sparkling blue eyes. Cindy greeted Matt with affection and another tight hug. A pack of young children surrounded him with happy squeals.

After politely refusing a glass of lemonade, Sienna quietly went outside to the back porch, allowing Matt private time for the family reunion. She didn't belong here in this crowd of Draicon. She sat in a rocking chair, studying her hands, envisioning them turning into jaguar claws.

If anything, she should have shifted into a wolf because of her Draicon half. Maybe it was emerging and manifesting itself in another form.

One thing was clear. The longer she stayed with Matt, the more her Fae powers dwindled.

Wind ruffled her long hair. She gripped the arms of the chair. This was a bad idea. If not for his insistence on sticking together, she'd have bolted for home. Demanded answers from Chloe. How could her aunt, who'd treated Tim like family, have pushed her out of the colony, as if Sienna were a stranger?

Grief shattered her and she slumped forward, fighting the emotion. Couldn't allow these Draicon wolves to witness her loss of composure.

A bank of moss-covered magnolia and live oak trees marked the edge of a murky forest leading to the bayou. Matt had taken her along the path earlier, their footfalls crunching dry undergrowth. He'd thought the woods would prove soothing after the terrible images in the city.

She smiled a little. Such a considerate guy. For a wolf.

Matt came onto the porch, the worn boards not even creaking beneath his weight. He leaned against the railing, thumbs jammed into the waistband of his jeans. A hank of dark hair spilled over his forehead. He looked weary.

"Sorry, didn't mean to ignore you. They insisted on talking, giving me a proper welcome."

Gone was the confident, poised SEAL, replaced by a polite stranger who looked as uncomfortable as she did.

"Proper welcome?"

"A proper tongue lashing, more like it." He rubbed the back of his neck. "All the females, my sister, her sisters-in-law, my sister's mother-in-law, hell, I think they rounded up a posse to gang up on me and nag me about settling down."

"Call in for reinforcements."

He gave a slight smile. "They're on the same side. It's like fighting a war armed with water balloons."

The back door banged again and Étienne came out, looking slightly sheepish. "I apologize, Sienna. We Cajuns are usually more hospitable. Seeing Matt, well, he threw us for a loop. We seldom get a chance to see him…give him a…"

"Lecture," Matt said dryly.

Étienne punched his arm. "Man, I've had your back all these months you went AWOL on us, not even a postcard. Dealt with Cindy's moaning and worrying about you and then after what happened in Afghanistan…"

He sighed and sat on a chair, hands on his knees. "It's safe now. The females have said their piece and we can get down to business. Why are you here?"

Matt told him about the missing Orb of Light. Étienne's jaw hardened. He stared at the forest.

"The Astra Orb wasn't half as powerful as its twin, the Orb of Light. And when those demons got their hands on the Astra Orb…" He leaned forward, his blue gaze serious. "You know what will happen. How can I help?"

"Tell us where a Fae would hide the Orb. How can it be concealed?"

Étienne shook his head. "Your grandmother had hidden it for years. I only saw it when Cindy showed it to me."

Sienna shot Matt a disbelieving look. "Your family stole the Astra Orb?"

"My grandmother did. She did it to keep it safe from a rogue Fae." Matt turned his full attention on Étienne. "If the two globes are twins, then they can be hidden the same. How would you conceal it from demons? Ward it with magick?"

The Draicon rubbed his chin. "No. Warding magick is something demons can diffuse and easily find. The spectral traces would be like glow sticks in the dark. I'd shrink it. Make it smaller and less obvious. Blend it into something that a demon would have trouble flushing out."

"Hide it in plain sight," she suggested. "They'd be searching for a hiding place, so why not put it in the open, but disguised? Part of the human landscape, something a demon wouldn't even guess at. If I were Tim, that's what I'd have done. Use my powers to conceal it, but keep it close at hand."

Both men turned toward her. Étienne looking surprised, Matt thoughtful.

"This Fae, he wanted to meet with you after hours?" Étienne asked. "Then he wanted your help. He wanted to confess."

"But he knew they were watching him," Matt mused. "He kept insisting the Orb was safe now. Hidden."

"Oh, dear goddess," she rasped. "The purse. There has to be a clue on the purse where he hid the Orb. It must have something, some message he knew I could read."

A hard edge lined Matt's jaw. "No. Not a clue. The Orb is on the purse itself. That's why Tim said it was now safe."

Sienna raced back upstairs to the guest bedroom, retrieved the purse and came downstairs.

"The Orb of Light reacts to anything Fae. Try touching it," Étienne suggested. "If the Orb is concealed in the purse, it will glow."

She ran her hands over it, desperate to sense anything.

Nothing. No hidden runes, no spark of light.

Matt crouched down beside her. "Maybe there's too much Draicon influence here. Take it farther away from the house to a more natural setting."

They walked several yards from the house to a pretty garden filled with purple and yellow flowers. Sienna sat on a decorative bench in the center.

"Concentrate. You can do it," he encouraged. "Open all your senses. Smell the forest of your home, hear the sounds of the Fae gathering…remember…"

Energy pulsed beneath her questing fingertips. Closing her eyes, Sienna held the purse in her hands, willing her Fae senses to the surface. She opened herself to the images of the past.

A tingle raced through her fingertips. Heart racing fast, she concentrated. Words danced in her mind. Old Sidhe.

Then just as quickly, the images vanished.

Matt regarded her with a mixture of sympathy and disappointment. Sienna let the purse fall from her lap and rubbed her arms.

Tension knotted her stomach. "I have to return home. Reconnect with my Fae self. If the Orb is hidden in this purse, I'll find it."

If nothing else worked, the Fae could find the Orb. But the thought filled her with sudden dread. If she needed help to find how Tim concealed it, wouldn't that only prove she was just a half-breed?

Maybe she could never return home. The thought was so horrible, it put a heavy pressure on her chest.

He rubbed his jaw. "Not an option. Not now. Can't you take the purse to the woods, concentrate harder?"

Typical man. Concentrate harder. Go someplace else. Easy solution. Nothing was easy for her when it came to the Fae life. Not anymore.

"Look, this isn't like fixing a car," she grated out. "It's this house, this land, these people, you. Draicon all around me. Every moment I spend with Draicon, I lose my Fae powers."

"And yet you are half Draicon."

"A half I don't like to admit."

His jaw turned to stone. "Sienna, accept what you are. You keep denying your wolf half, your wolf magick. You can't deny what happened on the road. That wasn't Fae."

She couldn't, but neither could she embrace her Draicon half. If she did, it meant total and complete shunning from the colony. The thought of being alone, alienated and without a place to call home was unbearable.

An image came to her…the lonely, wild mountains of her home. Snow-dusted mountains, the eerie call of elk in the fall, the miles of rich forest. "You claim I'm denying my Draicon half, but what about you? You're a wolf. Yet you loathe being around your pack, and you don't shift much. I've never seen you exercise your magick. You rely more on that—" she jabbed a finger at the gun he wore "—than you do as a Draicon. Even around your family, you remain armed. You're more SEAL than wolf. Why, Matt?"

His jaw tensed to rock. White lined the edges of his mouth. He stood, brushing off the back of his jeans. "I'm going for a walk. Keep concentrating. Maybe if you keep acting like a Fae, not giving a damn about considering others, it will come to you."

Her stomach churned as she watched him storm off, a man in a leather jacket, weapon at his side. Then she blinked, and iridescent sparks shimmered.

No longer a man. Or a SEAL. A muscled gray timber wolf stood in his place. The wolf stood in proud silence for a moment, giving her a mocking grin. Then it loped off toward the forest, not looking back.

Lungs squeezed out each breath, the pads of his paws hitting the soft ground as he ran. Scents of squirrels and rabbits invaded his senses. Matt ignored them, the man screaming inside with every pounding heartbeat.

She was right, oh, damn, she was right. And it hurt to know the truth.

He'd turned his back on his family, on his heritage, on his damn powers! All because he was afraid.

Afraid of being what he was—a wolf. A wolf bonded to his family and pack. And with that kinship came heavy responsibilities.

He'd been reminded of them, several times, ever since setting a boot inside the Robichaux house. His mother, father. Cindy. Even the damn Robichaux parents. And Étienne, his main support.

They thought he was a regular SEAL. No one knew of the existence of the Phoenix Force. Being a Draicon and a SEAL had blended together so well, he'd never considered another life. Never thought the day would come when he'd have to face the haunting truth.

He couldn't be a SEAL forever. And settling down, mating and producing offspring…how could he stay in the military? It was one thing for humans, who faced their own challenges of bidding goodbye to wives, husbands and children when they served overseas.

For a Draicon, his loyalties would be always torn between duty to country and team and duty to family and pack.

Matt leaped and snapped at a dragonfly skirting the air.

For years, he'd served the teams in blissful ignorance, sticking close to the unit and substituting it for his Draicon pack.

Pressure to quit had been tempered with the knowledge Matt was saving lives and keeping their country safe from enemy operatives, both human and paranorm.

Now a different pressure hounded him.

Guilt.

It ate through him like acid. He'd accepted the fact he could die in the field, slain by a bullet or a blast from a demon. But he wrestled now with the knowledge that if he died as a SEAL, no one would remember him.

He'd become a wraith, like Adam. His memory would be Matt, the happy bachelor Draicon.

Dying in a car crash, maybe.

None of their team had ever died. Until Adam. And then the grim reality of their ghostlike existence had crashed down.

He needed the team. Needed to be a SEAL. But he needed something else, as well, and meeting Sienna, spending time with her, had brought it raging to the surface.

He cared for her. Hell, the night they'd fallen into each other's arms, and nearly made love…

Growling, he ran faster, heading down the worn path leading to the bayou. At the bayou's edge, he scented something sharp and unpleasant. His senses warned he wasn't alone. He lowered his head, sniffed the ground and began loping along the waterline, trying to flush out the unfamiliar scent threading through the normal swamp smells.

He scented a familiar male behind him. Matt ground to a halt, paws digging into the soft earth, and whirled, jaws snapping.

The large gray wolf behind him skidded to a stop. Black alpha markings lined its proud muzzle. It grinned, tongue lolling out.

Matt shifted into his human form, waving his hands and clothing himself by magick.

"Damn it, Étienne, you more than anyone else should know not to sneak up on me."

His brother-in-law shifted back, as well.

"I caught wind of something foreign. Slightly metallic, tinged with something burned. When did you last ward this land?"

"Last month. Shield is a little weaker here, doesn't hold as well because of the swamp water. Something about natural decay."

"Ever check for intruders?"

"Always." Étienne's gaze went dreamy. "But it's safe here. I brought Cindy here for a miniescape last week. That metal smell is probably the grill we used while we camped."

Matt raised a brow. "Camping?"

A twinkle sparked in his brother-in-law's eyes. "When you have kids, you'll see. You grab every opportunity you can to be alone with your mate. I'm fairly sure we made another one last week."

Children. Family. Gods. Sinking against the trunk of a maple tree, he sat. Étienne joined him.

"You always liked this trail. Good for a long run."

"I plan one tomorrow."

"Good. Get it out of your system. You know I'm talking about the woman."

He opened his mouth to deny it, saw his face. Nodded brusquely.

"She's got you in knots, and your balls in a vise. It's a great feeling, and it sucks at the same time." His brother-in-law picked up a decaying leaf. "It's not us, Matt. Not the females nagging you to settle down. It's her. Sienna. You're falling for her, hard and fast."

"Don't want to talk about it."

"Then let's talk about something else. The Orb. How are the demons using the intel?"

When Matt told him, Étienne crumbled the leaf. "The unit has to be protected at all costs, Matt. The demons had a taste of the Orb's power. They'll do anything to get the real deal. That Fae is a damn fool for thinking he could trick them."

"Was. The Fae paid with his life."

"Listen to me." His voice was low and urgent, a sharp contrast to the peaceful woods. "If you find the Orb, you know it's not over. You can't rely on the Fae to guard it."

"I know." Matt stretched his legs out. "Sienna thinks she's going to march it back to her people, and they're going to host a parade for her, and welcome her back. But my orders—"

"Are different." Étienne gave him a look far older than his years. "And she doesn't know."

"She won't know. She'll show it to her people, and regain her place in the colony, and then I'll destroy it. I also have orders to take her memories when we're finished. She won't remember anything…." He drew in a deep breath. "Even me. I'll be a total stranger."

"*Merde.* There's no way around it?"

"Not that I can see." His chest compressed at the thought of Sienna's shining face, her earnest expression, shadowed by fear as he went to wipe out all recollection of their time together….

Étienne clapped a hand on his shoulder. "Cheer up, man. You'll find a way. I know you. You're a stubborn SOB who never gives up."

But this time, he knew the cards were stacked against him. He didn't have a choice.

When the mission was over, Sienna would never know he existed.

I can't fall for her, he thought desperately. *We have to keep our distance.* Because he knew what would happen eventually. He wouldn't be part of her life ever again after he took her memories. It would be as if he'd died.

Without being in her life at all.

Chapter 8

Sienna didn't want to be part of a big, happy Draicon family. But the Robichaux clan, with their friendliness and warmth, left her no choice.

They'd pulled her into the kitchen to prepare a huge meal of crayfish and vegetables. When Cindy found out Sienna liked greens, she made Étienne dash to the market. Sienna had sat at the worn oak table, snapping fresh green beans while the children helped. More beans fell on the floor than into the bowl, but no one cared.

Matt's family was loud, argumentative, and the males arrogant and yet tender. She found herself softening toward them. They weren't aloof like her people, or ready to ostracize because of blood. They'd welcomed her, half Fae and all, into their home with open arms.

She'd hated the Draicon for so long, it was hard to admit the truth. The wolves were tight-knit and it felt more comfortable cracking beans in their kitchen than chanting spells around the firelight in the colony.

She fit in here.

At home, she did not.

The thought kept circulating in her mind as she slipped a long flannel nightgown over her head. Miserable, she curled up in the single bed allotted to her in the attic. Matt had crashed in Étienne's old room. It was as if the Robichaux family knew she needed space.

She refused to feel sorry for herself. Somehow, she'd find her place in the world. The most important thing was keeping the Orb safe. Her needs came second.

A soft sound across the hardwood floor made her go still. When the bedcovers rustled, she attacked.

"Ow!"

Snapping on the bedside light, she stared at Matt. Barefoot, dressed only in a pair of low-slung fleece pants, he rubbed his side where she'd slammed him.

"You carry a hard punch, Miss McClare. Remind me to give a warning next time."

His crooked grin sent a funny flip-flop through her stomach. "What's wrong?"

"Nothing. Came to check on you. I thought you might feel alone, all the way up here."

"Check on me by sliding into bed with me?"

Matt rubbed his rumpled hair. "Was checking to make sure you had enough blankets. Gets mean cold in the attic. Even if you sprinkle plenty of pixie dust around."

He looked so sexy, his arms layered with thick muscle, his gaze sharp with sexual need. Sienna's heart pounded. Need arrowed through her, sharp as glass.

"And I know this house, how it creaks." He glanced at her. "How uncomfortable you might feel, in a den of wolves."

The pride she'd worn slipped off like a silk robe. Sienna

looked deep inside herself and felt ashamed. She seldom apologized, but knew she'd hurt him earlier. "What you said about me being Fae, and Draicon, it's hard for me to admit I'm half wolf. And that was no reason to lash out at you. I'm sorry I made those jabs at you."

"It's true." He walked to the octagonal window. "You only said what's obvious to my family. They pointed it out, as well."

Ouch.

"So you shifted to prove me, and them, wrong. And ran."

"Yeah. It felt good, running as a wolf." A wry grin tugged his mouth to one side. "Hard to do on base. Might raise a few brows."

Moonlight glinted his inky dark hair, sharpened his profile. He looked aloof and distant, but she sensed a deep vulnerability.

Sienna threw back the bedcovers and stood. Her hips swayed gently as she closed the distance between them. Matt's eyes darkened, his breathing increased.

"You're the bravest wolf I've ever known. No, the bravest male I've ever known." She slid a hand over his cheek, feeling the warm skin, the slight bristles.

"I want you," he said softly. "But I don't want to hurt you, damn it. I can't…"

A protest lost beneath the pressure of her lips against his. He groaned and slid his arms around her, his arms solid and strong.

Matt slipped his tongue past her parted lips, stroking softly. Oh, the wolf knew how to kiss, knew how to push past all her defenses. All she could think of was his strong body holding her close, making her feel safe and warm and cherished. He was honorable and solid, and yanked down every single misconception she'd harbored against the Draicon.

He slipped lower, cupping her bottom as he dropped to his

knees, kissing the soft indentation of her belly, the arch of her hip. There was a magnetism about Matt, a barely leashed power in those gentle, exploring hands.

Backing her up to the bed, he let her fall onto the mattress, caging her between his arms. Her lower body flared with anticipation as he pushed her gown up past her waist. Cool air touched her skin. She felt wicked and hot, her skin too tight.

His hands caressed her with exquisite tenderness. Sienna parted her thighs as he settled his hips between them. She felt the hard edge of his erection, sensed the driving purpose in his deep, passionate kisses. Sighing, she opened her arms to him.

Intent flared in his blue gaze. He wanted her.

She wanted him equally, but doubts niggled their way inside.

If she surrendered to passion, she'd lose herself and everything she'd worked hard to attain. Making love with this Draicon would erase yet more of her Fae side. She had to stay focused and alert, not give into this intensely sexual pull.

When she pulled away, he made a frustrated sound and rolled away. On his back, arms laced behind his head, he stared at the ceiling. His body was taut, his erection straining.

"What's wrong, Sienna? Is it this place?"

She turned on her side, hot with unshed need, drinking in the sight of the layers of hard muscles beneath smooth sun-darkened skin.

"A little. I want you, Matt. Yet I'm scared."

It took a lot for her to admit the truth. He turned on his side, propping his head on a fist, his expression tender.

"Don't be scared, pixie. I'll take good care of you. Is it because it's your first time?"

Heat flooded her cheeks. "A little. I think it's more because I'm afraid of what will happen. Maybe releasing my wild side. Wolves get a little wild in bed, don't they?"

Matt caressed her cheek. "Yes. It's in our nature. But I'll be gentle, sweetheart. And you're half Draicon. It's only natural for you to release your wildness."

"Natural for a wolf. Not a Fae. We're rather…restrained."

"Why can't you embrace your wolf instead of running from it?"

"It's easy for you. You get up in the morning, face the mirror, know who you are. If we make love, you'll still have your identity. And me—" her voice trembled "—I'll feel more lost than ever."

"I'll never let you feel lost, starshine."

The deep velvet of his voice stroked over her sensitive skin. How easy it would be to lose herself in him, give herself over to making love and the hot pleasure promised in his touch. She wanted to believe him, but too many years of hatred and bitterness lay below the surface.

"You can't make a promise like that. No one can."

"Do you want me to leave?" he asked quietly.

She wanted him to leave, knowing it was best. But she wanted him to stay. The strange house, and the strange Draicon scents with their pull, calling her to surrender to her wolf half, made her lonely and a little afraid. Matt was familiar and she felt comfortable with him. Safe.

"Stay. Please. It's a little spooky up here alone."

"I'll stay. Because you asked."

He snapped off the light. In the moonlight he looked strong, certain and fearless. But she caught a hint of vulnerability in his eyes, in how he jammed a hand through his thick, dark hair.

Matt slid to the bed's edge, turning his back toward her. Sienna ached to hold him, to draw close. Gradually she closed her eyes.

She dreamed.

Ghostly gray images filtered through a layer of mist insubstantial as wraiths. A deep lake, mirroring a leaden sky, ice floating on the surface. Trees wreathed the water, their branches stripped and stretching out like beckoning arms. She sensed the flight of small animals from something dark and sinister.

She felt heat, intense heat smoldering below the partly frozen earth. Not warm and welcoming like a hearth, but dangerous and volcanic. Sienna looked down and saw an area just below her feet, the size of a shoe box, glowing red.

Fear rippled through her, but she had to know. Had to see. Driven by a powerful compulsion commanding her, against her will, she dug at the ground with her fingers. She knew what this was, what it did.

Claws erupted from her fingertips. Alarmed, she tried to stop, but could not. Sienna dug with the claws, ignoring the small pebbles cutting her fingers.

Beneath the earth, she saw what made it glow.

The glow intensified, sending out a white-hot flame straight at her heart. She tried crab-crawling back, but it burned her, exploding before her terrified eyes.

The fire, it was burning her, searing her...gripping her with ironlike arms in its hot embrace...

Sienna screamed.

"Wake up, sweetheart, you're dreaming!"

The smoky fog slowly cleared, the pain abated as she blinked rapidly. A nimbus of moonlight wreathed Matt's dark hair. Warm fingers curled around her upper arms, digging into her skin. Waves of concern flowed from him. His scent was sharp and tangy, and somehow reassuring and familiar.

Sienna gulped down air. Her skin was cold and clammy.

"Easy now. Just relax," he soothed.

All she wanted was the strong comfort of his embrace. Shaking wildly, her heart skittering against her chest, Sienna fell against him, her palm splayed against his broad chest.

"Hold me," she whispered. "Make it go away."

Laying a hand on her head, he tucked her against his shoulder and stroked her hair, softly crooning to her.

For several long moments, he simply held her, giving her the sheltering comfort of his strong embrace as if he could vanquish the fiery images. Sienna curled against him, her head pillowed on his shoulder.

"What was it, sweetheart? What scared you?"

Drowsy, feeling more secure, she rubbed her cheek against his naked shoulder. "Demons. They burned me."

Matt made soothing sounds, but a nagging memory tugged at her. She had the oddest feeling the nightmare wasn't only a dream.

But a memory.

Matt had nearly taken her. All night, her scent teased him, seduced his senses both as wolf and man. Took all his strength to resist rolling her over, lifting her flannel gown to slide his hand over warm female skin, teasing her senseless. Then pushing open her legs and thrusting into that heavenly, velvet warmth…

When he'd heard her scream, he'd bolted upright, his heart beating erratically. He'd soothed her back to sleep, gave her the comfort of his sheltering body, even though it was excruciating torment. Sienna had slept against him all night. Hell on his body, but she felt good in his arms. And it felt good to know she felt safe.

He'd have fought an army of demons to protect her.

Bare-chested, wearing only olive-green shorts, he stood on the porch. Gray light filtered through ridges of magnolia and oak. Inside, the family still slept.

Matt stretched, doing several lunges, making sure to warm up muscles that had tensed all night. Barefoot he stepped off the porch and headed for the forest.

Dewy grass slushed beneath him. He took the path in a steady pace, breath easing in and out of his lungs. Hard earth and decaying undergrowth crushed beneath his calloused soles. The call of birds in the trees overhead scolded him as he ran, the cool air sliding over his body.

He didn't break a sweat until he'd cleared the forest and hit the bayou. A fine mist hovered over the swamp, cypress trees stretching out their ghostly gray limbs. Knee-deep murky water sucked at him. Startled by his presence, a dragonfly resting on a lily pad flew off. Matt slogged through the muck, not afraid of gators.

He was a far more fierce predator.

When he'd gone four miles and turned back, sunlight warmed the land. It felt good, pushing his body. Punishing, he thought wryly as he headed into the forest.

The woods were oddly quiet. A scent of hot, sharp metal and something burning stung his nostrils, made his eyes water.

Panting, he stopped and scanned the land. This wasn't a trace of Étienne's cooking grill.

He followed the scent, pushing through undergrowth and a tangle of branches, until reaching a small clearing.

Ringed by oak trees, a small deer lay on the ground, its eyes staring blindly at the sullen sky. Dead. No hunters did this. The magick shield warded off humans and paranorms alike.

Until now.

Freshly killed, the deer lay like a sacrificial offering. Matt took a step forward, then stopped. He smelled nothing at first but the tangy scent of fresh meat. Then his well-trained Draicon senses detected the faint odor of metal.

About two yards from the kill the scent grew stronger. Matt squatted down, searching the ground. A glint beneath the leaves.

Carefully, he brushed away the undergrowth, exposing the source.

Trip wire. His breath hitched. He followed the wire to a nearby pine tree. The earth looked normal, but he sensed newly turned earth. Twigs and leaves covered the spot. With extreme care, he dug, the metallic odor burning his senses. A splinter pricked his finger, drawing a bead of blood. Matt kept digging.

About a foot down, he found it. Strapped to four cylinders with duct tape was a small board rigged with wires and a firing pin.

Gathering his powers about him like a blanket, he let his magick swirl in the air. Then he cursed.

A dull crimson glow surrounded the device in response to the iridescent sparks created by Matt's power. He saw the gears of the firing pin begin to move.

Gods.

Matt backed down his magick, willed it back into his body. The glow faded and the firing pin went back to neutral.

That was too damn close. He covered the device and backed away slowly. Then he turned and ran to the house.

The others were up, congregating in the kitchen, as Étienne sat on the porch, sipping a cup of hot coffee. The welcoming smell of chicory washed away the sting of metal as Matt leaped over the railing. "I found something in the woods. Fresh kill. Rigged to a little surprise."

"What?"

"Trip wire, rigged to a stack of C4. Unexploded ordnance, hidden by leaves, very carefully. The kill looked natural, nothing suspicious. Set up to lure someone to the UXO."

He wouldn't have found it if not for his training. Étienne's jaw hardened, his eyes growing steely. "This land is warded for miles."

"And something very powerful infiltrated just the same."

His brother-in-law pushed to his feet. "I'll gather the other males. Show us where you found the deer. Rafe can disarm the ordnance with magick…."

"Afraid not. It's got a web laced through it that reacts to anything magick. Diffusing it with magick will set it off. There's enough C4 to blow up half the swamp."

"Damn. Then we'll have to do it the old-fashioned way."

"I'll do it." Matt caught his arm. "Wait. Has anything unusual happened lately? Any dark magick, any hints of something unnatural? Like a rogue demon?"

Étienne shook his head. "Gabriel and his mate, Megan, stopped by a few days ago. They've cleared the city and the surrounding lands, and our lands, of all demons."

His guts churned. "Then they followed us."

"They?"

"Pyro demons."

From inside the kitchen came the insouciant laughter and talk accompanied by the clatter of plates, the smell of frying bacon and eggs. Étienne cut a worried look at the house. "Damn it, Matt. I can call Gabriel and Megan, they can flush them out."

"And they won't find anything. They're playing with me. The deer wasn't meant for me, or for Sienna. It was a direct threat to your family." Matt drew in a deep breath. "The kids. These demons thrive on pain and suffering, not merely for their pleasure, but to distract."

If one of the children had been killed, all Matt's defenses would drop. Guilt and grief made a bad combination and would make him vulnerable to a direct attack. He'd become a sitting target. The demons knew just how to trigger his buttons.

Blood drained from Étienne's face. He swore lowly, clenched his fists. "I'll kill the sons of bitches."

Matt squeezed his shoulder. "I'm sorry. The threat is here

only because I'm here. Once I leave, they'll have no reason to stay, especially since the element of surprise is gone."

"It makes no sense. Why the sneak attack? If they think you have the Orb, or know where it is, they'd come at you, guns blazing."

The realization hit him like a hard punch to his gut. "It's not just the Orb. It's personal. They want me to suffer first."

Étienne's blue eyes widened. "By targeting anyone close to you. And that pretty little Fae at your side…damn, Matt."

"She's a target, too." He dragged a hand through his hair, glancing upward where Sienna still slept. "I tried to send her back, but she wouldn't budge."

"Tough little Fae. Then you have to be on your guard even more."

"I will." Mat set his jaw. But he wondered about Étienne's advice.

Who did he have to guard himself against? Fire demons? Or Sienna herself?

Accompanied by male Draicon who scanned the surroundings as they loped into the forest in wolf form, Matt led the way to the ordnance. When they reached the small clearing, they shifted. Raphael, the immortal Kallan and death dealer, kept guard with his brother, Gabriel, father, Rémy, Matt's father and Steve, a Robichaux cousin.

Étienne accompanied Matt to the site. The small, box-like device sat firmly in the hole. Matt set his tool kit on the ground.

Étienne squatted down to examine it. "I can disarm it."

"And you're a father and will leave Cindy a widow if it blows. Stay back."

"Matt…"

He tensed. "Look, Étienne, let's not play macho wolf. You

and I know this is no regular unexploded ordnance. It's laced with magick."

"Which is why you need my help."

Both men looked up to see Sienna standing over them. Wearing formfitting jeans, a soft red sweater and a determined look, she crouched down. She'd scraped her long hair back into a ponytail.

"All the women are back at the house," Étienne snapped. "How the hell did you get here?"

Matt glanced to where the other males stood guard. One Robichaux cousin was missing.

"Glamour. Your cousin Steve is still snoozing in his bedroom. She took his place." Matt shook his head. "Get back, Sienna. This is too dangerous."

The long fall of her ponytail swung as she bent her head to stare at the ordnance. Sienna reached out to touch it. Matt grabbed her hand, his heart kicking hard against his ribs. Sweet goddess...

"Get back to the house," he ordered.

"C4 torch bomb."

Matt's skin went cold and clammy.

"How the hell did you know that?" Étienne demanded.

"I don't know. It seems part of the dream I had last night." She rubbed her forehead. "But I can help. Maybe it's a Fae ability I haven't discovered yet. Please, Matt, trust me."

All his wolf and SEAL instincts raged to send her back. Matt heaved a deep breath, wrestling with the primal need to keep her safe.

The Fae were mysterious and aloof. Her magick was twinned with the earth, and its natural forces. Sienna might be able to help.

A thin thread of trust hovered between them.

Matt closed his eyes and made up his mind. "Étienne, you, beyond those trees. Sienna, keep back one hundred feet. Talk to me from there. If this thing starts to glow, run like hell. I'll take the brunt."

A heavy flow of curse words in Cajun French from Étienne. Sienna looked upset. Not for herself, he realized.

"Don't you dare let anything happen to you," she said softly.

Matt took a deep breath, and slowly lifted the UXO out of the ground. He set it between his crossed legs, blood racing at the thought of it so close to his balls. Hell, if it went off, wouldn't matter what happened to the family jewels.

From her vantage point, Sienna dreamily stared at the device. Her gaze was distant and unfocused. "Detonator won't be obvious. They like to toy with their bombs and fool everyone. You have to unlearn everything you were taught, Matt. This isn't a regular bomb. Think pyro demon and what they thrive on. Pain. Suffering."

Her voice went flat. "This device is designed to burn you alive, not blow you to bits." Then she gulped and seemed to regain herself. "But that doesn't make sense. Won't it just blow up?"

Matt considered. "C4 is very stable, hell, soldiers in 'Nam used to burn it for fuel. You need applied force, energy, to set it off. This is a trip-wire bomb."

His expert gaze swept over the device. "Increasing the tension on the line sets off the bomb by releasing a spring-loaded firing pin. The pin triggers the strike, giving the device the energy needed to explode the C4."

"How would you disarm a trip-wire bomb?"

He rubbed his mouth. "Cut the wire, remove the detonator. But most military fuses have dual functions to make disarming them trickier to the enemy. You cut the wire, the tension decreases and sets off the firing pin."

"So you're toast either way?"

"Burned toast." His hard gaze met her worried one.

"But this isn't military, it's a simple trip-wire booby trap, relying on the hidden element to target the victim. I cut the line, and it gets disarmed. Except for the incendiary trigger. That's not military." Matt gestured to the cylinders of plastique strapped to the detonator. "In this case, the plastique provides fuel to the fire. Like the C4 the soldiers burned."

She scanned the ground, muttering, "Has to be here, something to keep the person trapped, prevent them from running. Regular bomb blows up, torch bomb burns. Flames shoot up, person would get burned, roll to douse the flames or jump in the swamp. Not effective."

Sienna shuffled the ground near the device. Metal, hot and sharp, stung his nostrils. Matt hissed and turned his head. "Don't move," he said quietly. "Étienne, get over here. Step sharp and bring a big stick."

The Draicon snapped off a thick overhanging tree limb. Étienne bent down and brushed aside some leaves, then poked them.

The sickening crunch and snap of metal followed. Sienna went pale. The trap's triangular teeth sank deep into the tree limb.

That could have been Sienna's leg, mangled and broken. He whistled out a breath, regaining his cool.

Sienna started toward him. Matt gave an almost imperceptible nod to Étienne, who caught her arm, holding her back.

Lines of tension bracketed her pink mouth. The delicate fragrance of her mixed in with the decaying leaves scattered on the ground.

Sulfur and acrid smoke burned his nostrils as he studied a tangle of multicolored wires. Matt spotted exactly what he'd suspected.

There. A groove cut into the detonator and a thin yellow wire. The firing pin created the initial explosion, fueling the

C4, concentrating the flames so they would shoot out like a blowtorch.

He needed to snip that wire first. Knew these sneaky SOBs. Could smell their stench all over the yellow fire, the one they'd handled, lacing it with demon magick to make the device ignite. Matt picked up the pliers.

Étienne gently pulled Sienna away. "Matt," she said thickly.

He looked up, gave a crooked grin. "Don't worry, pixie. I can do this."

Throat muscles worked in her slender neck as she swallowed. "I know you can. You're hot stuff. Just don't become... hot stuff."

He smiled.

Then she broke free, bent down and gave him a soft kiss. Her mouth felt like warm silk against the bristles on his cheek. "When you cut the wires...there is a chance it will burn, anyway. Because it's magick."

Matt gently tugged her ponytail. "I know. Go."

They retreated to the trees. Sweat trickled down his spine, pooled in the waistband of his shorts. Matt took the pliers, carefully pulled free the thinner yellow wire, separating it from the other wires. Heart pounding like a war drum, he cut.

Snip.

Following the trip wire as it led from the device, he carefully opened the pliers.

Snip.

The device began to glow crimson, pulse with supernatural energy. With preternatural speed, he jumped up, sped to the safe zone. "Rafe," he yelled. "Now! Destroy it!"

The handsome Kallan raised his hands, directed a burst of energy at the bomb. It shattered beneath the impact, crimson waves floating to the surface. Then the pieces fell, dissolving into ashes.

The ashes vanished, leaving behind only the man-made steel trap, which Raphael destroyed.

Matt heaved a sigh, as Sienna wiped sweat off her brow. Their gazes caught and met, his filled with cool relief, hers with shining joy. "You did it!" Sienna jumped up, her ponytail bouncing. She looked exotically lovely, her oval face etched in a wide smile, a spark in her green eyes.

"Because you helped me," he reminded her. "We're a team."

He caught her in his arms and swung her around. She felt good in his embrace, all warm female curves and soft skin. Giving into temptation, he buried his nose in the crook of her shoulder and inhaled her fragrance. Wondering how she'd taste beneath his tongue, the heady scent of her filling his nostrils as he parted her thighs oh-so-gently and put his mouth on her...

"You disarmed it. Great."

The musical voice was flat and cold. Matt glanced up to see Gabriel studying them with a cool look.

In fact, all the Robichaux clan was standing closer, their expressions a little too aloof for his liking. Hell, he'd just disarmed the UXO, and they acted as if he'd planted it there.

Not you. Sienna.

The thought flitted into his mind like mist. Matt lowered Sienna to the ground, kicked dirt over the hole.

"Interesting how you knew exactly what kind of bomb it was, Sienna." Hard speculation, not respect, shone in Étienne's gaze.

The same thought shot through his mind. How had Sienna known so much about this type of bomb? And what did that mean?

Sienna stared at her outstretched fingers. "I dreamed about it last night. I saw the bomb exactly as it was in the ground, saw them planting it, laughing as they rigged the detonator."

"Mighty convenient timing," Raphael drawled.

"Where were you last night, Miss McClare?" This from Rémy. Usually friendly, but the Robichaux Alpha was now demanding and arrogant.

Gabriel's nostrils flared, as if he were trying to scent a trace of demon on her body. They surrounded her, making her look small and defenseless. The pack mentality, banding together against an outside threat.

Enough of this. Matt slid a protective arm around her waist.

"Sienna's a guest here. We arrived together and I was with her all night. Lay off. Or do I have to remind you of that famous Cajun hospitality you've forgotten?"

The Robichaux males didn't lose their speculative looks. Sienna looked troubled as they headed back for the house. She glanced at him, moss-green gaze huge.

"Thanks. I thought for a minute they might snap off my head."

"They're just protective of their family, and wary."

And even though he knew they'd spent the night together, Matt had his own suspicions.

For a Fae who was terrified of pyro demons, she suddenly had plenty of knowledge about how they operated.

Chapter 9

Matt leaned his hands on the porch railing. He'd showered and changed into a gray polo shirt and khaki cargo pants. His broad shoulders tensed as he studied the children playing in the yard. On a lawn chair, a grim Étienne watched over them. The other male Draicon were in the forest, patrolling the land to ensure no demons slipped past their notice.

Even though he'd defended her, she could see the mistrust shadowing Matt's eyes. She was Fae, with a murky past.

He turned, folding his arms over his powerful chest. "I need to find out how the demon gained access to our land. How could it slip past the warding?"

Her gaze whipped to the yard. "Your brother-in-law seems to think I had something to do with it."

"Étienne has suspicions, because he's worried sick about his children. He'd strangle whatever demon planted that device. I would, too." A furious flush suffused his face. "They could have killed one of the kids. The bomb was planted last night, because I took that path yesterday and there was no trace of it, or the kill."

The fact made him pause. "They're targeting me. But how did they trace us?"

"Who else knows where we went besides your C.O. and Sam?"

"No one. Even they don't know our full itinerary. I've kept that on the q.t." He fished out his cell phone. "I'm calling Shay."

She walked off to give him privacy. When she returned, he looked speculative. Hard.

"Tell me about your dream last night. You said it was connected to how you knew how to diffuse the bomb."

Her fingers curled around the post, feeling the solid wood. Strong and sturdy, like Matt. Pulse skittering, she watched him withdraw a knife from a sheath on his waist. The tip of the blade dug into the railing's worn wood. Bits and pieces flew as he traced a carving.

"I don't even know if it was a dream. Maybe a lost memory."

Sharp and cold, his gaze swept over her. "You're telling me you've diffused incendiary devices planted by pyro demons?"

She felt frustrated by the black hole in her memory. "I don't know. I wish I did! All I know is the dream felt so real, as if I'd been there before." She could still smell the scent of burning earth, hear the hiss of the flame as it spewed out, taste the charred ashes.

The knife sank deep into the railing, quivered there a minute. After jerking the knife free, he turned, muscles flexing smoothly beneath his jeans and tight shirt. "Been there before? As in helping a demon plant a bomb? Level with me, Sienna."

Sienna's heart lurched. He looked cool and lethal, a man

who could kiss you one minute and break your neck a minute later if you crossed him.

She suddenly felt very small and defensive. Sienna threw her hands out.

"It was a dream, but it felt so real. I can't explain. I know how this looks. But, Matt, I'd never plant a bomb, no matter how I felt about Draicon wolves. That's not me. I would never hurt your family, certainly not risk your nieces and nephews." Sienna bit her lower lip. "You've got to believe me."

Because no one else does.

But why should he trust her? He was a wolf and wolves stuck together. They were a pack, loyal to the core, and distrusted outsiders, just as Fae did.

Matt glanced at the other males who'd returned from the forest. Gathered on the lawn, they aimed her sullen looks. Emotion knotted her throat. The Robichaux family had aligned against her. Oh, the women were still friendly, but she'd seen their uneasy glances.

"Please, Matt. I'm telling the truth."

A heartbeat of silence quivered between them. Then he turned his back to the males. "I believe you. I don't know what's going on, but I believe in you."

Relief rushed through her. She felt giddy from it. "For a moment, I thought you would throw me to the wolves. Or the demons."

"My family is just being protective of their own. As for the demons…" A flash of sharp canine showed as his upper lip pulled back. "The pyro demons aren't getting past me and getting to you or anyone else."

The SEAL looked ready to take on a whole legion of demons. Not just for his family, but for her, the stranger, from a race he distrusted. Overwhelmed, she pressed her hands against his chest, feeling the steady beat of his heart.

"Thanks for sticking up for me," she whispered.

Sienna stood on tiptoe, meaning to kiss him in thanks. She slid her arms around his neck, and the kiss turned urgent and demanding.

Matt wrapped his arms around her, crushing her against his chest. So solid and firm, he smelled delicious, pine mixed with his own spicy maleness. Rough bristles slightly abraded her cheeks as he slowed the pace, lazily kissing her as if they had all the time in the world. She breathed in his scent, dragging it into her lungs.

When she broke the kiss, he smiled down at her, his gaze filled with erotic heat. He pushed a hand through her hair, the touch leaving a sizzling current in its wake.

Sienna traced a line over his wet, firm mouth. He was so different from anyone she'd ever known, a wolf who aroused her with touch, his scent so spicy and enticing…

Scent. "The demon, why didn't it leave a scent? It left a scent in the witch's house."

Interest flared in his eyes. "You noticed. Your wolf half must be emerging. Demons can easily cover their scent, especially in open, natural areas like the bayou."

"Sometimes I wonder which half of me is Draicon."

"The better half," he teased, tweaking her ponytail. "Have breakfast with me."

"Sprouts and green beans?"

He playfully tugged her ponytail again. "Breakfast in the kitchen, not the pasture. Real food. Bacon, eggs, sausage." Warm breath lifted a stray lock of hair as he bent close. "It's what wolves eat. And you, pixie, are half wolf."

A fact she could never live down. Or ever forget. Because back home, her family would never allow her to forget.

The realization saddened her. Even if—no, *when*—she brought them back the Orb, they'd still regard her with suspicion. Always wonder when the wildness would emerge, the beast would claw its way to the surface.

Matt had a home and a loving, bossy family.

Sienna wondered if she could ever have the same. Because right now, she wasn't certain where she fit in.

Anywhere.

A hot shower helped cleanse Sienna's confused emotions.

Sienna felt hopeful for the first time in years. Last night's dream indicated her long-buried memories were awakening.

But once she returned to the Fae, Matt would erase her memory of these past few days.

The Robichaux males were downstairs, discussing how pyro demons could have gained access to their powerfully warded land. She wanted to join their tight group. Show them there was nothing to distrust about a mixed breed. Prove she didn't have anything to do with the bomb. Maybe she could help them discover how it was planted.

A twist of gray Spanish moss lay on the pine bureau. She picked it up, cradling it in her palms. It had covered the bomb and Matt had taken it to try to track the demon down, though it proved fruitless.

It was time to try testing her full powers. The Fae could glean memories from the earth, using the energy the land emitted. From an early age, her aunt had taught her how to "read" an aura. "Anyone can do it," Chloe had insisted. "We Fae are more centered with the earth, so it comes more naturally to us."

Sienna closed her eyes, seeing the booby trap as she had in her nightmare. Feeling the crisp edges of the fallen moss, smelling the dank earthiness of the bayou.

The ugly demon planting it, eager to wreak havoc. Only this time, the murky swamp was a clear, mirrored lake, the sky overhead a sullen winter gray. Icy cold stung her bare skin as she watched the demon laugh.

The scenery felt familiar, looked familiar.

*Study the enemy. Get to know him as intimately as you
know yourself. What drives him?*

Matt's words echoed through her mind. Remembering the
mottled gray flesh of the demon who'd tried burning them in
the witch's house, she concentrated.

Sand in her lungs, burning sand. So many tiny granules.
Once she'd been powerful and feared. Now, a dry dust of
herself. No one remembered her, no one cared. She was dust
on the wind, part of the rocky, pebbled earth that blew red
against the sun.

Hungry, so hungry, craving fear, needing it to feed. Even
though her throat was parched, she managed to take form.
The form was wizened, barely enough to take shape and
blend. But she blended, dredging up every last droplet of energy to mingle with those who hated and killed. The killing
was good; it felt wonderful, feeding on the blood and fear.

Stronger now. Hatred boiled inside her, driven to hurt and
score flesh, burn those who'd imprisoned her, the paranorms
who thought they were invincible. She was the invincible one.
Track the SEAL to his home ground. She felt a mix of rage
and cold, lethal purpose. And then, as she sped through the
air on a warm wind, she felt herself being stopped by a cold,
invisible barrier, like a giant hand. Magick. The land was
shielded. Frustration glowed inside her, feeding the rage as
she bounced along the magick wall.

Near the swamp, she sensed a weakness where magick of
the Draicon flowed into the dark, natural magick of the murky
bayou. Natural magick. Natural…like smoke.

There.

A low, harsh cackle, like the screech of a banshee on
the night wind, came from her throat. She would burn, and
burn….

Sienna's eyes flew open. She gulped air, shivering at the
nasty images swirling in her mind. Talk about getting into

form…this kind of pure concentration, absorbing the mindset of the enemy, was dangerous. But here in the attic room, with the bright blue-and-white quilt covering the bed and the sprigged rose wallpaper reflecting the sunshine flooding the room, it didn't feel real.

Excitement surged. She knew what had happened. Sharing it with the Robichauxs would surely help defray suspicion from her. Sienna didn't know why she felt this was important, but she was going with her instincts.

She walked down the staircase, feeling hungry, starving almost. The hunger was almost a living thing, demanding and growling.

Her muscles felt weaker as well as she clambered down the steps.

Hearing the sounds of laughter and deep male drawls, she brightened. Wait until she told them what she'd learned. No, maybe it could wait until after breakfast. She was starving.

The hunger intensified. Her fingers itched, burned a little.

Power flowed through her, hot, dark and sweet, magick that stank of sulfur and yet tasted delicious in her mouth. A little scared, she hit the landing, holding her hands out.

Horror arrowed through her. The once-elegant fingers with their neatly pared nails, were long and spindly. Blood raced through her veins, hot and pulsing with magick.

This isn't me, she thought desperately. *What have I done?*

At the landing, she saw a mirror next to a bright red umbrella stand. Sienna raced to it, staring in dumbstruck astonishment.

A grimace stretched the red slash of a mouth. Her nostrils were flat holes, her skin gray and sickly. Burning crimson replaced the forest green of eyes that once sparkled. Now those eyes burned with hate.

Ugliness settled in her body, creeping through her like sludge, thick and vicious and nasty.

Someone help me. Please.

No Fae magick could fix this glamour. It had sunk its claws into her skin, refused to leave. She needed real power. Draicon magick.

Matt.

Sienna crept down the hallway, peeked into the living room. Matt's family sat in comfortable armchairs or sprawled on the carpet, talking and laughing loudly. All but Matt. He stood alone by the window, hands shoved into the pockets of his jeans. In a room filled with family, he stood alone. Solitary. His indifferent manner was a suit of armor, but beneath, she glimpsed a sense of bleakness.

He was part of them, yet not one of them.

The urge to kill, watch him burn, became overwhelming. With every ounce of strength, Sienna fought it.

I am Seelie Sidhe Fae.

But the rage burned deep inside. Ashamed, terrified, she raced into the living room.

"Matt," she cried out. "Help me."

Then a guttural grunt fled her lips.

Cindy glanced up. She screamed, grabbing her children, covering them with her body.

Sienna stretched out her hands in a plea. They glowed red, the tips flaming bright like lit matches.

Her quick reflexes helped her dodge the energy bolt Gabriel suddenly tossed. The males pushed to their feet, shifting into wolves. Teeth bared, growling, they advanced. All but Matt, who'd turned from the window.

Kill them now. Make them suffer. Make them scream.

No. Never.

"Stop it, guys," Matt said quietly, the tone of a man accustomed to command. "It's not a pyro demon. There's no way a pyro demon would ask me for help."

He held a hand out, keeping the snarling wolves at bay, and looked deep into her eyes.

"Sienna?"

A low cackle tore from her throat, a screech of nails over glass. The wolves whined in pain, but kept advancing as the women fled with the children.

"Sienna. Change back for me." Urgency laced Matt's voice. "They can't see anyone but a pyro demon. C'mon, little pixie, you can do it."

His voice was deep and soothing, a rope of sanity. Sienna grabbled for that rope, trying to recover who she was, what she was.

You don't even know what the hell you are, a nasty voice echoed. *Maybe you are truly a demon.*

"You're half Draicon. Look at the wolves. They're part of you, Sienna. Part of the Draicon deep inside. Shift into wolf. You can do it."

Uncertainty held her back, but she dropped her glowing fingers, the talons sharp as razor wire and glowing hot.

Footsteps, hard and fast. She glanced up, felt her blood race with terror. Raphael, the immortal Draicon Kallan. Death dealer. Remembering how he'd blasted the defunct bomb with a single hand wave, she shrank back. The cold expression told her he wanted to do the same with her. But he held his ground. Raphael glanced at Matt.

"She's not a pyro demon."

"Yet she terrified our women." Raphael's voice was soft, laced with threat.

"Back off, Rafe." Matt gave the order as if the immortal wasn't a powerful being who could kill with a single glance. But the Kallan stepped back, his cold gaze never leaving Sienna.

Matt gave her a gentle smile. "Sienna. Trust me. Look at me. Part of you is just like me, wolf. Feel the wildness of nature, the scent of the earth, the joy of bounding over forest and field. You can do it."

Taking a tentative step toward him, she hung on to his words as he kept talking. The wolves backed off, their wary gazes trained on her.

Slowly, the fragrance of freshly cut grass and the feel of a cool mountain breeze against her skin overrode the stench of sulfur and the acrid hatred. Sienna closed her eyes, seeing her forest home, a quiet lake, hearing the joyful howls of pack.

When her eyes opened, she stood on four paws, tail lowered, the scents of Draicon flooding her nostrils. Matt crouched down, stroked her head.

"I knew you could do it. That's my pixie."

Willing her exhausted body to change, she took on human form, clothing herself. On all fours, her face cupped by Matt's gentle hand, his blue eyes filled with concern.

The other males shifted back, their expressions furious, their concern for the women in the kitchen, protecting the children.

"I'm sorry," she told them, her voice hoarse, her throat dry. "I don't know what happened."

Silence thick and piercing, quivering in the air. Finally Raphael, the immortal, spoke.

"It's best you leave, Sienna. Now."

The curt dismissal shouldn't have cut so deeply, but she felt it like a slash against her chilled skin.

"I'll make the arrangements." Matt looked resolute.

Sienna struggled to her feet. He gripped her arms, his calloused fingers gentle.

"I'm sorry, Matt." Étienne looked uneasy. "But I won't risk Cindy and the kids."

He shot his brother-in-law a fierce look. "She's not dangerous."

The Draicon wolves lined up against them, like a firing squad. His family. She'd done this, put a barrier between them.

"I can find a place on my own. A hotel room, until we leave New Orleans," she began.

"We'll leave together." A firm statement, his glare directed at the men. "Better look after the women."

When the men had gone into the kitchen, Sienna exhaled. The pall of sheer anger hung in the air, clogging her throat, squeezing air from her lungs.

Matt looked down at her, his expression softened.

"I never meant to come between you and your family."

He trailed a finger down her cheek. "Forget about it. Now I don't have to suffer their nagging anymore."

"I don't know what happened. I was upstairs, thinking about the demon we'd faced in the witch's house. Trying to get into his mind. You know, trying to see his motives, what he wanted when he'd fled his sand prison. Next thing I knew…"

Stretching out her hands, seeing the pink flesh, she shivered. "I never intended to become one. That's not the type of glamour I ever want to assume."

"A very realistic glamour. Enough to convince several powerful male Draicon, including a demon hunter." Matt stroked her bare arms, sending a different heat surging through her body. A welcoming heat, like a fire burning merrily in a hearth.

Not the cold, dead hatred conjured by the demon whose form she'd assumed.

She collapsed onto the sofa. Matt disappeared into the adjoining kitchen, returned with a glass filled with water. Grateful, she gulped it, relishing the liquid easing her parched throat.

"This proves you're really Sienna. The preferred drink of pyro demons is gasoline, or flaming apricot brandy as an after-dinner cocktail."

The light teasing didn't lift the chill from her shaking shoulders. The glass rattled against the wood coffee table as she set it down.

"What am I, Matt? Fae can glamour and I'm the best, but not like this. Not…" She gulped down a breath. "Not something evil. When I walked into the living room, I saw the children and all I felt was…need. I wanted to hurt them. I couldn't help it. My fingers itched to shoot flames at them."

Settling beside her, he cupped her cheek. His palm was warm and rough against her icy skin.

"You're Sienna McClare. Half Draicon, half Fae. A woman of extraordinary ability who would hurt herself before laying a hand on an innocent. Especially a child."

"Then explain what happened, because everyone in that kitchen is thinking I'm dangerous."

"What do you think happened?"

She blew out a frustrated breath. "I don't know! All I know is I felt consumed by the images I conjured. It wasn't a mere glamour, but as if I were possessed by what I desired to understand."

Matt gave her a steady look. "Possessed. Like an actress so consumed by her role, she becomes the character she portrays."

Sienna sank against an embroidered cushion. "Exactly."

"But you became wolf. Because deep down, it's the heart of you. A part you've refused to acknowledge and pushed aside. It's your safe zone, Sienna."

The blue of his gaze was warm and understanding.

She didn't want to be wolf. Not a creature with fangs that tore and killed. A kaleidoscope of violent images flashed through her mind, colors swirling, inky dark blood pooling on the ground, thick and viscous. Nothing natural, only a brutal malevolence that sought to maim and kill.

"I know how the demon gained access to your land." She

glanced at the portrait of the proud wolf over the fireplace mantel. "That's what I was rushing to tell everyone."

Matt looked interested. "Go on."

"I concentrated, saw the form of the demon, and dove into his mind." Digging into her jeans pocket, she withdrew a few crumbles of the dead moss. "This is the moss you took from the bomb site to try to track the demon. I used the moss to connect to his thoughts. His memories. Connecting with the residual energy, something the Fae taught me. But this..."

Troubled, she tossed down the moss. "I turned into a demon, Matt. Not glamour. It didn't feel like glamour. It felt real. Why is that? What's happening to me?"

His touch was soothing and calmed her jagged nerves. "I don't know. But we'll find out, eventually. The important thing is, you connected with your wolf when you needed it most."

That knowledge disturbed her, too. She was Fae. Why couldn't she shift back into her Fae form? Was it the Draicon influence of the Robichaux den?

It wasn't important now. Other priorities mattered more.

"He knew how to find your family, Matt, knew you would come here because they'd gained information from the Orb."

Skin drawn tight over harsh cheekbones, he nodded. "Go on."

So calm and collected. But cold fury burned in his blue eyes. Sienna gathered her strength.

"Tim didn't just give out information about you and Adam being SEALs." Emotion clogged her throat. "When I became the demon, I got into his mind, how he operates. And I realized what happened. Tim must have given the witch all your personal information, as well."

Muscles went rigid, his hands clenched into fists as if Matt wanted to pound someone. But his voice was calm. "How did the demon break the warding around this land?"

Sienna rubbed her hands on her jeans, trying to erase her revulsion. "He tested the shield. Found a weak spot by the bayou, the edge of the Robichaux territory. The swamp is diffuse with life and dark magick. You can sneak in using a natural element. He came into the land by setting a small fire and then dousing it when he gained access."

Tensing, he braced his hands on the railing. He looked angry enough to race into the woods and beat the demon to a pulp.

"They want me. Targeted me in Afghanistan. Now they're targeting me here. Threatening my family." He turned, brushed a finger down her cheek. "And you. Not on my watch. I'd let them cut out my heart before I'd let that happen."

"A little drastic, don't you think?"

A wan smile, steely purpose in those eyes. "Go upstairs, pack your things."

Anxiety churned in her stomach. Sienna lifted her chin, refusing to show her fear. "I'll move out right away. Just point me toward a hotel. I even have my own credit card. I may be a hybrid, but hey, I've got a great credit score."

He gave a gentle smile. "I'm taking you with me to the French Quarter. And you'll be safer there. Here, you're a moving target."

"What about your family? Can't they help?"

A terrible bleakness shadowed his face. "You heard Rafe. I'm on my own."

She pressed the flat of her palm against his chest and felt his heart beat solid and steady. He was a tower of strength, and yet she sensed the vulnerability. Here, among his family, he, too, felt like a stranger.

"You're not. I'm here."

Matt picked up her hand, brushed a kiss on her knuckles. "I want you safe, Sienna."

"I can take care of myself. If I run into a demon, I'll just kick him in the groin. Or glamour myself as a fire extinguisher."

"I'd rather you glamoured yourself into a fireproof safe. I'd teach you to use a gun, but guns don't work with these bast…sorry, these guys."

A faint blush reddened his sun-kissed cheeks. Matt looked like an adorable, abashed schoolboy caught smoking in the boys' room. She found his old-fashioned courtesy charming.

On impulse, she kissed him. His mouth was warm and firm beneath hers. Matt framed her face with his large hands and deepened the kiss, his tongue plunging into her mouth. Delicious heat curled through her body, pulsing between her legs. He groaned and pulled himself away, his body rock hard, his eyes dark and gleaming.

"Whoa. Watch it, little pixie," he murmured. "Keep that up and I'll lock you in my bedroom instead of that fireproof safe. Nothing between us but bare skin, my mouth tasting you…all over."

The hot throbbing increased beneath his heavy-lidded gaze. Sienna tried to control her breathing, set her desire on a back burner. "Where are we staying?"

He traced her lower lip, heat filling his gaze. "A place in the Quarter, an apartment called the Dubois Arms. We were going there today to meet a contact. We'll crash there, fly out tomorrow. To your cabin."

"Who are we meeting?" Sienna leaned into his touch.

Matt pressed a finger against her lips. "Secret."

"Tell me, wolf. We're in this together, remember?"

"Shay. Quick briefing." Desire surged, hot and thick, as she rubbed her lips against his finger, her gaze heavy-lidded. "Don't do that, pixie. No matter how much my family scowls at me, you'll delay our departure by tempting me to take you upstairs." Footsteps sounded, and he stepped back.

Cindy came into the living room, her eyes red-rimmed. She'd been crying, and it broke his heart.

"Hey, sis," he said softly. "It's okay. I understand. Don't worry."

She crossed the distance between them, glanced at Sienna with an apologetic look. "I can't help but worry about you. You're my brother. You're a SEAL. And now, this thing you're battling…"

His sister's lovely blue eyes clouded. "I know how powerful the Astra Orb was, Matt. You're fighting demons. I wish I could help."

"We'll be fine," he assured her.

Her gaze darted to Sienna, and she offered a tremulous smile. Cindy stuck out a slim palm. "I wish we'd had more time to get to know each other. I'm glad Matt found someone, finally."

As she shook hands, Sienna opened her mouth as if to protest, but Cindy shook her head. "I know. You're in a state of denial now. But in time, you'll see. And please know this, no matter what they say…" She rolled her eyes as she glanced over her shoulder. "Despite that their DNA tells them we females can't protect ourselves, those overprotective males need to accept that you are always welcome in our home."

Sienna flashed a grateful smile. "Thank you."

"If you need our help, Sienna, we're here for you."

Gratitude swelled inside Matt. He encircled his beloved sister in his arms, gave her a tight hug. "Thanks, sis."

Cindy kissed his cheek. "Take good care of yourself, Matt. And her."

As she left the living room, Sienna gave a real smile. "I guess I'd better go pack. I like your sister. I like her a lot."

He watched her run upstairs, admiring the curve of her strong legs. Scenting someone familiar behind him. Matt clamped down his temper.

"Nice of you to stick up for me."

"Don't start on me. Cindy already did. But I have a family to protect."

"And Sienna's not dangerous. You dislike her because she's not one of us. She's Fae and you think Fae are devious and self-absorbed." Matt turned and faced his friend, the man who'd urged him to join the navy and undergo the rigorous BUD/S training to become a SEAL. The man he'd trusted above all others.

Who did not trust the woman he was starting to care for.

Wisdom filled Étienne's gaze. "What about the reason you gave for loathing the Fae, Matt? Now you've changed your mind?"

Damn. "She's not fully Fae. She's half Draicon, as well. She's…"

Different. Fascinating. Complex and funny, and tough. Matt's heart gave a funny jump.

"I told you, she's got you in knots."

"I can take care of myself."

"I know you can. But be careful, Matt," Étienne said softly. "She's shown us she definitely is not what she seems. That's mighty powerful magick. She wants the Orb, too. So watch your back, because in the middle of the night, you might find a knife sticking out of it."

Chapter 10

The apartment complex was in the French Quarter near Jackson Square. Iron latticework grilles adorned the picturesque balconies lining the cobblestoned street. Sienna looked up with wary resignation.

"Terrific. Iron. If the demons don't get to me, the iron decor will."

"Don't touch it. Stay by my side."

He pressed a worn brass button set on the gate below. The door opened soundlessly. Matt pushed it in. The wood steps creaked beneath their footsteps, and dust motes floated in the streaks of sunshine glinting the watery glass windows. The air was musty and she caught a faint scent of mildew. If anyone did live here, they seldom used the quarters.

On the second floor, a faded Oriental carpet lined the dimly lit hallway. Matt produced a key from his pocket, and unlocked the door that read Apartment 666.

The door opened to a small apartment, a kitchen squeezed

into a former closet. A small faded blue rug covered the scuffed hardwood floor. Faded but serviceable furniture sat near a wood coffin that served as a coffee table.

"Where's Shay? In the coffin?" she quipped.

"Not here yet. We're early. Under the circumstances, I thought it best to leave as quickly as possible."

Because of her and the tension she'd created. Sienna felt a sharp stab of regret. "I'm sorry. I didn't mean to create friction between you and your family."

Something flickered in his eyes she'd never seen before, as if a barrier had dropped between them. "Hey, it's not your fault." Matt touched her nose playfully. "I needed a good reason to escape them, anyway."

"They're your family. You don't like being around them?" Gods, she'd give anything to have a tight-knit group who cared about her welfare.

"I love them, but they don't understand the life I've chosen with the teams. Why I want to remain a SEAL. They're all about pack and pack loyalty."

"And your loyalty is to your team and duty. You're different." She was beginning to understand his fierce devotion and the isolation he felt.

A silent communion flared between them, as if they were bonded together in the moment. Sienna knew with complete certainty that Matt had known the deep loneliness she'd felt.

She reached out and laced her fingers with his. He looked startled a moment at the contact, then his heavy-lidded gaze met hers.

A brief knock pulled them apart. Matt glanced up, his expression puzzled.

"Shay?"

A man shuffled inside, wearing jeans and a red-and-orange Hawaiian shirt. He closed the door with a firm click and locked it.

Sienna aimed him a genuine smile. "Hi, Sam."

"Hey." The SEAL grinned, and jammed his hands into his pockets. "So sweet to see you again, Sienna. You're looking mighty fine."

He kept staring at Sienna worshipfully. And ignored Matt, who was watching him with narrowed eyes.

"Shay."

The Mage blinked. "Oh, yeah. What's up?"

Matt gave his teammate a long, thoughtful look. "Check the coffin lately?"

"What's in there, a vampire?" Sienna asked.

"Better. It's our goodie box," Matt said.

Sam opened the heavy black lid. Inside were enough weapons to outfit a small army of vampires. Sienna's blood went cold. She knelt down, touched the blue steel of a gun that looked powerful enough to take out an elephant.

But not a pyro demon.

"Wouldn't happen to have a fire extinguisher in here? Because none of this will work." Sienna sat back on her haunches, rubbing her hands on her faded jeans.

Sam laughed as he fished out a lethal-looking submachine gun. "Don't worry your pretty little head about details. Leave it to us men."

His patronizing tone accompanied another worshipful stare. Matt closed the coffin lid.

"We should move these out to a safer location. Did you bring the fire extinguishers?"

"Nope, but I know where I can get a water pistol." Sam winked at her.

"Inventory all the weapons and move them back to base. I don't want them falling into the wrong hands," Matt ordered.

Then the SEAL blinked. It was so quick, she might have blamed her imagination. Sienna's blood froze in her veins.

"Maybe we should leave for a bit, Matt, while Sam takes inventory. Get a bite to eat. Because I am awfully hungry."

Sienna dug her nails into her palms, desperately hoping Matt would understand.

Running a finger along the coffin, Matt considered the cache. He glanced up at Sam and suddenly went still. Sienna took a step back at the chilled look on his face. If he looked at her like that, she'd turn and run away as fast as she could.

"Been working out lately, Shay? How much did you bench-press? What was it last time, two hundred pounds?"

Sam looked wary. "Around that. More like three hundred. I like variety, Matt."

"I do, too. But not with my closest friends. Sienna, get back."

Shuffling backward, she watched the two SEALs face off like sparring partners. Sam gave a small, ugly smile, ruining the handsome contours of his face. He had the fine-tuned muscle of a long-distance runner, while Matt was taller with more bulk. But none of that mattered. Not in this kind of fight. Matt unsheathed the knife at his ankle.

"What the hell are you doing, Matt?"

The SEAL's voice became thinner, high-pitched. Matt held his ground.

"Shay stopped bench-pressing three hundred pounds last year when he got shot in the shoulder. And he never, ever calls me Matt."

With a virulent hiss, Sam shifted. His body became taller and longer, the sandy-brown hair parted down the middle turning white-blond. Hazel eyes turned dark, cold gray.

Sienna's breath caught. Darksider Fae.

"Fucking bastard. You're going to die. I can make it quick and painless. But when my masters get here—" he gave an icy smile "—you'll fry."

The Fae pointed the weapon at Matt, pressed the trigger. Nothing happened. Cursing, he checked the gun.

"Never bring a gun to a knife fight," Matt drawled. "Especially when it's unloaded. We never leave loaded weapons in the apartment in case someone breaks inside."

The Fae dropped the gun and dematerialized. Sienna ran for the door as the Fae teleported, but he caught her from behind, wrapping a sinewy arm around her throat. Desperate for air, she gasped, but the Fae dug sharp claws into her throat. She fought against panic, struggling to draw a breath as he squeezed.

"Where is it? Tell me where the Orb is and perhaps I'll let you live."

"Orb?" She choked out. "I'm more the crystal-ball type."

"Bitch. Ever feel the insides of your organs cook slowly? My master will make them boil. I'll make you scream and beg to die."

"I'm begging you now," she wheezed. "Shut up. Your breath smells real bad."

The Fae raised its hand. "Your eyes go first."

He released a loud shriek. Blood splattered as Matt sank the knife deep into its back. Sienna twisted hard, shoved her elbow into its soft, concave stomach and broke free.

Like an avenging angel, Matt stood over the Fae writhing on the floor. He withdrew the knife. Blood coated the black blade.

"Sienna, get out," he ordered harshly.

"Matt…"

"Now."

The cold look in his eyes did it. She left the apartment, sinking down to the floor in the hallway and hugging her knees.

Low murmurs came from inside, and then the Darksider Fae screamed. Sienna squeezed her eyes shut. She didn't want to think about what was happening. It was ugly, but necessary. She wondered how it affected him, and if each time something like this happened, Matt lost a little piece of his soul.

His family could help him decompress and regain himself. But he was isolated from them.

Did either one of them truly belong anywhere?

The door opened. Matt leaned against the jamb. He looked tired. Red splattered over his clothing.

"Is he…?"

A rough nod. "He shifted back into Shay. In the end, it almost felt like dispatching my teammate."

Dear gods. She imagined the terrible moment he'd faced.

"You okay?" she asked softly.

Matt gave a wry smile. "I've had worse. Give me a few. I need to rinse off."

After he'd showered and changed clothing, he joined her on the living room sofa. The Darksider Fae was gone, his body disintegrated into ash.

"He told me his 'masters' knew something was missing from the shop, figured Tim had hidden the Orb and wanted to see if he had given it to us. They gave orders not to touch us until after we'd arrived in New Orleans because they wanted us to think we were still safe, and keep the element of surprise until they could plant the bomb, which explains why we were able to leave so easily. The demons thrive on fear and pain and wanted to make me feel as much as possible. They couldn't touch us on Robichaux land, so they planted the bomb on the outer fringes of the bayou. And then that failed."

He paused, his gaze darkening. "This one thought he'd gain points by getting to us before the others did."

Her stomach churned as she thought about the extreme means he'd been forced to use to gain the valuable information. "How did he know we'd be here?"

"Don't know. The leak is worse than I thought. Or it's Shay."

"It can't be him. There's got to be something else."

"I don't know who to trust anymore. It's you and me, Sienna. No one else. Not even my team. We're on our own."

Seven quick knocks at the door, followed by eight. Matt withdrew his sidearm. "I doubt it's the delivery guy. Stay back. And make a note of the time."

When he opened the door, Sam stood in the hallway, a wide smile on his face. "Dakota."

Fisting his hand in Sam's collar, Matt dragged him into the room, kicking the door shut with a boot. He slammed him against the wall, his eyes wild, breathing ragged, as he shoved the gun beneath Sam's jaw.

"L.T.! What gives? Chill out!"

"Talk. Tell me the code."

Sienna bit a knuckle, her heart racing.

To his credit, the young SEAL didn't flinch beneath the heavy pressure of Matt's hard hand. "To country. To comrades. To protect. To defend. To conceal. To silence. To the death."

Silence hung thick in the air. Matt remained tense, but lowered the gun. "What's my name? What am I to you?"

Lines furrowed the Mage's brow. "You're Lieutenant Dakota, although right now I'm tempted to call you a complete and total asshole. Did you forget your meds?"

Matt turned to Sienna. "Keep your eyes on him. If his body even flickers, tell me and I'll put a bullet in his brain."

"Hey." Sam's eyes widened.

"Shut up. If you're Shay, tell me who gave you that scar on your left shoulder."

"You did. Saved my ass during the voodoo priestess op in Grenada."

"Why?"

"She was sucking out my life force, and the bullet broke her hold. Damn it, L.T., what is this about? Want to get off me now? People will think we're in love."

"Time, Sienna."

She glanced at her watch. "Ten minutes."

Matt lowered the SEAL to the floor and holstered his gun. He blew out a heavy breath. "Sorry. Had to make sure. Even our team code...I had no way of knowing if it had been leaked, too. The Darksider Fae teaming with the pyro demons can't hold a glamour long. And there's no way they knew about your being shot."

His big shoulders remained tense. "No one knows details about your little gem, except you and me."

"What the hell's going on?" Sam's gaze whipped between them both. "You look worse than yesterday's leftovers. And why are you already here? ETA was 1500 hours."

Sienna crossed the room and laid a gentle hand on Matt's back, rubbing circles to calm him. She knew what it was like to not trust anyone, to suddenly feel the entire world was your enemy and could kick you in the stomach any time.

"We had a surprise visit from your evil twin. A Darksider Fae."

Sam's expression narrowed. "Son of a... How did it know we were meeting?"

"I don't know." Matt rubbed the back of his neck. "Unless it picked up our phone call. But the phone is clean. I scanned it."

"Tell me everything."

Matt did. Sam paced the room, his gaze glacial. "There's no chance anyone knew where you headed?"

"Only you and I knew. And Sienna."

"Damn it! You've got a bug, Lieutenant."

"Can't be me. I did a total and complete warding before setting out on this op. It must be..."

Her blood ran cold as both men's gazes turned to her.

Matt's jaw turned to granite, while Sam's expression turned cold and lethal. "Run a scan on her?"

Minutes later, Matt ran the cylindrical device over her body. Nothing beeped. The two men exchanged glances.

"Change the setting for our psi chip."

Shay's eyes widened. "You serious?"

"Do it."

He made an adjustment, then ran the wand over her again. This time it flared red and beeped.

"Son of a…" Shay lowered the wand, astonishment widening his eyes.

"It's inside her," Matt said tersely. "Someone left a little calling card in your blood to track you. A psi chip, which was designed to track all SEALs on the Phoenix Force in case we run into real trouble."

Something evil and nasty was swimming inside her body. Sienna fought against the nausea rising in her throat. "Get it out of me."

"We need Stephen," Sam told her.

"Who's Stephen?"

"He's a vampire. We've used him before to remove unwanted objects from contacts."

The men exchanged meaningful glances.

Holding out her hands like a traffic cop, she backed off. "Whoa, whoa. No one's touching my blood. What are you going to do, cut me and drain me dry?"

Fear skittered along her spine as Matt stalked forward, his jaw tense. But his blue eyes were filled with compassion as he gathered her hands into his. "No one's going to hurt you, pixie. I swear to it. Stephen's ex-military. Loyal and discreet."

"I'm not going to be someone's blood bank."

He pressed a gentle kiss to her battered knuckles. "He's

very good and I'll be there the whole time, keeping watch. Painless as possible."

Over his shoulder, Sam's expression tightened. "If she is infected, we need to move. Now, before those bastards hunt you down."

The street was narrow and lined with charming building façades. They stopped before a brick building where iron lacework balconies marched across the second floor.

The building's gate opened to reveal a small courtyard with a sparkling turquoise pool and a disorganized garden filled with small blue wildflowers. As they mounted the steps to the second floor, Matt explained that the vampire was Gabriel's neighbor. The Robichaux demon hunter owned a French Quarter home he'd turned into apartments for paranorms.

They went down a narrow hallway flanked by polished brass lamps outside each apartment door. Sienna glanced around as Matt knocked on a door. "If he's a real vampire, won't he be asleep?"

The door swung open, revealing a pitch-black apartment. Matt entered first, giving a wolf whistle.

"Damn it, you lupine bastard, do you know what time it is?"

A light snapped on. Sienna blinked, her eyes adjusting to the warm, soft glow of lamplight. She hung back, just in case the vampire was a grumpy riser.

On a cocoa leather couch, a chestnut-headed man stretched out, his bare feet dangling over the end. He was bare-chested, wearing a pair of leather pants slung low on his hips. The man sat up, tousling his thick, short curls.

"I had a rough night. Too much tequila from Gabe's bar. And you come waltzing in, disturbing my beauty sleep."

"You're beautiful." Matt tossed him the rumpled striped

shirt draped over an armchair. "Shay, check him out. Make sure he's the real thing."

Stephen narrowed his eyes as he shrugged into the shirt. "Imposters running amok?"

"The worst."

Shay took Stephen into a bedroom as Matt explained. "All of our contacts have a small, secret marking. It's an identifier just in case someone decides to impersonate them."

When the pair emerged into the living room and Shay was assured the vampire was the real thing, they sat.

"We need your help to check out a blood wiretap," Matt said.

"Someone got the upper paw on you, wolf? Hard to believe."

"Not him. Her." Sam jerked a thumb at Sienna.

Matt drew her forward, his hand reassuring. "She's got a psi tracker in her blood."

"Aw, crap. I knew I should have stayed in bed." He rubbed his face and yawned.

"Stephen, meet Sienna. Sienna, this is Stephen."

The vampire's chocolate-brown eyes studied her. "Hi, there, Sienna. What are you? I can't get a read on you."

"Right now? I'm pretty scared," she admitted. "But as much as I don't want you sucking my blood, I want to get rid of whatever's inside me."

For a creature so fearsome, he looked gentle as he knelt by her, gave a warm smile. "I'm good at my job. Did this a time or two before for them."

Matt's gaze narrowed as he pulled Sienna to him in a clearly possessive move. "Take it through the wrist, Stephen."

The vampire looked amused. "Feeling a little territorial, wolf? I'll see what I can do."

Matt sank into a comfortable easy chair, spread his legs open and pulled her between them. The heavy weight of his strong arms wrapped around her as she sat. A frail bond of trust wove between them. He wouldn't let anything happen to her.

Putting a knee upon the floor before her, Stephen gave a reassuring smile. "Just relax, Sienna. Think of this as a trip to the dentist, without the expensive bill."

His fingers explored her wrists, quickly and efficiently. Blood pulsed through her veins, seeming to echo in the room as his dark eyes widened. Then he slid a hand up to her throat, long fingers pressed against her jugular. It was like facing a large tiger considering a meal, a tiger with a wealth of chestnut hair and a sexy smile.

Matt tightened his grip around her waist. "I'm here, pixie."

Tension eased a little in her tight muscles.

Stephen's upper lip curled. "Can't tell this way. I'll have to take her from the neck."

"Okay," she managed. "Let's do this."

Matt swept back a length of hair from her left ear as Stephen tilted her neck to the side. The Draicon began whispering reassuring words as the vampire's warm breath feathered over her skin. It felt a little scary and erotic.

Fangs lengthened and descended in Stephen's mouth. Tension knotted every muscle. Hypnotized by the deep lull of Matt's voice, she tried to avoid looking at the avid hunger in the vampire bending over her neck. Instead, Sienna stared at artwork on the wall. Reproduction of the birth of Venus. Only, the woman rising out of the sea on a half shell in this painting featured a lush, naked blonde with a shy smile that clearly displayed shiny white fangs.

"Nice painting," she whispered. "Never knew Botticelli painted vampires."

Oh, goddess, he was going to do it, take her blood. It was too intimate.

Then Matt turned her face toward him. "Look at me, pixie," he said quietly.

As she felt a sharp prick, like a needle's sting, Matt kissed her. His mouth was warm and authoritative, tongue plunging past her lips and claiming her mouth. Sienna moaned, desire igniting her blood. The sensual feel of the vampire suckling at her neck and Matt's possessive kiss as he stroked a gentle hand over her cheek was the most erotic sensation she'd ever felt.

When it's time, I'll kiss you all over, Sienna. Every inch of you beneath my tongue. You'll be mine.

Words he'd spoken in the past? Or a voice echoing with pure male intent? She couldn't tell. The line blurred between reality and fantasy with each languid stroke of Matt's tongue, each pull of the vampire's lips.

As Matt broke the kiss and gazed at her with deep tenderness, a tongue lapped slowly, sensually, over the puncture wounds. Matt drew his eyebrows together and growled low.

"You didn't have to enjoy it so much, Stephen."

The vampire didn't answer. Sienna languidly turned her head and saw him make a face.

"Blech." Stephen spat into his hand. "Tastes like ashes. Here's your damn tracker."

Thumb and forefinger pinched, Matt took the device, the size of a bead. It blinked a steady pulsing red.

"Kill it, Shay," he directed, tossing it on the floor.

The SEAL flung out his fingers. White light sizzled and sparked, incinerating the wiretap. "Nice fireworks," she said drowsily.

One knee still bent on the floor, Stephen gave her a speculative look. "You're different. I've never tasted anything like you before…."

"And you never will again," snapped Matt. His arms tightened around her, the move filled with primal male possession.

Sienna leaned back against him, more tired than she'd ever felt. "I'm half Draicon, half Fae."

The vampire arched an elegant brow. "So you say. I've had both. Fae aren't to my taste. Too bland and dull. No real sustenance. Like drinking carrot juice. You're much richer, like a full-bodied red wine. Maybe it's the mixture in your DNA, but your blood is off the charts. Savory, rare…very delectable."

The New Orleans drawl turned into a sensual purr. "Delicious."

As Stephen ran a tongue over wet, reddened lips, the hard male body behind her tensed. She could almost hear a rumble reverberate through his powerful chest. Matt swept back her long hair and pressed a singularly sweet kiss on her nape. Sexual heat flared at the warm pressure of his mouth.

He stood and lifted her as easily as a child. She laid her head against his chest, too tired to resist, and closed her eyes.

"She needs rest." The commanding tone of his voice rumbled against her ear.

"Guest bedroom's to the left."

Sienna relaxed as he carried her inside. She heard the snap of a light switch and opened her eyes. Black drapes covered a set of French doors. The room was gothic and elegant, with framed paintings hanging on crimson silk wallpaper. Sienna blinked.

"Those are nudes," she said drowsily.

"Stephen's guests have, ah, interesting tastes. Fortunately, it's been cleaned since his last party."

"Don't you mean orgy?"

Matt smiled. He laid her carefully on a bed big as a football field with black satin sheets. She stared at the ceiling.

"Mirrors? Guess the myths are false."

"He's a vampire. Vanity runs in the veins."

A drowsy smile touched her mouth. "Very funny, Matt. I'd laugh if I weren't so tired."

He parked a hip on the side of the bed and closed her eyes with a brush of a hand that could crush an enemy but felt infinitely gentle against her skin. "Sleep, Sienna. Sleep."

Chapter 11

When he was assured that Sienna was asleep, Matt joined Stephen and Sam in the living room. The vampire was sipping from a crystal goblet. He handed a glass to him and Sam.

"It's a very fine vintage."

"From the vineyards of Buxom Blonde 2009?"

The vampire gave a mocking smile. "You know I wouldn't waste fine blood on a wolf. I'd give you something less erudite, but the corner store happened to be out of jug wine."

Matt sank into the leather armchair and sipped. "Not bad, vamp."

"Now tell me, what the hell is going on?" Stephen swirled the liquid in the glass. "How did she get infected with your own damn psi tracker?"

"Sienna was mugged in the subway. Assailant used the opportunity to plant a demon hitchhiker worm. Tracking device was on the knife. The worm was a decoy to deflect attention."

Matt felt a slow rage building. The psi tracker had been

implanted in every SEAL in the Phoenix Force to safeguard them. After Adam's death, the other SEALs disabled their devices should they fall into enemy hands. Except it had been too late.

"How the hell did demons get their hands on a psi tracker?" the vampire asked.

Fists clenched, Matt stared at the floor. "They took it out of Adam, before they burned his body to ashes. They used our own technology against us."

Shay swore. Stephen's brow furrowed. "Who is Adam?"

Throat tight with emotion, Matt shrugged. "No one in particular."

Once he and Adam had sat in this very parlor, drinking a six-pack, blowing off steam after they'd successfully eliminated a ring of international blood slave dealers who were kidnapping young girls to ship to South American vampires. Stephen's spies had cracked the intel on that one, and the smuggling ring had been broken. Adam had challenged the vampire to an arm-wrestling match, lost, and bought him a case of vintage wine. They'd joked long into the night. And now Stephen didn't remember his name.

Changing the subject, Matt asked, "Tell me, vamp, what do you have for us?"

Stephen set down his glass, his expression serious. "The pyro demons are planning something. There's talk about doing something major out west and using that to fuel their energy."

"What about me, and my team?"

"The real act comes after they grab the Orb. Then all hell breaks loose. You're the only ones who can stop them."

ST21, the only protection standing between the demons and the world.

Matt rubbed the heel of his left hand into his eye, fighting fatigue. Nothing compared to the rigors of Hell Week, the toughest week of SEAL training, but back then, it was physical and mental trials.

Not the grinding challenge of fighting an enemy who could melt bullets, kill your best friend with a blast of heat and turn him into ash. Bile rose in his throat. Seeing the Darksider Fae with Sienna in its grip, ready to claw at her, had made him nearly mad with rage. The Fae had paid dearly for laying his ugly hands on her.

Shay twirled the glass, running a long finger over the stem. "We need a handle on what they're planning. Who's the true target?"

Stephen flexed his bare toes. "Info is very tight. But whatever it is, it's big. And nasty and involves a big explosion. The intel is limited. I can't gain anything else. Only found out because I hooked up with a pretty minion with a penchant for pillow talk and threesomes. Her regular lover is an aspiring member of the Ring of Fire, albeit a very minor demon on the food chain. Some redhead in New Mexico named Alberta."

"Was an aspiring member."

The vampire glanced up, interest flaring on his face. "You tangled with her?"

"I put her out of action, permanently." Matt drained his glass of wine. The delicate stem snapped beneath the pressure of his fingers. He set it down. "Sorry."

"No problem. I can get another set at Walmart." Stephen sat up, glanced at the guest bedroom. "And what about Sleeping Beauty? I sensed her pulse skyrocket when you locked lips with her. She was scared of me, but when you stepped in, it wasn't fear."

The kiss was smooth and silky, her lips soft beneath his. He'd felt her pulse leap, as well. His own. Hell, if he were alone, he'd climb into her bed, hold her close and she'd be in his arms when she awoke. Maybe wake her with a nuzzle along the sensitive spot of her nape…a slow stroke of his tongue over her pulse…

"Yo." Shay waved a hand. "Dakota, you look hungry and it's not for rare hamburger."

More like a rare Fae, sweet, delicate and yet tough inside and braver than any female he'd ever encountered. Thinking of Sienna lying on the satin sheets within a few footsteps made his blood race, his heart pound.

His cock grew hard as stone.

She would be his. Soon.

Yet she still refused to acknowledge her Draicon half. Matt rubbed a hand over his face.

"Ah, the wolf grows restless. And I doubt it's the demons holding your leash. Must be the Fae asleep on my bed. She does taste very exquisite. Maybe I should have seconds."

A low, deep growl rumbled from Matt's throat. He was on his feet, fists clenched, as he started for the vampire.

Stephen looked amused. "Damn, you've got it bad."

Nearly the same words his brother-in-law stated. Matt forced down calm, kept the wolf at bay. Must not lose focus. Something big was at stake here and his instincts couldn't pin it down. The bomb back at the Robichaux land. The way Tim had been tortured.

"Your contact, is she still in the area?" Matt persisted.

"Left yesterday. Something about opportunity knocking with a legion of lesser demons, and Darksider Fae. Tried to read her mind, but she had it sealed shut. All I know is something big and bad is backing it."

"The pyro demons," Shay mused.

Interest flared in the vampire's gaze. "You suspect they're planning a barbecue?"

"They need one. Pyro demons soak up energy through fire or the thermal equivalent. The more destruction they cause, the more energy they have. So why haven't they set a huge fire to gain more power?"

Stephen shook his head. "Their options are limited. It's not 1871, like Chicago, when they burned down old lady O'Leary's barn and watched the city fry. With modern fire-fighting equipment, there's little chance of a blaze that big."

Something kept nagging him. "They're not interested in small infusions of power. They're planning something bigger, more methodical. Something requiring an army."

The vampire's eyes went bloodred. "A demon army? Could wipe out every living thing. But there's not enough of them. Unless you failed to close that bolt hole."

"No chance of that." Shay's expression tightened. The Phoenix Force knew every demon bolt hole in the world and had sealed them all, but the Darksider Fae had discovered one and opened it, releasing the pyro demons. After Adam's death, Shay had spent a draining forty-eight hours pouring his Mage magick into resealing the tampered bolt hole so no more demons could escape.

Stephen looked thoughtful. "What about other bolt holes? Dormant and hidden, needing a little juice to revive them?"

The possibility was one the team had already considered. "Sealed long ago." Shay pushed a hank of hair away from his forehead. "There's only four others in the world, including another in the good old U.S.A."

The Mage's gaze went flat. "New Mexico. That one is already sealed. You know where it is, vamp."

The vampire gave an elegant snort. "Always thought that was an asinine idea, building a base with the largest underground stockpile of nuclear warheads directly on top of a demon bolt hole. But that was before we organized."

"It's tight," Shay stated. "Kirtland has the tightest security in the world. The bolt hole is in a highly secured area. The air force has state-of-the-art security and you can't even blink without them arresting your ass. Every member of our Phoenix Force warded it with enough magick to seal it against anything nasty getting inside."

"Indeed." Stephen set down his wineglass. "But the magick is tied to all of you while your team lives. And if something happens to your unit, Mage? The magick will die and leave the base unprotected."

"No one's leaving anything unprotected. If we're KIA, Admiral Byrne will appoint other paranorms to ward the base," Shay argued.

"Even Byrne can't mobilize another top-notch unit that quickly. You'd have a window where the base would be unprotected," the vamp retorted.

Matt's blood ran cold, his mind racing.

"You're acting like the base is a big-box store and anyone can stroll inside. The bolt hole is secure."

"Against most paranorms," Stephen shot back. "Not against an army of pyro demons."

Shay snorted in derision. "Right. The only thing that could free a demon army would be—"

"Nukes," Matt cut in. "From the biggest stockpile in the world."

All three stared at one another.

"Oh, hell," Shay said, horror creeping over his face. "That's what they wanted all along. Why they need the Orb."

His mind raced over the possibilities. "I need a map."

They went into Stephen's office. Sophisticated computer equipment lined an elegant oak desk. On the wall was a large map of the United States lined with pushpins. Matt took a red pushpin and stabbed it into the map.

"You said they planned something big out west, east of California and Nevada. They're running out of energy, can't hold a glamour for long. They need fire." He tapped the map with a forefinger. "Here's the base."

He traced a line from the air force base. "They wouldn't set a fire here, anywhere near the base. Too much suspicion. They'd need it in a deserted area, forest, where it wouldn't cause suspicion and could burn for hours, fueling their energy. Here in southern Colorado…"

Matt stared at the map, breath constricting in his lungs. "Acres and acres of forest and mountains."

Shay cursed. "They want the Orb to hunt us down and kill us so the warding would drop around the base. And then, they'd gain access to the base and the nukes."

Just one nuclear weapon could free an army of fire demons.

The images emerged with blood-chilling precision. Pyrokinetic demons slaying SEAL Team 21's entire Phoenix Force, then using the energy of the fire to assume a longer-lasting glamour. Gaining access to the base once the warding ceased and blowing it up to free a demon army.

Nothing to stop them. Countless demons freed from the netherworld, getting their talons on the country's nuclear arsenal…watching all humanity burn.

A bloodcurdling hiss came from the vampire. Stephen's talons emerged from his hands. He ran them across the wall, scoring deep gouges.

Shay flexed his fingers, as if itching to release his powers. "I'm hightailing it out to New Mexico. Double the warding around the air force base."

"No," Matt said. He turned and fiercely regarded the younger Mage. "Your hide and the rest of the teams' are on the line. You're returning to Little Creek. That's an order."

"No way in hell. *Sir*. I'm not leaving you alone. I'm with you on this. All the way. You go, we all go. We're a team."

Emotion thickened his throat. "Your job is to stay alive and keep those nukes secured. If something happens to me, you and the team are the only ones who can protect the base."

He drew in a breath. "I'm going with Sienna back to the

Fae colony. It's safer for her there. I need to access the Orb. And destroy it."

The room fell silent. Resolve filled him. Damn it, he might die, but he'd go down fighting before he let a single demon talon touch a nuclear weapon.

The room fell silent.

"You'll need to refuel before you leave. All the energy you can ingest, wolf. My fridge is stocked." Stephen sighed. "Nukes and demons. It was much simpler back in the days when all you had to worry about was the black plague and drinking contaminated blood."

In the kitchen, Stephen went to the sleek stainless-steel refrigerator and withdrew a carafe of crimson liquid. He considered it, then downed the contents and wiped his mouth with the back of one hand. "Came from a downtown blood bank. Plebian, but will suffice."

Matt dug into the freezer, removed two thick steaks and put them into the microwave to defrost. He found some fresh vegetables and began chopping them.

Shay leaned over him. "What's this? You never like anything green, except money."

"Sienna likes fresh salad."

"You've got it bad. Just saying," Shay noted.

"When a wolf turns into a chef from a cable cooking show, you know Shay is right," Stephen drawled in his laconic New Orleans accent.

"I saw that kiss. I haven't seen you that involved since—"

Shay's next words were cut off as Matt pinned him with a look that could slice steel. The SEAL shrugged.

"She seems very nice. Trim form, nice curves...very nice taste." Stephen ran a tongue around his lips.

The vampire was pinned against the wall by Matt's hand on his throat before Stephen could blink. Stephen laughed.

"Guess this proves it. You're smitten."

Matt relaxed his hold. "I'm smitten about getting dinner."

Stephen slid down to the floor, pretending to gasp. "Oh, he touched me! The wolf touched me. I'll never wash this throat again."

"Never do, anyway, vamp." Shay chortled.

As they all laughed, Matt felt piercing regret that he'd lost his best friend and might lose his team, as well. Were they doomed to the same fate?

And Sienna? His appetite vanished.

Was she next? *Not if I can help it.*

He finished preparing the food and went to the bedroom, trying to ignore his racing pulse. He wasn't involved.

And then he stood in the doorway, mesmerized by the woman lying on the black satin sheets, one hand curled beneath a pale cheek.

Aw, hell.

The bed dipped beneath his weight. He brushed a finger over her soft cheek, tucking back a strand of silky hair. She sighed and rolled over, her eyes opening, a languid smile on her sweet mouth.

Need became a barreling force, driving him forward. Matt leaned down and kissed her. Her lips parted beneath the gentle pressure of his. One hand slid down her shoulder, curling over her arm. He thought about what the pyro demons would do if they caught her. Never. He'd strangle them with his bare hands before they stroked one talon over her skin.

Chances were he would die soon. But hell, he wasn't going to die without truly living first. Plunge headfirst off that cliff. Like his first jump from thirty thousand feet, he was both exhilarated and scared.

It's a fool who isn't scared, he remembered Étienne saying. *It's the brave man who admits he is strong enough to be damn terrified, but pushes on despite that fear.*

He kept kissing her, framing her face now, drinking in her

sweetness. She was driving him wild, this sensual half Fae who tugged at his heart.

"Matt," she breathed between his urgent kisses. "I've never felt like this before."

Sienna's tongue tangled with his. His breathing grew heavy as his heart pounded. The sweet scent of her desire filled his nostrils. It would take so little to join her on the bed, slowly divest her clothing...

"More," she whispered.

He pulled back, his cock hard as steel, blood racing through his veins.

"Not here."

Huge moss-green eyes stared at him, desire and disappointment smoking their depths. "I want you, Matt. Please. I'm not afraid anymore."

She sounded breathless and sultry, her natural sensuality rising to the surface.

"It's not private." He lifted her chin with a finger, drowning in the sweetness of her face. "I want you, Sienna. I want you like I've never wanted a woman before. And I will have you. But now isn't the time."

He needed a soft bed, privacy and a locked door.

Matt lowered his head, breathing in her arousal. "Not here, for a few quick minutes. I'm going to kiss every inch of your body, and taste you all over, until you beg me to stop. Or not stop. And for that, little pixie, I need privacy."

Red flushed her skin, her eyes growing huge and wide and dark. "So no one can interrupt?"

His mouth nuzzled over her neck where Stephen had bitten her. He gently nipped the healed skin, leaving his own mark. "So no one will hear you scream."

Chapter 12

The rental car had a flat tire. Matt said nothing as he fished in the trunk for a spare and a jack. They'd left the warmth of New Orleans to head back to her Fae colony. Though the temperatures in this part of Colorado had dipped well into the fifties, he'd removed his jacket. He tightened the lug nuts as she stood watching him.

The muscles in his forearms flexed with each movement. Sienna's heart did a funny jump in her chest.

Almost the same as when he'd told her they were heading back to her home.

She cleared her throat. "It's only a few miles to my cabin. I could glamour us a ride. Or maybe test my powers of flight. Fae once did have wings. Though I suppose I'd only have half wings, since I'm a hybrid."

He straightened, rubbing his hands on his jeans. Such big hands, strong and square, dusted lightly with dark hair on their backs.

After he'd shrugged into his jacket, she caught his hand. "Matt, level with me. You haven't said anything since Sam hustled us to the airport. What's going on?"

Instead of answering, he cupped her chin with thumb and forefinger. His blue gaze seemed distant and haunted.

"You'll be safer with the Fae."

Then he turned and walked to the trunk, tossing in the jack.

Safe? She didn't want safe. She wanted answers. She wanted to ride this out-of-control, crazy feeling she had for this strong, brave wolf who suddenly turned mute. Something big was at stake and she had to find out. Sienna climbed into the car.

"Safe from what? Demons? Or wolves? Talk with me. I can't read your mind. What do you want, Matt? Should I start waving semaphore flags? Maybe then we can communicate?"

He shot her an amused look as he slid behind the wheel, started the engine.

"Or maybe I should just change into something more comfortable for you."

"Sienna." He cut the engine with a sigh as she shifted into a six-foot soldier in olive drab, sporting a pistol similar to the one on his belt. "Stop it."

"You don't like the new me? Then talk to me."

She tried to shift into her Fae self, needing connection with her roots, but instead found herself in human Draicon form. Squashing the panic that rose in her throat, she faced him.

Matt quietly regarded her, sunlight glinting his hair, picking out the light brown streaks. He had an arsenal in his duffel bag, and another on his body. Two deadly knives sheathed at each ankle. Gun on a holster at his side. Instead of a belt, a length of steel cable threaded through the loops of his pants. Another weapon, she guessed.

He looked relaxed, but with the air of a dangerous wolf

on alert for prey. Gone was the teasing look in his deep blue eyes. They were watchful and aware.

"Tell me about the Los Lobos colony. How big is your territory?"

Surprised, she gestured to the land. "We crossed into it ten minutes ago. The Fae consider this part of their protective custody. The colony is guarded and gated, but they keep watch over all the land, including the mountains."

He drove, glancing constantly at the rearview mirror. "Not many people out here."

"They bought the land years ago under the pretense of a large land developer. Then as time changed, they assumed the glamour of a New Age religious cult who wanted to harmonize with nature. It's been the best masquerade so far, and it's worked."

"No services like water, sewer, infrastructure, police or fire protection?"

She shook her head. "Outside the colony, no. My cabin is modernized. They built it to defray suspicion and used it for the occasional tourist who wanted to play nature lover. It's on the side of a mountain with a steep hiking trail. But it's so remote few people come here. They prefer more touristy areas with restaurants and shops."

His expression turned stony, making him look dangerous and hard.

"No fire protection," she repeated, and then suddenly the aspen, oak and pine trees took on an air of menace. "Are we safe here?"

"Safer than back in New Orleans." His gaze flicked to her. "Your people will protect you, Sienna."

"Because you think I can't protect myself? Or because you're leaving and heading back east to deal with whatever new threat surfaced?"

At his stubborn look, she sighed. "Just tell me, okay? I need to know what's going on. I deserve as much."

"How good are the Fae at protecting their turf?"

Images flashed through her mind in rapid succession. Wolves leaping and snarling, teeth bared, screams, the glow of crimson...the terrified pleas to live...

Heat scorching the earth as she watched from her little hollow, a fist stuffed into her mouth to stop her own screams...

Sienna drew in a deep breath and looked straight at him. "Their weapons are glamour and connecting with the earth. They can create storms, which isn't effective against fangs and claws. But they're fierce and will defend their own to the death."

He pulled onto a small dirt road, almost hidden by a thick overhang of sweeping branches. "How did you know the way?"

"Followed your scent." His eyes were very blue, a deep persuasive blue. He gave her an intent look, as if he wanted to absorb that particular scent, rub it deep inside him while he buried himself deep inside her....

Sienna sucked down a breath. Whoa.

Pine and aspen flanked the dirt road. Matt ignored the fork to the right and kept driving straight. He drove for a mile until reaching a wooden gate. A hand-painted sign, hanging crookedly on a tree, read Rustic Haven Ranch. No Trespassing.

He parked, shut off the engine and climbed out. Sienna followed as he approached the gate. Matt waved a hand in front of him, and drew back, lines furrowing his brow.

"The scent." He rubbed his eyes, shook his head as if to rid himself of it.

"The Los Lobos community incorporated the scent to discourage other paranorms, except wolves. It fades for Draicon after a while." Sienna rested a hand on the crude gate. "They warded it with magick to repel the humans."

A few minutes later, they arrived at the right fork. Matt followed it, dust and pebbles kicking up beneath the sturdy tires. In a few minutes, the narrow lane opened to a sweep of open, flat land, neatly swept and free of brush. Matt pulled up to the pine cabin.

"Stay here," he ordered, and climbed out.

He was checking out the area for intruders. Sienna fisted her hands. Once, she'd had that ability. But now she couldn't even summon her Fae image. It felt as if something drained her powers.

Then the SEAL turned into a gray wolf, teeth bared, every muscle tensed as he loped over the yellow grass meadow, sniffed the ground around the cabin and vanished up the mountain.

A few minutes later, the wolf leaped atop the big granite boulder before her cabin door. He looked proud and dangerous, a wild creature belonging to this land. She felt an unexpected lump of pride. Her wolf.

Not really hers. He was going to erase her memories and leave her soon. And she didn't know how she'd deal with his departure.

Matt shifted into his human form. Naked, he stood proud and straight. Her mouth parted as she gazed at his broad-shouldered body. High on his left shoulder was a small black tattoo of a wolf running with a lightning bolt in its mouth.

A small but nasty pink slash marred the other shoulder. It looked like a knife wound.

Her hungry gaze traveled the length of his back, the ridges of thick muscles on either side of his spine, marching down to a trim waist and narrow hips. Two small dimples indented the skin above his buttocks. Sienna admired the taut roundness of his rear and, when he braced his legs apart, she caught a glimpse of his sex dangling between his opened legs.

Then Matt turned and stretched his arms to the sky. His

mouth moved as he began a lyrical chant. Fascinated, she watched him walk around the cabin and a wide perimeter. Iridescent sparks trailed in his wake like fireflies as he quietly patrolled the meadow.

When he returned, his face was pale, and he looked tired and drained. Sienna jumped out of the car, but he waved her off.

"Energy shield. Powerful enough to ward off a legion of demons."

Then he turned and seemed to get his first real look at her cabin. His eyes widened. "This is your home?"

Sienna felt a twinge of shame at his incredulous tone. "It's not big, and looks a little run-down...it's not what you expected."

"No," he said slowly. "It's exactly what I imagined."

A distant look entered his gaze. Sienna couldn't gauge it. "I guess you've slept in worse places as a SEAL. I've tried to make it comfortable."

He rubbed his jaw. "It'll do. It'll do just fine."

Matt had slept in places she couldn't even imagine. But he'd never slept in any place like her cabin. The pine cabin was quaint and homey. It featured a wide front porch with a small stoop, and a flagstone path wending from the dirt drive to the porch. Pots of red geraniums swung from the porch rafters. A small heart on the wall declared Love Makes a House a Home.

Emotion closed his throat as a painful longing surfaced. This was the cabin of his dreams, the place he'd imagined on those long nights when enemy fire raged, when he wondered if he'd ever make it out. The cold nights in the desert when he'd look up at the stars and wish he had someone special when he returned.

She kept giving him apologetic looks, as if she thought

he hated the place. "I know it's small, but there's a pull-out couch in the living room. I bought it just in case…" She gave a little laugh. "As if I had friends. My people want nothing to do with me. I'm a Fae leper."

She looked forlorn and sad, the long fall of dark hair cascading over her slender shoulders. Sienna was tough outside, but inside, damn, he knew she had to hurt.

"Let's get inside," he said gently.

She unlocked the cabin door. Large picture windows looked out to a sweeping view of the valley below and the mountain above. He gazed about the living room, with its plush forest-green recliners and matching sofas. A stone fireplace had a welcoming log on the heart and a milk jug filled with dried flowers on the mantel.

Sienna set the purse into a safe in the hall closet. She spun the combination and locked it.

Matt headed for a sofa. Warding the perimeter had sapped all his valuable energy. He closed his eyes.

"Just need a minute to recover."

"Liar. You're exhausted and you need food. Stay here and don't move."

Opening one eye, he gave an amused smile. "Aye, aye, sir."

In minutes she hauled inside their luggage, and the food he'd purchased at a grocery store a few miles back. Matt watched her through hooded eyes.

Soon she had a fire burning merrily on the stone hearth and two steaks sizzling on the gas grill outside. He sat up, looking around with interest. Sienna went to the couch, gently pushing him back into a prone position.

"Now it's your turn to rest. Stay there."

"Just a quick nap."

He closed his eyes.

The image sharpened into focus. Adam, hanging by the Hummer, one hand resting against the tough exterior. Joy exploded through him. His buddy was back. Matt laughed and punched his arm. "You sly Wildcat. We thought you were dead. Should have known nothing could take you down. You're too damn stubborn."

The jaguar slapped the vehicle. "It's like you, Dakota. Tough and built to take the pressure. But even a Hummer can explode under the right circumstances. Let go, Matt. It's time to let me go. You can't hold on forever. It was meant to be."

His best friend leaned a shoulder against the vehicle, giving his cocky smile. "Hang tough, but don't hang on forever. I'm gone, and I'm never coming back."

Then the smile faded, replaced by a solemn look. Adam shimmered like sunlight hitting water, a glistening, crystalline figure. "You know that bullet was meant for me. I saw it."

"Wait," Matt begged hoarsely. "Come back. I have to tell you…"

Adam vanished like a light snapping off.

Sweat dripped down his temples, dampening the microfiber beneath his cheek. Matt's eyes flew open. He rubbed his face and sat up, heart pounding against his chest.

Never coming back.

A delicious smell of grilled meat teased his nostrils. Matt glanced up at the adjoining kitchen. Sienna hummed a little as she set out plates and glasses on the table, along with an etched-glass bowl filled with greens. Next she carried inside two thick steaks on a platter.

"Dinner's ready."

So pretty, so cheerful and upbeat. Her face flushed a pretty shade of pink from the heat of the grill. She'd changed into a turquoise-blue sweater. Her toes peeped out from beneath the hem of her faded blue jeans. She'd painted her toenails a matching turquoise blue. He grinned, admiring them.

Blue toes. Very unconventional. Very Sienna.

"The steaks are for you." She gestured to the salad. "I'm sticking with grass."

The meat was grilled just right, barely seared over an open flame, tender and delicious. He dug with zest into both steaks, concentrating on the meal, but aware of her picking at the salad. Odd. She'd consumed meat with zest when they were together, but here in her cabin she seemed adverse to it.

Sienna looked up, her gaze suddenly clouded with emotion. "The Fae look down on eating meat."

A loud protesting rumble came from her stomach.

"Yet you're still hungry." He cut a piece of beef, placed it on her plate. "Eat it. You need your strength."

Sienna gulped it down and wiped the plate with a napkin, throwing it out. Disposing of evidence.

Matt gathered the plates, dumped them into the sink and began washing. Keeping his thoughts to himself, silent and guarded.

"You mentioned his name when you were sleeping." Sienna picked up a towel, dried the plates and put them into a cabinet. "Adam."

A glass shattered beneath his clenched fist. Shards flew into the air. Sienna cried out, grabbed his wrist. Blood streamed from his palm.

She picked out a few shards, wrapped his hand. But the wounds had already stopped bleeding and would soon heal.

Not so the jagged wound in his heart, ripped open by the constant guilt.

She studied him with a thoughtful look. "You never had a chance to say goodbye. That's it, isn't it?"

"Part of it."

"Would you like to talk to him again?"

A short, bitter laugh. "Unless your magick conjures the dead, that's impossible."

"It doesn't. But I can glamour myself to appear as him, so you can talk to him."

Was that hope making his pulse race? A second chance. Release the awful pressure sitting on his chest since that terrible day.

"I can see it on your eyes, Matt. You can't let him go. Please let me do this for you."

Never had he felt this vulnerable. Didn't like it. But the sincerity shining on her face, twinned with the tender concern, shot past his defenses. She wanted to help.

He knew the damages guilt could inflict. If he were to carry out this mission, he needed to be sharp and alert. Regret was too distracting.

"I need to go for a walk." He threw down the dish towel. "Be back in a few."

Hurt flashed onto her face. Matt cupped her chin with a gentle hand. "Thank you for your offer."

The back sliding door closed firmly behind him. On the patio, two hummingbird feeders hung from a rafter, along with a hand-painted sign proclaiming Peace to All Who Enter Here.

Peace. Nice concept. Not with a passel of nasty demons who'd love to fry his ass. And Sienna's, as an added bonus.

Not on my watch. He clenched his fists, and began a short run up the pathway that wended through the mountain.

Stalks of yellowed grass crunched beneath his boots. Jagged boulders edged the mountain, and the wind blew through pine and aspen trees. Matt ran upward, relishing the feel of his powerful muscles, the rhythm of his heartbeat. This was familiar. This was good, comfortable.

Her voice soothed and stirred his blood. A rush of protectiveness overwhelmed him as he thought of dark forces preying on her. Then again... He grinned, remembering how she'd stood up to the Darksider Fae with such courage, and jammed her elbow into his stomach.

Beneath all that soft female skin and delicate bone structure beat the heart of a true warrior.

He ran a good two miles up the mountain. Not wanting to leave her alone for long, he backed up when an odd scent floated on the wind. He was a creature of nature, and wolf instincts surged. Matt stopped, surveying the mountain below him.

The faint scent of wolf drifted up from the dead grass. Scent of a powerful Alpha who'd placed his marking scent on this mountain. Matt crouched down, splaying his hand over the dirt path. Not Draicon like him, but not animal, either. Very odd. Almost like a hybrid.

The wolf inside him snarled with possessive intent. Matt unzipped his jeans. He erased the foreign scent by covering it with his own. Marking his territory.

She's mine. Stay away. The message was clear.

He zipped up, bothered by these intense feelings more than the old scent.

When he returned to the cabin, Sienna was sitting by the fire, staring into the flames. Firelight cast her hair into burnished shades of amber, drawing her face into shadow. She glanced up, uncertainty in her eyes. He felt a twinge of real regret. He'd shut her out, and felt the distance as if a giant chasm yawned between them.

She was right. If he didn't get this out of his system, it would eat him alive. And he wanted the peace she offered him.

"All right," he agreed. "Let's do it."

She released a deep breath. "I'll need a photo of Adam."

They sat on the sofa. Matt dug a worn photo from his leather wallet. He and another man dressed in battle gear faced the camera. One wore a wide grin as he held his gun aloft. Adam. He showed it to her.

"All evidence of Adam's existence as a SEAL was destroyed. I was allowed to keep one small memento."

Sienna took his hand, her small palm warm. He wanted the comfort she offered, needed it, but damn, he couldn't do this. Had to be strong. A tightness settled in his chest. He felt bottled up and wanted to scream.

The palm holding his hand turned larger, stronger and calloused. Matt looked up and recoiled.

Dressed in his BDUs, hefting his gun in that cocky way of his, Adam sat beside him. Matt jerked his hand away.

"Never were the touchy-feely type, were you, Dakota?"

It was Adam's rasping voice, Adam's Midwestern twang. He rubbed his eyes, knowing the illusion was a gift.

This was so tough. What did you say to a buddy who sacrificed his life for yours? A SEAL who left behind a grieving widow who thought he died in a car crash because no one had any memory of him as a SEAL?

Except me and the team.

"Wildcat. Damn, you look good for a dead guy."

Adam sat silently, cocking his head exactly as the photo depicted.

Matt couldn't look at him. He stared at the carpet instead. Then he sensed the magick shimmer a little. Sienna couldn't hold the illusion long. So he gathered all his courage.

"I miss you, man. I miss you so much. I miss your stupid jokes, the way you mocked me for being so serious." Matt gulped down a deep breath.

"How you always watched my six. You were solid. I never trusted anyone like I trusted you, Wildcat. Not even my family. We were tight. I don't understand why you kept it a secret what was going to happen? You knew, damn it. You knew what we headed into. It was a suicide mission! Gods, you knew one of us was going to die and you never told me. I've been thinking and thinking about why you insisted on riding up top and then I realized, it was because you knew what would happen. That's why you insisted on riding up top. You took the hit and took away the choice from me!"

He slammed a fist into his thigh, feeling his chest constrict. "There's not a day that's gone by that I haven't questioned why you were killed and I was left alive. Not a day when I regret what happened to you. Why you did it, when you had Tatiana to live for and I had no one. I guess I just have to accept that you did it for a reason. And I'm not meant to know that reason. Not now."

Grief roughened his voice. It poured out of him in a tidal wave of emotion he couldn't hold back.

"Thank you, Wildcat, for what you did for me, for all those you saved, for all you did for your country. Miss you, man. You'll always be here—" he touched his chest "—and I'll never forget you. The world has, but I never will. Until we meet again, on the Other Side."

Adam's form began to shimmer. Matt pushed on, knowing he had to get this out. Say it now before he lost his nerve.

"Another thing, Wildcat. You always teased that the teams were everything to me. Being a SEAL meant more to me than anything else. Even a woman." He smiled a little, remembering Adam's mocking grin. "It was. But I've met someone now. And I understand why you had to have Tatiana. Why you took that risk and fell. I've fallen, too. It feels like I've taken a HALO jump without a chute, but funny thing, I'm not afraid."

Tears glistened in Adam's eyes. Matt never took his gaze off his friend. "Sienna's gotten to me. She's special. You once joked that I'd take a hit for the team, but if a woman tried to spend the whole night, I'd be outta there faster than an insurgent facing an army of SEALs. Not anymore. I'd bleed for her. I'll do anything to keep her safe. She makes me crazy and happy at the same time. I love seeing her smile, love the way she wakes up, with that sexy little smile that makes me tumble off that cliff all over again. I'd do anything to make her happy, give her the moon and the stars."

He paused, a lump rising in his throat. "I'd give up my life for her, if it came to that."

Adam's form shimmered and disappeared. Sienna stared at him, eyes luminous with unshed tears. She cupped his cheek. He turned into her touch, relishing the softness of her palm.

"You're amazing, Lieutenant Matthew Parker. You have the true heart of a hero. Thank you for everything." Sienna's mouth wobbled. "For everything you did, and everything you said. Because you have the courage to say it aloud, what I'm feeling, as well."

He kissed her. In gratitude partly, but the man in him longed to taste the softness of her wet mouth, chase away tears with pleasure. Matt framed her face with his hands. Keeping the kiss gentle and unhurried, not wanting to startle her. Accustoming her to his touch, breaking down her natural apprehension.

She made a humming sound of pleasure and leaned into him. Beneath the light pressure of his lips, she opened her mouth.

The invitation was there. He plunged on, drinking in the sweetness, tasting everything that was this exotic, sensual Fae-Draicon who'd freed him from a prison of guilt. She was warm and delicious and he wanted to savor her, but the need became hot and pulsing.

When she shyly reached up to toy with his hair, he deepened the kiss. As whisper soft as his mouth had been, it became firm and commanding as he sought to teach her true pleasure. Sienna arched her body as his hands spanned her rib cage. Her breasts were full and lush, and fit perfectly into his palms. Matt gently thumbed her nipples, feeling them harden. Hearing her excited whimper, he kept ravishing her mouth. Loving the sounds she made, catching the surging scent of her arousal. It was heady and spicy and tunneled straight to his cock. He hardened to granite, his body responding to the sweetness of the woman in his arms.

Mercy.

No mercy.

The wolf in him clawed to the surface, demanding and urgent. He was caught in the maelstrom, his feelings spiraling free. He needed Sienna, wanted her so badly he shook from the need.

A growl tore from his throat.

Panting, Sienna pulled away. His body was painfully hard, sexual need sharp as glass. The sounds of their ragged breathing filled the cabin, mingling with the crackling flames in the hearth.

Her eyes were wide and clouded with passion, her mouth smudged and swollen from his passionate kisses. She was scared.

Immediately, he tried to reassure her. "It's only natural, sweetheart." He framed her face with his warm palms. "It's an expression of my desire for you."

"It's your wolf coming out...Matt."

"You can. I know it's inside you. Don't fight your nature, Sienna. Let the wolf inside you break free."

"I don't know if I can," she whispered.

Chapter 13

Matt rubbed the back of his neck, struggling with his feelings. Her mouth tasted like ripe berries, soft and sweet against his. He wanted her badly. He couldn't get enough of her. The twin ropes of desire and need coiled together like snakes, rubbing against each other. The raw eroticism of his wolf clawed to the surface, demanding to mate with her, mark her as his own.

He had to get out, break free, grab control.

The front door banged behind him as he walked outside, restless and edgy, wolf scratching to the surface. A cool wind caressed his cheeks, ruffled his hair. Wolf smelled the redolent pine, the raw earth and the wildness of forest. Overhead, the silver gleam of the waxing moon filtered through the boughs of tall, thick pines.

Claws erupted on his fingertips. Matt surrendered to the beast.

Up the mountain he ran as wolf, senses exploding with

knifelike awareness. He roamed the meadow, bounding off the trail to explore the outcroppings of granite peppering the mountainside. Muscles stretched and flexed with each movement.

He loped through the forest. Leaves and dead undergrowth littered the path, which dipped and curved and led down the mountain. He relished the freedom, the pull of his strong muscles, the sharp awareness of wolf.

After a half mile, the path ended. He ground to a halt, disturbed by an intense tickling in his head. As if someone ran a feather over his muzzle. Matt growled, pawed at the ground and snapped at the air. The tickling bothered his nostrils, dug into his sensitive ears. Hell.

He shifted into human form, clothing himself in soft leather boots, black jeans and a black T-shirt, and the sensations immediately subsided.

Very odd. He must be on the edge of Fae lands. He continued on, finding the path easily, and following it, drawn to it like a lodestone.

Then the path vanished, giving way to thinning trees. Matt looked up at the nearly full moon, large and pregnant in the glittering velvet sky.

Voices rose on the wind, soft and coaxing. Their music enchanted him, wove around him like a cloak. He continued on, hovering on the edges of a large glen.

The clearing was ringed by the forest. In the middle were twelve large granite stones, pointed and phallic, thrusting to the sky.

A dozen people wreathed the stones, their skin luminous and pale. Their ankle-length robes shimmered silver beneath the moon's caress. Six men and six women were dressed the same. But he saw the men had short hair, and the tips of their ears were pointed. They raised their hands to the sky, chanting lyrical words he could not understand. They pivoted as they chanted, and began to dance, their bodies swaying in sinuous grace. Matt swayed, naturally responding to the music, the sweet melody of the voices. Entranced, he watched the Fae celebrate the approaching full moon.

Suddenly their robes became pale as starlight and vanished. The twelve naked Fae continued to dance, then paired off. Male and female joined together, arms winding around each other, the couples backing up against the stones. The air grew heavy with musk, the erotic scent winding around Matt and holding him immobilized. He could not move, only watch, a helpless prisoner to the sensual play.

One male lifted a female and positioned her against a stone. Moaning, she clung to him as she opened her legs, revealing the glistening pink of her sex. The musk of her arousal floated on the wind. The male smiled with satisfaction, his phallus jutting and strong. He positioned himself against the female's center and thrust. She flinched, then moaned as he began to piston his hips, pounding hard and fast into her.

His blood ran thick and hot. Matt's body tightened, his own sexual need pouring through his veins. He closed his eyes, seeing the woman as Sienna, her long, slender limbs spread wide for him, the hot spice of her own arousal perfuming the air. Her eyes would be soft with desire, a flush pinking her cheeks, her mouth swollen and smudged from his hot, possessive kisses.

His erection throbbed with painful intensity as he lifted her by the buttocks, holding her easily against the stone, the symbol of nature's fertility. Slowly, so slowly, the tip of his arousal prodded the sweet entrance to her body. Then the tight, hot feel of wet silk as he surged forward, feeling her clench tightly around him.

It was heaven, oh, gods, it was intense; he shook with the pleasure of it. It was raw and exciting, the jagged pants of his own breath, her tiny, excited cries…it was…

His eyes snapped open.

The scent had shifted, lined with something foul and dark, like sewer water tainting perfume. Matt's erection faded.

This was all wrong.

The couples writhed and moaned as they made love, but their moans began to sound like hideous cackles, vacant of the enchanting whispering music they'd created earlier. It was no longer lusty and earthy, but crude and base.

Even the molecules of air shifted, carrying a faintly sinister heaviness. Then he realized what was missing. No night sounds of the forest. Even the crickets were eerily silent.

A cloying metallic scent slammed into him like a freight train. Matt went still.

Blood.

He swept the circle with his gaze, searching for the source. There. In the center of the stones was a pile of furred carcasses. Dead animals. Squirrels, rabbits, beaver. They'd been slaughtered and left like small sacrifices to the stones.

It made no sense. The Fae protected, not killed, the forest animals. Even the rare times when they did kill, it was purely defensive.

This looked sinister, like a blood sacrifice.

Had to do recon while they were distracted. As the Fae couples continued to make love, he slipped among the trees, his feet making no noise.

A crackle of branches. He went still, searching the air. Twenty yards in front of him, something moved in the bushes.

Interesting.

As a SEAL, several missions had involved insertions into enemy territory. He used this training now more than his wolf, trusting in it more than wolf's abilities to slip through the woods. He made no noise as he followed the odd scent to the base of a tall cliff.

Stunned, he watched the grayish creature fly into a small

recess in the cliffs. Suddenly a vivid orange glow came from the recess. A fire?

Matt glanced around, the cold air tightening his muscles. He had no equipment, no resources. And no time, either.

He placed a hand on the rock, feeling it cold and hard beneath his fingertips. He could scale the cliff. Wouldn't be easy, but he could do it.

And then his blood chilled as he thought of Sienna, alone and vulnerable back in the cabin. Unprotected.

If something sinister were afoot, he had to ensure her safety first. No way in hell could he leave her. He didn't know their customs or culture that well. But every Draicon instinct warned something was wrong with these Fae.

Torn, he glanced upward, itching to follow. Finally his hand dropped in frustration and he clenched his fists.

Matt turned to find the path to Sienna's cabin. He trotted through the woods and gained the path. But at the section demarking the Fae territory, he ground to a halt.

And then he stared in shock.

The trees had closed in like a fence, barring the way. Magick.

Heart lodged in his throat, he tried to make his way back, meeting only solid pine trunks, brush lodged between each one, making an effective barricade. Matt kept following the line, trying to find a way past. Brambles scraped through his clothing, cutting his chest and arms. He was forced to turn back.

The Fae's defense system had detected his presence. His jaw tightened.

No choice. Had to shift.

The change came slow, pain riding his bones. He gritted his teeth, riding through it, realizing Fae magick also prohibited the shift. Finally, success. On four paws, he prowled, muzzle lifted, teeth bared in a snarl.

The trees parted before him like a crowd respectfully making way.

He loped through the woods until finding the dirt path again. Wolf raced through the woods, alert and watchful, as he followed it to the invisible barrier dividing Fae territory from the acres ringing Sienna's cabin.

Only when he could see the golden glow of lamplight coming from her cabin did he stop and shift back. Matt ran back to the cabin. Even though he'd barely run two miles, he felt as if he'd raced twenty. Wheezing, he bent over, hands braced on his knees. The Fae magick was powerful and clever, suctioning out his energy.

When he caught his breath, he went into the cabin. Sienna sat in a recliner before the blazing fire. A book was in her lap, but she stared instead at the flames.

She glanced up, her eyes widening at the blood on his shirt.

"I got caught in brambles."

The book fell to the floor. "Fae brambles. I recognize the markings."

Matt glanced downward in surprise. The scratches on his bare arms had a distinct outline in the shape of a wolf.

Sienna went to him, gently traced one of the marks. "The woods near the border of Fae territory are warded with magick to allow in all animals, and paranorms who appear as animals. They mark you to identify your animal form. The marks will fade, but reappear if you cross the border again."

Her touch felt soothing as she ran a finger over the reddened scratch.

"Tell me about the standing stones."

Her hand rested on his skin. She looked surprised. "You got through that far? The warding must be fading."

"I saw a ceremony." He watched her expression. "Fae ringing the stones, chanting, as they danced. Then they removed their robes and made love."

Her eyes widened. "The autumn harvest moon dance. They celebrate the fecundity of the summer for a final time, planting the seeds that will slumber through winter and awaken in the spring." Her eyes darkened and he caught the sweet scent of her arousal. "Six couples trying to conceive are chosen for this honor. It's a celebration of conception. It's said the standing stones aid in fertility."

Blood surged, hot and thick, through his veins as he thought of his earlier vision of Sienna. Matt frowned.

"Do they sacrifice animals, as well?"

She blinked. "Never."

"I saw animal carcasses in the center of the stone circle."

"Oh, that. They were probably animals killed by predators. We put them in the center of the circle as a symbol of the circle of life and death…as the couples make love, to create new life."

"Interesting tradition," he murmured.

A delicate flush tinted her cheeks. "The dance is filled with magick, and makes the night come alive. The Fae celebrate the ritual as a sacred tradition." She gave a little sigh. "I was to participate when I chose a mate, but…no dance for me."

She looked so wistful, it tugged at his heart. Matt went to the stereo system, flipped through a few CDs. He inserted one. As the lyrical melody filled the cabin, he stood, holding out a hand.

"Dance with me instead, Sienna."

No refusal brooked in that husky command. Matt's palm was warm as he pulled her to him. Sienna rested her cheek against his broad shoulder, feeling the heat of his body through his clothing. Beard stubble shadowed his jaw. He looked wild, like a wolf.

Yet this wolf had been only gentle with her. She kept finding more sides to him, the considerate man hiding beneath a protective layer of warrior and wolf. Matt was strong, fiercely loyal, courageous and would fall on his sword before harming her.

Holding her with ease, his steps were sure and light as he guided her around the room. She felt the tensile strength of him.

"Let go, Sienna. There's nothing to be scared of. Let go of all your inhibitions." His deep whisper sent a delightful shiver coursing down her spine.

The promise of sex gleamed in his blue eyes. Her body hummed instinctively to the sultry call of his demand.

A small moan escaped her as he kissed the underside of her ear. Sienna clasped his shoulders, her fingers digging into his wide shoulders. She explored the length of his body, dropping a hand between them to the front of his jeans. The rigid length of his arousal met her palm. She stroked, fascinated by this wolf's desire for her.

A low growl reverberated through his deep chest, but this time, it didn't scare her. Sienna leaned closer. Fisting a hand through her hair, he crushed his mouth against hers. It was no gentle, teasing kiss, but a wolf staking his possessive claim. His tongue boldly thrust past her lips, tasting her, exploring the wet cavern of her mouth. Moaning, she clutched fistfuls of his shirt as she sagged against him.

He kept at it, exquisite sensual torture, the tension simmering just below the surface. As if his life depended on her, his next breath.

Heat and masculine lust radiated from him. He nipped her bottom lip, then licked it in a lingering caress. She opened her eyes, startled at his hot, intent look.

Sex with Matt meant more than surrendering to his sexual dominance.

It meant forging a physical link between them, tying her physically to this strong, courageous wolf. Making love would be intimate and emotional, digging past all her defenses she'd erected since leaving the colony.

As if he knew, Matt slowed and stopped. He cupped her cheek tenderly.

The look shattered her. He gazed at her as if she were the most precious thing on earth. As if nothing else mattered, not his being a SEAL, nor a wolf. Only her. The sheer tender longing crumbled her resolve. No Fae had ever made her feel like this, had wanted her this badly.

He was a covert wolf, who risked his own life to protect others. All her life, she'd lived a covert life as a Fae, secluding herself from the world. Suddenly she wanted to throw herself headfirst into all he offered in the promise of his soft, seductive smile. Sienna shook with her own longing.

"Make love to me, Matt," she whispered. "Make me yours tonight. I don't care about anything else right now."

They were only a man and a woman, with this burning need between them.

He took her into the bedroom, snapped on a light. Matt tugged the shirt over his head and shed his boots and pants. Breath caught in her throat.

"Um, wow. You were right. Commando," she managed to say.

He looked up with a grin as he kicked his clothing aside. Dark hair covered his chest, stretching from nipple to nipple. Muscles layered his flat abdomen, his biceps. She glanced down at his genitals. His thick shaft was long and erect.

The thought of taking his hardness into her body filled her with anticipation and slight fear. Curious, eager to explore his body, she went around him, touched the small marking of a running wolf.

"What's this?"

"The mark of our team. A member of the Phoenix Force gets branded with it after the first time he goes on an op."

Muscles quivered beneath her touch, then he shuddered as she kissed the mark, tasting the salt of his skin.

Heat smoldered in his gaze as he turned. Never had anyone looked at her with such fire, such stark craving.

"Undress for me," he said softly.

Slowly she removed her clothes. Her body tingled with arousal, hungering for the contact between them. She was naked, shivering as cool air caressed her breasts. Self-conscious, she covered them. Gently, he placed his hands over hers and guided them to her sides.

"You're so beautiful."

Tremendous heat suffused her beneath the warmth of his gaze. Sienna arched beneath his touch as Matt thumbed her cresting nipples. When he bent his head and took one into his mouth, she clung to him, dizzy with need, her core growing wet and throbbing. He swirled his tongue over the taut peak, then suckled her. She was growing hotter now, a fire stoking inside her as the sweet tension braced her body.

They fell onto the bed, as he kept kissing her breasts. She whimpered, her hips rising and falling off the mattress, driven by instincts of her own.

"Soon," he soothed her.

Gathering her close, he ran a hand over her silky skin, marveling at her softness. Matt kissed her deeply, his hand drifting over her belly, down to her feminine curls. She made a startled sound, which he soothed with his kisses, as he slid a finger across her wet cleft.

Sienna gripped his wide shoulders as he began playing with her, easing her into passion. His wolf howled at the heady scent of her, but he grimly focused on her pleasure. Not his own. Matt slipped a finger inside her, drew it out. Tight. She was so very tight. The thought of her surrounding his cock made him nearly lose it.

Slowly he began to pleasure her, loving her little moans,

the way she squeezed around him. He wanted to absorb her, brand her with his mark of passion.

Because this wasn't destined to last. Nothing ever could with him.

Pushing aside the thought, he teased and stroked. Naturally sensual, Sienna would discover her own wild nature, and release the wolf inside her.

His fingers lightly circled her center, feeling her tense beneath him.

It was consuming, setting her on fire, every inch of her body crying out for something more. Sienna strained toward him as he teased and stroked, his hands sure and skillful. The ache between her legs intensified and she pumped her hips upward, desperate for something she didn't understand. Every stroke and whorl sucked air from her lungs until she gasped for breath, ready to burst out of her skin. Tension heightened, spiraling her upward and upward. And then the feeling between her legs exploded. Sienna screamed, crying out his name as she dug her nails into his wide shoulders.

Her eyes fluttered as she fell back to the bed, spent and dazed.

Finally, her breathing eased and she lifted her head. A hint of untamed danger lurked in his eyes. The wolf barely held at bay.

Then he gave a dangerous smile. "Again."

Matt knew she was shy. So many new experiences, and with a wolf, yet. Teaching her about the pleasure between a man and a woman would erase those emotions. He dropped to his knees as she lay on the bed, breathing heavily.

"Trust me, Sienna. Will you trust me?"

When she nodded, he smiled reassuringly. "Good. Now lie back, and just relax."

Deeply moved at her absolute trust as she did so, he leashed the wolf howling to mate. Her pleasure first. Always. Once was not enough. Matt splayed her thighs wide open with his hands, the feel of her soft, silky skin driving him wild.

He stared at the wet, pink flesh of her center, scenting her arousal. "Gods, you are so beautiful," he said thickly.

Then he put his mouth on her.

The first touch of his warm tongue made her jerk backward in delighted shock. He slid his tongue between her folds in slow, steady strokes.

Hot, delicious honey slid down his throat. Her sweetness ran for him as he stroked her. Matt swirled his tongue, absorbing her scent into him, marking her with the taste of arousal. Going to push her harder, and faster. Sienna cried out, her hands fisted in his hair. He could feel her excitement gathering, the crescendo of sweet tension ready to shatter her once more.

When she screamed his name, he stayed with her until the shudders ceased. Then he looked up with a small smile, backhanding his mouth. His cock ached with the need to penetrate. He opened the drawer and withdrew the condoms he'd placed there and sheathed himself.

She was ready now.

"Give in, pixie," he whispered. "Let me inside."

Mounting her, he felt the enormous strain of his muscles from trying to take it slow. He kissed her. Over and over, his tongue stroking her inside, imitating what was to come with his body. Nudging his hips between her legs, he braced himself on his hands.

"Look at me," he commanded.

Slowly he pushed slightly inside her. Trust filled her wide green eyes. Hellfire, it felt so good, her tight, wet core squeezing his cock. Matt strained to hold back. Sienna needed tenderness and good loving.

She needed to know that a wolf knew how to love, and not hurt.

His heavy weight covered her, pinning her to the bed. Silky hair from his thighs sensually rubbed against her legs as he lay between them. This was the moment, then, when she shed all her cares and thoughts and joined with him.

Needing this closeness, wanting to share herself with him.

Matt laced his fingers through hers, his gaze fierce and glittering. Slowly he pushed into her. He felt huge, thick and invasive. She wriggled, trying to find ease as he penetrated.

Matt dropped tiny kisses over her face, soothed her with a whisper. Then he thrust forward again. Slight pain accompanied the odd fullness. He stayed still, watching her. Waiting for her to make the next move. A drop of sweat rolled off his forehead, splashed upon her like a tear. Sienna became aware of just how much control he exerted, how much this meant to him.

Experimentally, she wriggled her hips as the pain gradually faded. She relaxed, opening to him, marveling at the unique feeling of him joined to her so intimately.

He pulled back and began to stroke inside her. His muscles contracted as he thrust, powerful shoulders flexing and back arching. This was Matt, who cared for her, who would lay down his life for her. Not a vicious wolf who cared only about his own needs. Deep inside, her long-neglected wolf answered his call to mate. Sienna's natural sensuality took over as she rose up to meet his rhythm.

The delicious friction was wonderful, the closeness of his body to hers, his tangy scent filling her nostrils. She pumped her hips, as he taught her the rhythm, feeling the silky slide of the hair on his legs. He began to move faster, his gaze holding hers as he claimed her with every thrust into her untried body, with each soft word of reassurance he murmured.

She could fall in love with this brave wolf. Maybe she already had. Emotions crowded her chest as she gripped his hard shoulders. It felt as if he locked her spirit in his, a closeness she'd never experienced.

His thrusts became more urgent. Close, so close… She writhed and reached for it, the tension growing until she felt ready to explode.

Screaming his name, she came again, squeezing him tightly as she arched nearly off the bed. Above her Matt growled deeply, but this time she wasn't scared. Sienna welcomed the sound, welcomed his wolf's call. He threw his head back with a hoarse shout. Collapsing atop her, he pillowed his head next to hers.

For a few minutes they lay tangled together, the sheets damp with perspiration, the cool night air sweeping over their bodies. Then he rolled off.

Matt gathered her close. Never had he spent the night with a woman. He'd always left afterward, not wanting any entanglements or complications. Not with Sienna.

She deserved to be held. All night.

He stroked a hand through the hair tangled on his pillow. Matt curled his big body next to her slender one, and draped a muscled arm about her waist to anchor her to him. She snuggled against him with a tiny sigh.

She was his, and he always took care of his own.

No matter what.

Chapter 14

With his long, jeans-clad legs stretched out before him, Matt lounged in a chair on the back porch. Sun streaked the mountains in rose and lavender. As Sienna watched from the kitchen door, he took a long pull of coffee from a mug.

Chipmunks and birds scavenged for seeds at the bird feeder. After the Fae had banished her to this cabin, she'd installed the feeder to lure the animals as company. Some days she was so lonely their noisy chatter helped fend off the desolation.

Not alone now. Not after last night… A flush ignited her cheeks. Warmth filled her as she remembered the gentleness of his lovemaking, the fierce pleasure he'd coaxed her to feel. Her body felt sore in places she'd never felt sore before, her muscles tingling with a pleasant ache. The piercing loneliness had vanished with this muscled wolf.

Sienna pressed her nose against the glass, staring in avid hunger at the big Draicon on her back porch. He was relaxed, yet she sensed an alertness that never fully left. He looked good in her home.

It felt right to have him here, as if he belonged.

Yet he did not.

The warmth faded, leaving her shivering. Last night's fantasy of warmth and acceptance had sharpened into the cold facts. Matt was Draicon, and these woods belonged to the Fae. Just as she did.

But for these few precious days they had left, she would grab everything life gave her, and cherish it. Sienna opened the sliding door and stepped outside, pulling her fleece robe tight. Feeling shy, remembering his big body as it covered hers last night, his soothing murmurs as he'd entered her untried body. The intimacy they'd shared, and the feverish pleasure he'd coaxed her to feel.

He glanced up, his smile warm. Matt patted his lap. "You look freezing, sweetheart. Sit."

His arm curled around her waist as she settled into his lap. Sienna pillowed her head on his broad shoulder. He stroked her hair in slow, tender caresses.

"You okay?" he murmured.

The earlier shyness returned. Sienna nodded, her throat tight.

Together they sat in companionable silence, watching the sunrise paint the mountains.

"Twilight used to be my favorite time of day," she mused. "When the sun sets and the light grows rosy. There's a stillness in the air of the world settling down. I'd sit in my secret place in the woods. Knowing I could go home and there'd be a big meal and laughter, and dancing by the night fires."

A lump clogged her throat. "That's all gone. Now I like dawn, because it's a new day. Fresh hope. And it means the night, and all the loneliness, is behind me for a while."

He rubbed his cheek against her head. "Yet they allowed you to stay here."

"It's a two-step program. Give me a home close enough, a chance to find a job and be on my own. Sometimes I thought it was best if I left for good. Went east, or anywhere, away from here."

"Why didn't you?"

Sienna stared at the wood rail fence. "Because I kept feeling there's unfinished business here. Something happened in these woods. It's buried deep in my memories, but I can't retrieve it. And until I do, I'll never feel whole. I'll always have half a life. And I'll always wonder, What's my purpose? Surviving? It's not enough. There's something mysterious in my past. I have to discover who I am."

Matt cupped her chin and gently turned her toward him. "I know who you are, Sienna. You're beautiful on the outside, but it's your inner strength and beauty that are strongest. I don't know why your people insisted on abandoning you. I do know this. You're a survivor. No matter what happens, where you go, you'll do just fine. I have faith in you. You're going to keep kicking life in the butt and winning, because that's who you are. A woman who never gives up, and each time someone slams you down, you'll get back up and keep fighting."

A reassuring smile touched his mouth. "You'd have made a helluva SEAL, if they allowed females on the teams."

His kiss was warm and tender, a promise of heat. She leaned her forehead against his, running her fingers through the silken strands of his dark hair. "You mean, if they allowed Fae on the teams."

Matt's smile slipped a notch. "Half Fae."

"The half that matters most to me."

A chill frosted the air that had nothing to do with the bitter wind. "You're half Draicon. And you still want nothing to do with your wolf."

Her heart gave a painful tug. "My wolf half is the half that hurt my mother. I have bad blood inside me, Matt."

"How can you be sure? Your memories may be tainted."

"I remember a cruel and evil father, and what Chloe told me. The Fae inside me needs to grow stronger. How can I ever find a place among them if I embrace my Draicon half, the blood inside me that caused so much pain?"

"You're not cruel. Sienna, you're compassionate and strong. Whatever memories you have of your father may be tainted. And if they aren't, what he was doesn't mean you're the same." His eyes were a fierce blue. "Don't deny your Draicon heritage because you're afraid of what you'll find."

She sat up straight. "I'm not afraid. I just know what I am. Where I belong. They raised me. They're my family. They're a part of my life and I can't let them go."

"Yet they let you go."

The old hurt stabbed her in the heart. "Because it's their way. I needed to prove myself."

"You don't need to prove anything. Not to me. Or any Draicon." His gaze was intense. "I would never let you go, Sienna. When all this is done, break free of the colony. Accept your wolf nature instead of pushing it aside. Until you do, you'll never find peace."

As she pushed off his lap, an icy cold settled into her bones. Matt looked expressionless, his big body tensing. He was alert and watchful like a wolf. Dangerous. Her gaze roved over his big body, remembering how skillfully he'd made love, bringing her from one height of pleasure to another. He was a consummate warrior who knew his own strength, could snap a man's neck with his bare hands, but he'd been gentle and tender with her.

She'd thought Draicon wolves were nasty and cruel, thinking only of their own base needs. Not Matt. He was different. With a startled pang, she realized she was falling for him.

Panic clogged her throat. She couldn't risk giving her heart to Matt. It meant giving up everything she'd known her entire life. Tough, courageous Matt with his quiet strength and raw sexuality did not fit into her world.

Matt was a shooting star, brilliant and fiery, but temporary. And he was wolf, enemy to the Fae.

"I'm not wolf. I'm Fae. I'll prove it and drop this glamour. It's nothing more than glamour, Matt," she said.

Closing her eyes, she culled the image of her Fae self. No more Draicon glamour. Sienna thought of quiet forest glades, the serenity of her people, their chants and music and history.

She raised her arms and concentrated with all her might.

And opened her eyes. Sienna glanced at her hands.

Her skin wasn't pale, like a Fae's. Reflected in the shiny glass of the sliding door was a woman who looked exactly the same as before.

Sienna staggered back, putting her hands to her face, touching her eyes. Not large Fae eyes with a slight slant and delicate arched brows. But Draicon eyes.

Ashamed, she went inside, into the bedroom. Studying her reflection in the mirror, she tried to analyze what happened. If she couldn't summon her Fae self, then how could she return to her people?

She'd have nowhere to go.

The sliding glass door opened and shut again. She felt two strong hands settle on her shaking shoulders.

"I can't do it. My glamour is fading. I can't even assume my own form anymore."

"It's okay, Sienna," he murmured. "It's okay. You're perfect just the way you are."

She offered a small smile. "You make me feel that way. You're pretty special, Lieutenant Parker."

She wanted to lean against him, soak in the comfort he offered. Gods, she was tired of trying to be strong on her own.

When they separated, he studied her. Eyes blue and piercing as lasers locked on her. A hank of hair fell into her eyes. Gently, he brushed it away.

"You're amazing and lovely, and have so much to offer. Your people are stupid for letting you leave. I'd never let you go."

Words from a strong warrior who admired her. Self-confidence flared again. Matt wanted her. Someone of great worth desired her. Her eyes tracked the bulge and flex of biceps, the wideness of his shoulders stretched against the tight T-shirt, the body of a hardened warrior. Intense longing shivered through her. She wanted to draw close and achieve what they'd shared last night. He'd made her feel special and cherished.

"Make me forget, Matt. Just for a while, I don't want to remember anything," she whispered.

Sienna slid her arms around his neck, feeling tensile strength in his wide shoulders. She parted her mouth as he bent his head. Warmth surged through her as his tongue thrust past her parted lips. Never before had a kiss felt so arousing, possessive and intense. Sienna closed her eyes, losing herself in sensation. She craved the closeness of last night, the fragile bond they'd created in the flesh.

She concentrated on the hot plunge of his tongue, the casual, skilled strokes he delivered.

He kept kissing her, his hand drifting up to her breast. He cupped it, gently kneading. Then his thumb drifted lazily over the tightening nipple. Sienna gasped as sharp, delicious pleasure speared her. His hips rocked gently, his rock-hard erection pressing against her, indicating his need.

Lips moved against hers, kissing with arrogant authority. He sucked on her bottom lip, released it with a faint popping sound. Whispered into her mouth.

"I'll make you forget, starshine. Make you forget."

Ragged need made his voice deepen. She bit her trembling lips. "I think—"

He laid a finger over her mouth. "Don't think. Just feel. No excuses, no changing your mind. Because if I don't have you, right now, I'm going to die."

A shaky hiss of breath escaped her lungs. He pulled her to him once more, kissing her, forcing her thighs open as he wedged himself between them. Palming her breasts, cupping and squeezing. The slow slide of his hands intensified the deep ache between her thighs. She felt empty. She wanted him to fill her, completely. Wanted to chase away the horrible feeling of failure. Matt made her feel feminine and desirable.

The fever built, scorching her with each stroke of his hands. Burning hotter as his fingers drifted lower, teasing lightly as he cupped her mound. She made little moaning sounds against his mouth, opening her legs wider, trying to get closer. They writhed and tangled with each other until her back met the wall and he caged her there with his body.

He tore himself away, his breaths ragged, his firm lips parted. Matt groaned as she licked his collarbone, tasting the salt of his skin. She lightly bit.

"Please. Now." Her voice trembled.

Parting her robe, he slid a hand beneath the fabric. Surprised pleasure dawned on his face as his fingers caressed the tangle of damp feminine curls. Sizzling heat bit as his fingers explored lower. He lightly stroked a finger across her wet, throbbing cleft. Her body arched, muscles squeezed. Sienna cried out, pushing her hips frantically against his exploring fingers.

"Easy," he soothed.

His fingers parted her folds, found her slick wetness. Rubbed slowly, lightly, stoking the fire to unbearable tension. Sienna moaned, throwing her head back, tunneling her fingers in his silky hair.

She nearly sobbed in frustration when he broke contact. He quieted her with a soothing whisper, then swept a hand across the nightstand, fumbling for the condoms he'd placed there.

His hand dropped between them. She heard the slide of a metal zipper unfastening, latex slipping over hard flesh. The jutting length of his erect penis indented her soft belly.

Sienna braced herself for the full impact of that rigid cock.

Matt cupped her bare bottom, kneaded and squeezed. With seamless ease, he lifted her. He positioned himself. The hard, rounded knob of his penis settled against her wet, throbbing cleft.

He pushed himself slowly inside. Pleasure etched his face as his eyes closed, as if he relished this moment of exquisite contact. Her core tightened in agonized need. Muscle and sinew in his shoulders tautened beneath the digging pressure of her fingertips. "Please!" Her voice rasped in a hoarse cry.

"Tell me what you want," he demanded, opening his eyes, his gaze fierce and glittering.

"You," she gasped.

"Look at me, Sienna," he commanded.

His ragged breath rasped. With a powerful thrust, he fully entered her. Sienna arched, gasping at the smooth, hard thickness of his penis. He was huge, thick and almost impossible to take. She wriggled around him, the discomfort turning to alarm. Immediately he withdrew slightly.

"Shhh," he murmured soothingly.

Holding her still, he pushed forward again. The feel of him between her thighs was like having a hot, thick bar pushing past the quivering muscles of her tight sheath. She clung to him, wetness dripping out of her, readying her for him as he withdrew.

He coaxed her mouth to his, stroking her bottom lip in long, sensual caresses. Sienna eagerly accepted the deep strokes of his tongue. Desperate to have him move again, she whimpered, making rocking motions with her hips.

Matt leaned his forehead against hers tenderly. "I know," he whispered.

He adjusted his position and pushed deep inside her, his gaze intent on her face. Sienna gripped him as he began to thrust deep and hard. She writhed helplessly against the smooth glide of his penis. He pumped steadily into her, driving upward as harsh groans rumbled from his deep chest. Sienna bucked her hips against him, feeling the delicious friction, the building tension as he penetrated. Closing her eyes, she surrendered to her body's needs. The grip of his strong fingers kneading her bare bottom, her legs tightened around his lean waist, the delicious thickness sliding in and out of her wet sheath. He was muscled, hard, controlling her with each demanding stroke of his thick shaft. His breaths came harsh and ragged. She burned. Oh, close, so close it was…

"Come on, pixie," he panted. "Let go. Come for me. Come for me, that's it!"

Stifling a cry, she climaxed, her core squeezing and milking him. She sagged against the wall bonelessly. Matt groaned, his powerful body bucking and shuddering against hers, head tossed back, jaw working violently.

His lungs bellowed air, mingling with her own rasping breaths. Slowly he pulled free, lowering her to the floor, then he ripped off the condom.

Escaping into the bathroom, she closed the door behind her. Sienna braced her hands on the sink. The face staring in the mirror had wide green eyes, a smudged and kiss-swollen mouth. No dignified Fae here. Only the wanton, flushed sensuality of the wolf looked back.

Sienna emerged, the earlier euphoria faded into stricken guilt. She'd just had more wild, abandoned sex with a Draicon werewolf. A navy SEAL, no less, who'd admitted his lifestyle was too erratic to settle down. Driven by her body's demands, she'd forgotten. Oh, yes, he'd done as she asked. For a few moments of incredible pleasure, she'd forgotten. Reality crashed down around her.

Matt waited in the bedroom. Sweat glistened on his brow, and his shirt hung open, showing a tantalizing glimpse of hard chest covered with dark hair. So sexy and powerful. The longing shooting through her hurt so badly, she shook from it.

Grappling with lost composure, she pulled the lapels of her robe tight.

"Hey." His expression grew troubled as he scanned her face. "You okay?"

When she nodded, he cupped her cheek. "What's wrong, sweetheart. You look upset."

"I was thinking about the Fae." She gulped down a breath. "Every time I get closer to you, I grow farther apart from them. I feel like I'm wandering in a forest without a way home."

He grew quiet a minute, as if gathering his patience. "I know how confusing it must feel. But I'm with you in this."

"For how long?" she blurted out. "Until you leave, and then I'm alone again."

Matt sighed and she saw the damnable truth on his face. "We'll work it out. You're different, Sienna, too good for the Fae. Just give it a chance. My people have a lot to offer you, too."

She had to steel herself against his soft words and tender promises. Sienna pulled away, throwing up every emotional barrier to keep him at bay.

"If they have so much to offer, why do you deny them, as well? Your family, Matt. You rarely see them. Your life as a SEAL means more than your own Draicon heritage. You can't give it up, can you? You're more bonded to the navy than your own pack."

Inwardly, she cringed. A flash of hurt entered his gaze, then it became guarded and distant. He rubbed the back of his neck.

"Probably true."

He turned to leave the bedroom. Matt glanced over his shoulder, the mouth she'd adored kissing now a straight, firm slash.

"But know this, Sienna. You can run, but you can't escape what you are. Because sooner or later, it will catch up to you. And when it does, you'll discover what you've been running from is what you've been searching for all this time."

The door closed with a firm, decisive click as she puzzled over his words.

Chapter 15

That afternoon they removed the purse from the safe.

The mood was strained with the morning's tension. She stole a shy look at him. "The nicest gift anyone ever bought me. Thanks, Matt. It was beautiful."

Then they began stripping off the decor. Each bead and stone was carefully removed and examined. It was methodical, tedious and slow. Nothing happened. Finally, when they'd stripped the purse of its decorative covering, she undid the clasp and peered inside.

Nothing.

Sienna laid her hands on the purse, closing her eyes. If Tim had cloaked the Orb through Fae magick, it would be revealed through Fae magick. But as she strained to connect with her roots, she felt only blackness and despair.

Opening her eyes, she shook her head. "It's impossible. I can't do this. My magick isn't powerful. I'm not good enough."

"You can."

"Maybe I should just give up. Give it to Aunt Chloe. A pureblood."

Gods, she hated admitting that.

Matt was silent a moment. When he spoke, his gaze was distant.

"When I was going through Hell Week, the hardest week of training to become a navy SEAL, there came a time when I wanted to give up. I'd broken my leg. Draicon heal fast, but because I had to run on it so soon, it didn't set right. The pain was…bad. We had to run five miles down the beach, in boots. I didn't think I would make it."

Sienna glanced at him. "How did you do it, then?"

"Adam. Wildcat was my swim buddy, refused to let me ring out, which means quitting. He told me, 'It's not your body that's letting you down. It's your mind. It's a mental game, wolf. You have to want it badly enough to ride out the pain.'"

A ghost of a grin touched his mouth. "Then he called me a pussy, hooked his arm around my waist and helped me finish the run."

Gratitude swelled inside her. He'd shared a part of himself he'd kept private. "Adam was special, like you, Matt. Courageous and strong, able to persevere through pain. It must have been very important to you."

Matt gave her a steady look. "That's what it's all about in life. Determination and endurance when you're chasing a dream you want to come true. How much do you want it, Sienna? Because it doesn't matter what kind of blood you are. You just have to want it badly enough."

He was strength and steadfast determination, and his presence gave her the courage to admit it aloud. "I want it more than anything. I need to find out the truth."

"Then do it," he encouraged.

Sienna fingered a bead. "I'm sorry I snapped at you. I feel

so confused. Maybe that's why finding the Orb is so important. It's not just returning it to my people. It's hoping I'll find it and realize the truth of who I really am."

"This magick rock can't give you all the answers, Sienna," he said quietly. "Some people search for their whole life for those answers, and never discover the truth."

Sienna closed her eyes and laid her hands on the purse. A faint vibration shimmered through her. Then it faded as quickly as it began.

But this time she felt a tugging inside her, like a child yanking on his mother's skirt. Insight hit her, along with fresh hope. "This cabin is blocking the magick. If Tim used a spell to hide the Orb, he drew on the elements of nature to fuel his power. There's a lake sacred to the Fae. If we go there, maybe it will help clear the air. And my mind."

Shifting his backpack, Matt concentrated on the hike to the Fae lake. Wind blew through the Olympia pines, rustled through the valley as they ascended the steep path. The narrow trail was a straight vertical climb, accented by glimpses of heart-stopping views through the sun-dappled pine boughs. Huckleberry and juniper shrubs clustered along the pathway and the outcroppings of granite.

Sienna climbed steadily on. He admired her determination, her toughness, as she scampered over rocks and through small caches of muddy earth. The blue jeans stretched tightly over her round bottom. He ground down his arousal, remembering how he'd clutched her ass, lifting her for his mighty thrusts as he'd slid into her hot, tight wetness....

"The lake at the summit is lovely," she called over her shoulder. "But this time of year, it's well below freezing."

He could use a dip in an icy lake.

He'd sealed her to him, bonding to her in the flesh. And for the first time, he wanted more, craved more. Craved her in his bed, coaxing a smile to her face as he pleasured her, yes. But waking up with her in the morning, teasing her, laughing with her....

Dream on, he thought grimly.

Some time later they reached the summit. Sienna led the way around the oval-shaped lake, to a fallen log on the shore.

Wind skittered across the deep blue water, pushing it into waves of shimmering ripples. Leaden clouds scudded across the sky. Near the fallen log, granite rocks marched across a small clearing like a fence. Long, narrow slashes gouged a dead tree.

Dense stands of ponderosa pine and Douglas fir ringed the still waters. Sienna sat on the fallen log, scuffing her hiking boot heel in the pebbled ground. Lily pads floated on the clear water. Through the trampled, yellowing grass, he saw paw prints.

Not deer, but wolf. Matt squatted down, examining it, detecting a fragrant scent.

"No wolf packs in these mountains. Not for years. Odd, a lone wolf, pausing at the lake to drink. Same set of prints, but here more than once. Several times. A favorite habitat."

Sienna stiffened.

"Come here often?"

She turned, defiance flaring in her green eyes. "It was a good place to practice my glamour."

Beneath the scrutiny of his steady gaze, she crumpled. Shoulders sagging, she slumped over, tracing a pattern of odd symbols in the earth. Fae symbols.

He sensed the inner war, the struggle for identity. Matt's heart ached for her. Damn, he knew the kind of struggle, trying to find your footing in a world where you didn't know quite where you belonged.

He was a respected navy SEAL, but considered mysterious and aloof, left alone by all outside his team. He was a Draicon werewolf, but to his family, bewildering and foreign.

"It is a good place to practice. I can see why the Fae revere it."

Sitting beside her, he placed a hand on her shoulder, gave a reassuring squeeze. Gratitude shone in her eyes.

"This place, it calls to me. There's something about it, so serene and yet riddled with memory."

"You shifted into wolf to try recovering those memories," he said gently.

"It hasn't worked in Fae or human form. In my dreams, I see this lake, hear the wind pushing at the tree limbs. I've known this place a long time." She looked up, and her anguish cut him like a hot blade. "A place of serenity and violence. Something terrible happened here long ago. And I can't remember anything. Tim came here, as well, but never shared anything with me."

After removing the purse from her backpack, she set it on her lap and concentrated. A few minutes later, she opened her eyes. "Nothing still. Maybe there's something here that Tim left that can help. Something he touched, that I can touch and channel his energy."

She paused, her eyes huge and beseeching. "Matt...I need your help, as wolf, your sense of scent. Can you please shift and search? I don't know if you recall his scent..."

"I remember," he said shortly.

Never would he forget the traitor's scent. It was stamped into his mind like a brand.

The change came swiftly, man to wolf. The breeze drifting over the lake ruffled his thick fur. He pawed at the ground, senses exploding with awareness. The earthy scent of animals hiding in the brush a mile away, decaying vegetation. He concentrated, pushing aside the scents, digging beneath the layers. Tail pointed straight out, chest thrown out, muzzle to the snowcapped mountains, he inhaled.

Smelled pure, white magick, mingled with dark. Yet overriding it was a dark scent, tainted and foul. He caught Tim's scent, but out in the lake. Odd.

Near the shore, a small granite boulder sat in the frigid water. Matt leaped from the shore to the rock, paws scrabbling for purchase on the slippery surface. The Tim scent was stronger here.

Something else as well was present. Faint and masked partly by bird droppings and mud.

Blood.

He drew his nose closer and studied a thin streak that blended into the natural red striations of the rock.

Something died here violently, fought for its life and fought hard. Trace elements of old magick lingered in the stone. Powerful magick to have survived this long. Like a marker.

He gazed into the clear water. Seemed normal, unthreatening. Only one way to tell.

Matt jumped in.

"Wait," she cried out. "It's freezing."

Intent on searching for clues, he pawed through the muck, silt muddying the clear water. The frigid water bit through the thick layer of muscle and fur. But the cold to a wolf was nothing compared to hours in the Pacific in human form he'd endured during BUD/S training.

Concentration at maximum, he focused on the objects buried in the mud. Something was down there, and he'd find it. He pawed furiously, spraying droplets and mud over his muzzle, his fur, the rock surface.

Then, something solid. Not a rock. Very carefully, he loosened the object with a paw.

Bracing himself, he shifted into human form. Needles of ice stung his naked skin as the wind howled down the mountain. Teeth chattering, he dug into the soft muck and pulled free the object.

Matt lifted it out. Hard and yet porous. Water cascaded from one end, plunking like raindrops into the lake. Covered with a layer of fine grit and silt, it was small, but unmistakable.

A human bone.

Sienna threw a wool blanket over Matt's shaking shoulders. The temperature dropped as the sun began to slide downward into the ice-capped mountains.

If she didn't get him warmed soon, he'd slip into severe hypothermia.

Yet he seemed steady on his feet, no sign of the disorientation or the wobbly muscles. Matt grimly marched down the dirt pathway, clutching his backpack, now hiding the object he'd retrieved from the lake.

He didn't show her what it was. She was afraid to find out. Anxiety coursed through her as she followed him down the path. Dark secrets lived in the lake. Matt had just unearthed one.

The icy wind cut like a knife. Sienna knew the land, didn't fear it, but this wind mocked and howled, as if whatever Matt found had unleashed dark forces.

A branch overhanging the path slapped her face, bringing hot tears to her eyes. She heard an eerie sound, like a low cackle. Enough of this.

She turned, facing the winding pathway leading to the lake. The wind was howling with a banshee cry, sending grit and dirt into her eyes. Tree limbs snapped, flying toward her.

Sienna dodged them and held out her hands. She closed her eyes and spoke the ancient Sidhe words to calm the weather, restore peace to the land. But the words were a babble now, their cadence not lyrical, but a stutter.

The wind still howled, an angry vibration humming in the air. Matt frowned. "Let's go. It's not safe here, pixie."

But it was. She wasn't sure why.

Sienna held up a hand. "Please," she told the wind. "Stop. Be at peace. I will find what happened here."

The wind began to die. And then she heard a faint whisper coming from the direction of the lake, echoing through the valley in a ghostly whisper.

"Sienna. My beloved."

"Are you all right?" Matt asked as he came into the living room. The hot shower had felt good and finally warmed him.

"Did you hear it? Someone called my name on the path," Sienna said. She'd changed, as well, and was now wearing the long, flowing dress of the Fae, her hair pinned up in a severe twist. Armor, he realized. A defense mechanism.

He shook his head. "All I heard was the wind, and then you calmed it."

"Maybe it was an ancient Fae spirit, watching over the land." She rubbed her cheeks. "What's up there, Matt? What did you find?"

"Let's sit at the table." When they did, he unwrapped the bone.

Blood drained from her face. "A human bone."

"Part of a hand. It's been buried there for a long, long time."

"I don't understand. This mountain, and the valley, they've been Fae territory for over two hundred years. Are you saying someone got murdered and the body was dumped in the lake?"

Matt covered the bone with the napkin. "Not a human. Someone who was in human form when they were killed. Or they shifted back to their human form just as they died. Maybe as a message."

"A Fae? One of my people?" Sienna shook her head. "Aunt Chloe would have known of it. She would have buried the body and cast a cleansing spell on the lake."

Matt intensely disliked Sienna's aunt. What kind of ruler kicked out an innocent because of her mixed blood? The woman wasn't a Fae, but a witch. The Hollywood kind that rode broomsticks and cackled.

"Tell me about the lake. How long has it been since anyone but you visited?"

She tilted her head. "Longer than I can remember. The Fae said it was a sacred place, but never went there. Maybe because it was outside their colony."

"Or too damn hard to climb up that path in those fussy robes."

The joke failed to coax a smile from her. "What's going on, Matt? You felt it, as well. Something's at the lake, dark and ancient."

"Someone lost their life up there, and the residual energy, combined with the long-buried magick, surfaced when you went there."

"I haven't been to that lake since I was shunned from the community."

Things were starting to make sense. "Most paranorms come into full power when they turn twenty-one. Maybe whatever is buried up there reacted to your powers."

"Or maybe it's part of a memory I'm starting to regain."

Their gazes caught and held. In hers he saw a flare of hope mixed with deep worry.

"What if I can't recall this memory, Matt? What if it's something I don't want to recall because it has something to do with..." she pointed at the bone "...this?"

The only way was to pull that memory free. Remembering the nightmare she'd suffered in New Orleans, he hated the idea, but perhaps it might work.

Matt gathered her hands into his. "Sienna, I can help. I'm a telepath. If you'll allow it, I'll go into your mind and pull these memories free."

Her skin felt cool beneath his palms. "Invade my mind?"

"It won't hurt. I won't try unless you give me permission."

Her gaze darted around the room like a hummingbird. "You'll pry into my memories. All of them. What if you find something dark?"

"I won't change your memories, Sienna. Only free them."

Tension knotted her body as a trickle of perspiration beaded her temples. Damn, this wasn't turning out as he'd hoped. "It's not easy, I know. But it's the only way to find out what happened. Do you trust me?"

When she nodded, they settled on the sofa. Her eyes were huge and anxious. Gently he closed them with his palm.

"Just relax. Think of something pleasant and soothing."

Matt laid a hand on her forehead, keeping contact. He tunneled into her mind, connecting their thoughts, and saw them last night on the bed, tumbling together in erotic abandonment.

Then he pushed on, deeper and deeper, digging out her years like a miner with a shovel, tunneling deeper until he met with a dark dead end. A wall, solid as granite.

With extreme care, he pushed at the wall, seeing glints of light. He picked at the fragmented edges, and then saw another glimmer of light.

Burning orange, flames, the intense heat seared him, it was growing closer, it was...

"No!"

Tears streamed down her cheeks. Matt pulled out.

"It's okay," he soothed. He gathered her close, rocking her against him.

For a few minutes he held her, until she pushed away. A wildness surged in her eyes, and she seemed almost panicked.

"I have to get out of here. It's too much. Let me go, I need air."

He shook his head. "It's not safe out there, Sienna. Not alone. You need to walk and get air. I'll go with you."

"No. I don't want you with me. I have to be alone. You were there…inside my mind." She gulped down a breath. "I just need to walk, feel free. Let me go, Matt."

He thought of what he'd seen last night. "Until I find out what's happening with your people, you're not setting foot outside the cabin alone."

Blood drained from her face. "You can't be serious. I know these woods, these people. When you were in my mind…it was as if I were wolf."

"Is that such a bad thing?"

"It is for me."

"Are you saying that because you're scared of what happened when we made love?" he asked quietly.

Her lovely mouth wobbled. "Last night was so…wonderful. You're an incredible lover. I'll always cherish the memory of making love with you. I've never felt like that before. But you're…"

The look said it all.

Matt checked his irritation. "I'd never harm you, Sienna."

She didn't answer, but her gaze darted to the bedroom door. "Maybe we should walk. I'll get my coat."

As she went into the bedroom, his cell rang. Great timing. It was his C.O. Matt explained about the Orb. His heart dropped to his stomach as he listened to Curt. Report back to base in twenty-four hours and bring the purse with him if he couldn't uncloak the Orb. They'd destroy the purse.

The orders were from top brass. Entire squad was on standby. No specifics, but it had to do with intel regarding the missing explosives, the Semtex smuggled out from Libya, and homegrown terrorists planning to blow up a civilian compound.

They were navy SEALs first, paranorms second.

Matt hung up and heard a distinct thump. He glanced out the window to see Sienna racing away from the cabin. Damn it!

A possessive growl rumbled from his chest. Wolf clawed to the surface. He tried to repress it, calling on his icy control, but it spilled past, rumbling like a volcano. It was this forest, the wildness, the heady scent of Sienna in his nostrils, the quivering need inside him to mate and claim.

The calm and levelheaded SEAL vanished, pushed aside by the male werewolf who scented his headstrong and stubborn female endangering herself. Matt bounded out of the cabin, shifting as he ran.

Chapter 16

Sienna had to get away. From Matt. She felt invaded, dominated by the powerful Draicon. In danger of losing her identity.

You're a coward, a small voice taunted. *Running from the best thing that's ever happened to you.*

But she needed space, needed to break free. Running, Sienna followed a trail through the heather until she reached the open plain. Pine and yellow aspen flanked the edge. This had been a favorite place as a child. She loved to sit here, entranced by the quietness of the mountains rising like ancient guardians of the forest and its inhabitants.

The granite boulder was still there. A cool wind teased her hair, ruffling the hem of her gown. Sienna sat, hugging her knees.

The forest was the same, yet different. She couldn't place it.

It no longer welcomed her, felt like home. Something dark tainted the land, or perhaps it was her. She was no longer the same.

I don't know where I belong anymore.

The thought pierced her like a steel blade. A physical ache began in her chest. Sienna rested her cheek against her knees, lost and alone. Just like the day when her aunt had gently, but firmly, ordered her out of the colony.

You do not belong to our people any longer. The time has come for you to find your own way, my beloved daughter of our spirit.

Thanks, O Mighty Ruler. Say, can you give me some postage-paid envelopes so I can drop a line and let you know I'm still alive and kicking?

Not that you give a damn.

A dirt trail wended through the flat meadow, flanked by thick pines. Her senses pricked with awareness. Undergrowth rustled. A large timber wolf stood in the path. Her stomach churned with anxiety as the wolf bared its teeth, threw its chest out, its tail standing straight.

Its dark gaze locked on to hers, and then he growled. The sound was unmistakable. Mine. Maintaining that proud, arrogant stance.

She'd run away from Matt. And he was very angry.

Sienna's palms flattened against the rock.

Suddenly the wolf stopped. Sparks floated in the air. In the wolf's place stood a man, more than six feet tall. Wind ruffled his thick, dark hair. He was naked.

Emotion glittered in his blue eyes.

"You're mine," Matt said softly. "You won't run from me again, Sienna. Understand?"

Dry-throated, she could only manage a nod. Arousal pumped through her as she gazed at him, the proud, straight limbs, the wide shoulders and chest. Sweat glistened on his muscles. A powerful man whose concern was for her and her safety.

No Fae ever made her feel this wild yearning. No Fae ever

sent heat spiraling through her, making her center moist and ready for him. Only this Draicon did, with his spicy scent and the hard edge of sexuality, sharp as a knife blade.

Matt's nostrils flared. He'd caught the scent of her arousal. From the nest of thick, dark hair at his groin, his erection jutted out as stiff as a thick tree limb.

Sienna trembled with sexual anticipation.

This time, there would be no turning back. Wolf that he was, he would hunt her down like prey until he claimed her, naked and writhing with pleasure beneath him. A wildness flowed from him, intensified by the rawness of the land.

Intent smoldered in his steely gaze. He crossed the distance between them and leaned forward, caging her with his strong arms.

Breathing heavily, he looked as wild as the mountains ringing them. Tension threaded through his body.

"You said you don't belong anywhere. No one will accept you, Fae or Draicon. I'm telling you now, you do belong. With me. I don't give a damn about your origins, your bloodlines. Your people. They don't matter. All I care about is you."

Thickness lodged in her throat at the blazing sincerity of his declaration. At the raw emotion etched on his harsh features.

"The wolf inside me wants to mate. But the man just wants to love and cherish you."

Matt pushed a hand through his thick hair.

"Every time I catch your scent, it drives me crazy. All I can think about is you. I don't care what you are—Fae, Draicon— hell, all I care about is *who* you are, Sienna. My Sienna."

Captivated, she stared at his mouth, the firmness of his jaw, the dark stubble shadowing his cheeks.

"Love me. I need you." Sienna slid a palm over his stubbled cheek.

As she lifted her mouth in total surrender, he caught her in

a powerful embrace. The kiss was brutal, savage, and she welcomed it, sliding her arms around his neck to draw him closer.
His mouth worked over hers savagely, his tongue thrusting
deep inside as his hands slid down the small of her back,
cupping her bottom. Matt lifted her skirts, his hands sliding
between her legs, and made a growling sound of approval at
finding her naked and wet for him.

For all his need, he was gentle as he lowered her to the
rock, pushing up her skirts. He mounted her, catching her
wrists in his hands as he settled his hips between her opened
legs.

"Now," he said thickly, and pushed forward.

A gasp fell from her parted lips as the head of his penis
made contact. He was hard as steel, soft as velvet. He nudged
farther inside, his gaze locked to hers as cool air flowed over
their bodies. She laced her fingers through his, holding on to
him. Wildness flared in his blue eyes as he thrust hard. He
lifted her and changed his position, angling his thrusts. Heat
built inside her, a gathering tension. Tightening her fingers
through his, she stared at him gazing fiercely down at her.
The tension wound higher and higher as she wrapped her
thighs around his pounding hips.

Her cries of release echoed through the meadow. Matt
growled, arching as he spilled himself deep inside her. Wild
emotions raced through her, a kaleidoscope of thoughts spinning past…

*Gotta make it good for her, damn, she's tight, so good, so
good, my Sienna…*

Then the thoughts faded, along with the warmth. She felt
emptied and drained, and oddly alone. Matt pulled out and
glanced down ruefully.

"Oh, hell," he said softly. "No condom."

A smile quivered on her lips. "It's okay. I'm in the safe
part of my cycle."

He rested beside her, touching her cheek. She turned to him.

"Did you feel that? It was like...we were bonding. Sharing our intimate thoughts. Just for a minute. It was amazing. Intense, and I felt like I was a part of your mind."

Heart racing, she watched his expression. "A little. Maybe. I lost myself for a while." He gave a twisted smile. "Kept feeling my wolf wanting to take over. Down, boy."

Sienna ran a hand over his flank, feeling him shiver. "Maybe you should put some clothes on. It's cold out here."

Intent flared on his face. "I'm not done with you. Yet."

Matt slid an arm around her waist, loaning her his strength, his vitality. She rested against him, admitting the truth. The Draicon she never wanted, the man she feared, had burrowed into her heart.

Wind ruffled their hair, rustling the brilliant yellow aspen leaves. Snow lay like powdered sugar sprinkled on the mountaintops. There weren't words, only emotion as she turned to him, lifting her face to his. He loved her slowly this time, savoring her with each kiss, each flick of his tongue over her skin. When they'd clung to each other, shuddering as they climaxed, she felt an odd tingle race down her spine. A spark of magick and energy.

Then it faded like the sun winking below the mountains.

They returned to the cabin. Her tiny home seemed cold and desolate.

The earlier euphoria of making love faded as she went into the kitchen to make coffee. Matt helped, his expression thoughtful.

"There's something I need to check out tonight. Before you set foot inside the Fae compound again."

He told her what he'd seen last night, the odd orange glow from the cliffs, the scent of malevolence coming from the standing stones.

"I haven't been inside the colony since leaving." Sienna

studied the distant cliffs of the Fae territory. "Take me with you, Matt. I can help."

His jaw turned to stone. "No. If something happens to you…" As she started to protest, he cupped her cheek. "I know you can take care of yourself. You're a tough, kick-ass female. But I've also seen a grown jag die screaming in pain when pyro demons burned him to death. Adam was a SEAL. He seemed invulnerable, like me. We used to joke that nothing could stop us, the dog and the cat. And then…he died."

Silence draped the air. She understood. Matt was part of an elite team of commandos with paranormal powers. He'd felt invincible. And then the illusion was burned forever by a stream of fire.

She wasn't a SEAL. But she knew the land, knew every ravine, rock and tree, and the Fae customs and habits. Matt didn't.

She placed a hand over his wrist, feeling the steady rhythm of his pulse. "I'm not going to die. They're my people and if something strange is happening, I need to know."

"You will know after I do some recon. I've warded your cabin with enough magick to blast a legion of demons straight to hell. You're safe here, until I return."

"And what if you don't return?"

"I will." His expression hardened. "It'll take more than Fae to bring me down. But there's something going on in that colony of yours. And I intend to find out what it is."

Matt dressed in black BDUs and strapped on the MC-4 parachute. The cliffs of the Fae compound stood tall and jagged. He could easily rappel down, but a niggling instinct nudged him into taking the chute.

Never knew when a night crawler with sharp teeth and claws might cut your rope.

He loved jumping out of planes during a HALO dive. Some

of the guys had to conquer fear of heights. Matt craved the thrill of free-falling, arms and legs spread as the wind slapped his body. It felt like flying, a pure rush of adrenaline-fueled excitement before he pulled the cord.

Guess I'm a junkie.

And you think you can settle into mundane pack life as a wolf?

Matt shoved aside the thought.

He gave a backward glance at Sienna, asleep on the bed, one hand tucked beneath her cheek. The ache in his chest went deep, speaking of feelings he didn't dare acknowledge.

He went outside, quietly closing the door behind him.

Crisp, cool pine-scented air greeted him. The sky was lit with starlight and the nearly full moon. He headed toward the Fae colony, wending through the trees, cursing the brilliance of the moonlight. Rather have full darkness for concealment. A deer grazing in the brush looked up, flicked its large ears, immobilized by fear as it apparently caught his wolf scent. Matt's lips twitched.

"You're safe from me. I have different game to hunt."

He found the path, and as he crossed the border, a tingling raced along his upper arm.

Matt glanced downward. On his right biceps, where the brambles had scratched him, the mark of a wolf glowed white. It pulsed with magick, a good, clean feeling.

He crossed over the invisible border, and it faded. Interesting. A pass of admission. He followed the path to the clearing where he'd seen the Fae sing and dance. He gazed upward at the cliffs.

Something was up there and he was going after it.

After he assembled his rock-climbing equipment, he scanned the forest. Nothing. Not a scent of Fae, only the dead embers of last night's fire. No birds, insects or animals rustling through the undergrowth. This area seemed dead of wildlife.

For a colony of Fae that cherished nature, it was mighty odd.

His instincts honed to razor sharpness, Matt kept alert. Even the rock here seemed lifeless, drained of energy.

He climbed steadily toward the rock recess where he'd seen the flickering light, muscles flexing with each step. Matt reached the small ledge where he'd seen the Fae vanish last night and pulled himself up.

The sharp tang of sulfur and decay slammed into his nostrils. Hugging the shadows, he investigated the small cave. Matt squatted down, studying a ring of stones surrounding burned embers. Something long and white poked through the gray ashes.

Revulsion churned inside him. He picked up the bone with gloved hands. Not human, but close. This bone was lightweight, almost hollow, like a paranorm capable of flight. Like a Fae...

He set the bone down, stooped down to peer deeper into the cave. Hair stood on the nape of his neck. A low growl rumbled from his throat.

He wasn't alone. Matt unsheathed his knife at his ankle.

A rush of hot air, a low, piercing scream broke the silent darkness. He dodged just as the creature rushed him. It pivoted, turning, holding out its hands.

The pointed ears, slender body and pale skin indicated Fae. But this was no ordinary Fae. Malevolence tainted its scent, turning it foul. Red lips pulled back in a sneer, the Fae displayed prominent teeth, sharp and pointed.

Two wings protruded from knobby points on its back.

The creature shrieked again and rushed him. He stabbed, and heard the blade snap cleanly off. Damn Fae had skin tougher than Kevlar. Swearing, he lunged forward, wrestling with the creature. One silver claw slashed at him. Burning pain raced along his arm. Matt breathed through it.

Enough of this. Time to say buh-bye. He wrapped his hands around the thing's neck and twisted hard.

A sickening crack ensued. The creature dropped to the ground.

Matt edged out of the recess and examined his arm. Blood bubbled up like acid. The silver acted like a corrosive, eating through flesh and bone. He opened his pack, applied a healing salve. Damn, this was a slash. What the hell kind of demon could do this?

A faint noise sounded behind him. He whirled, dodged as the creature stood. Hell, it straightened its neck as if adjusting a tie, then spread two sinewy wings, the skin thin and threaded with red veins.

Giving another shriek, the creature ran and dove off the cliff.

Damn it.

His heart lodged in his throat. Twenty feet down, Sienna was climbing upward. She saw the batlike creature and jumped on its back. Riding it like a damn horse.

Then she let go, spinning down to the earth.

He leaped off the cliff in a trained free fall. Matt spread his arms and legs to aerodynamically guide him. She was falling fast. He imagined her hitting the hard ground and panic lodged in his throat. He forced it down, folded his arms and legs to speed his descent.

There.

Matt grabbed her around the waist with one hand, deploying his chute with his other. The move jerked them both upward violently, yanking hard against his chest. Her panicked gaze sought his, then he yanked her tight against his chest. Adrenaline pumped through his body, making his heart race in a crazed rhythm.

He could tango with a dozen demons and never sweat, but seeing her jump on that demon had nearly given him a heart attack.

She wrapped her arms around his waist as he pulled the chute chords to guide them over the treetops. Then he heard a distinct, terrible shriek.

Bat Boy was back, riding the air currents above him. A ripping sound, and suddenly they were falling fast.

Matt withdrew his Sig. Damn if this thing was going to touch Sienna. He'd loaded the trusty weapon with an extra-special treat.

"*Sayonara,* ugly face," he shouted, and pulled the trigger.

The armor-piercing bullet hit the creature straight in the chest. Moonlight showed Bat Boy's nearly comical look of surprise, accompanied by a thick stream of black blood. It gave a last shriek, and spilled downward. Shocked, he watched it shift into a large bird, and fly away.

The ripped chute still kept them aloft, but they were losing altitude fast. If they hit the earth, bones would break. He spotted the thin ribbon of river through the trees, and pulled the cords to guide them to it. Farther downstream, jagged rocks poked above the water. If they hit there, they were dead.

"We're going in the river above those boulders," he shouted to her above the rushing wind. "Take a deep breath before we hit and let go. The current is wicked, so ride it until I get you."

"Got it," she yelled back.

The river rushed up at them, and he braced himself. "Now!"

He dropped Sienna and the chute before they hit, water splashing around them. Icy needles dug at his exposed skin, his cheeks. He knew the navy was gonna be pretty pissed about him losing a chute worth a few thousand. Screw it.

He struggled to the surface. The water was freezing, but

he'd experienced worse. He rode the current, scanning for Sienna.

Damn it, where the hell was she?

There. Her wet hair plastered like a helmet to her head, she bobbed up and down like a cork. *Good girl,* he thought silently, and began powerful strokes.

Matt circled an arm around her waist and began towing her to shore through the vicious current. The jagged boulders came into view, and he swam harder, dragging her upward as his feet touched bottom. Lying half in the water, Sienna coughed, shivering violently.

"My muscles, they feel locked tight," she said through chattering teeth.

As her teeth chattered, he swept her into his arms, studied the tree line, the position of the stars.

They were out of Fae turf, closer to her cabin. Somewhat safe.

Not safe enough.

Matt began the walk back, keeping a sharp watch for flying objects, just in case Bat Boy had friends.

After getting her to the cabin, he removed her clothing, bundled her in a woolen blanket and set her before a roaring fire. Matt stripped off his gear and clothing.

"What the hell were you doing back there?" Matt asked.

"Saving your ass." Sienna huddled deeper into the blanket. "And since it's a mighty fine ass, I thought it worth saving."

"My ass can take care of itself. What I can't handle is you following me, and then watching you fall. You would have been killed!" He struggled to leash his rising temper. "You think all of a sudden because you're back on their turf, you'd sprout wings?"

From beneath the curtain of her wet hair, she looked up with big green eyes etched in misery. "All Fae have wings. They're hidden in the shoulder bones. Once they were muscles and tendons, like regular appendages, but evolution changed that after hundreds of years of disuse. I had them when I was younger. I even tested them when jumping off the roof of my cabin when I was six. But now…they don't work."

The hurt stamped on her face and the uncertainty tugged his heart. Damn it, he'd almost lost her. The thought twisted his heart.

Naked, Matt sank onto the floor beside her, tunneling his fingers through her wet hair. "I'm sorry, pixie. That must hurt."

"I didn't mean to make you mad. But after you left, I remembered something. I only wanted to warn you. I couldn't bear it if anything happened to you."

She gave him a beseeching look, and he felt an odd mixture of joy at her words and dismay at what they meant. Because he wasn't certain where this was heading. He'd known how to cut his losses.

Not with her.

Warming her cold body with his, he pulled her tight. "I've made seven hundred and eight jumps in my career as a SEAL. I've fallen out of airplanes at thirty-three thousand feet. And what I felt was nothing compared to seeing you fall a few hundred yards. After jumping on Bat Boy."

"Bat boy? Oh, the gargoyle. That's what I came to warn you about. I was only trying to force it to change." She pulled away, made a stabbing gesture with one hand. "You stab it through the back with a knife and the shock makes it shift into a vulture. More harmless that way."

He felt sick to his stomach. "You knew about that thing?"

"I saw one once, when I was very young. Aunt Chloe told me about them. The Fae took them in, as their guardians, when the gargoyles began to die out, hunted by other paranorms for sport."

"It tried to kill me."

"It was protecting its nest. It could have killed you if it wanted to."

"Does its nest contain Fae bones?"

Sienna's eyes widened. "Maybe old bones. Gargoyles feed off scraps of carcasses of other paranorms. That's why shifting into a vulture suits it."

"These are the things best known before setting out on a mission," he said dryly.

She looked abashed. "I'm sorry, Matt. I only thought about it after you left. That's why I came after you, to warn you."

He felt restless and edgy, filled with a nervous energy. Matt took out his cell phone, glanced at it, pocketed it.

"What is it, Matt?"

"My orders were changed. I head back to base in less than twenty-four hours, so we don't have much time."

Shock widened her eyes. "You're leaving me?"

Gods, he hated this. "No. I'm taking you with me and plan to leave you somewhere safe. On base, or with a friend."

"I can't leave my people," she whispered. "But that doesn't matter. What about you? Where are you going?"

"I can't tell you."

"Another mission, right? A mission where you can get killed. I feel like I'll never see you again after you leave." Sienna looked frail and suddenly very small. "I won't remember you, anyway, even if I do see you. Because you're going to take my memories of you, right?"

Reluctantly, he nodded.

Tears bloomed, hot and bright, in her mossy green eyes. Matt gently wiped them away with the edge of his thumbs.

Matt cupped her face, the sweetest face he'd ever seen. She was so lovely, with her exotic features and a mouth that could tempt a saint. But it was her inner courage, her strength, her determination, that sealed her to him.

It was the memory he'd carry for always, of Sienna, and

her shy smile, her sass, her lion's heart and her sheer determination.

One night together would not be enough.

He bent his head to her. "Be with me tonight. I need you, pixie."

He had never wanted to make love like this before. Never had this shaking, uncontrollable need to be with a woman. They would make love and Sienna would forget him. And if he survived his mission, some nights he'd gaze up at the stars, and think of her.

And know she would never recall his name.

But he needed tonight. He craved her in his arms, her sweet mouth on his, her soft body to hold close. Primal male instinct rose, to stamp her with his scent, send his seed deep inside her. Leave something of his behind, because in less than twenty-four hours, he wouldn't even remain a memory.

He'd be a ghost.

"Say yes," he whispered, drawing his arms around her. "Tell me you want me as badly as I want you."

She looked up, and the passion darkening her gaze made him lose it.

"Take me," she whispered. "Take me as a wolf does. As a wolf claims his mate."

Whoa, boy. Words that sent the beast inside him loose. But the fierce desire glittering in her own eyes assured him she was ready.

Ready to acknowledge her wilder side.

They stripped and rolled on the bed together, kissing. They tangled together in a frenzy of passion. Dimly he thought of protection, but she pushed aside his hand, her eyes flashing with erotic abandonment.

"I want to feel you inside me, like before. Skin to skin," she breathed.

Then he rolled over, coaxing her to lie on her stomach.

Sensing she was a little afraid, he ran a hand over the curve of her back, murmuring praises. Her ass was sweetly rounded, and he caressed her, drawing a finger over her soaked cleft.

Matt drew her back on her knees and positioned himself, shaking with excitement. This was it. He pushed his cock slightly inside, moaning with pleasure. She resisted slightly, then her tiny muscles relaxed, allowing him to slide fully to the hilt. Damn, it felt so good, wet silk encasing his cock. His beast growled to the surface, the wolf clawing eagerly for more. He gripped her hips, thrusting hard and fast, the bed banging against the wall.

She pushed up against him. Startled, he realized she growled, a low, deep sound of excitement. Matt's excitement intensified and he licked and bit her neck. Sienna bucked beneath him and he sensed her approaching climax. A flurry of thoughts and images flickered in his mind, colors and sparks, and he was dimly aware they were not his own.

Emotions crowded him, the feelings overwhelming in a cresting flood. He felt her emotions, her wonder.

Her love.

"Come with me, darling," he rasped. "Now!"

Shrieking, she tightened around him, her orgasm making him buck and shudder, Matt felt his seed shoot into her, hot and demanding.

Then he felt himself thicken inside Sienna, growing harder. Stunned, he tried to pull out. Could not. Sienna fell to the bed, gasping.

She lay splayed beneath his sweating body, sweat dampening her dark hair. He raised up on his elbows to avoid crushing her as she turned her head in an awed expression.

"Matt, what is this? I feel everything inside you, all your emotions, not just mine."

He marveled as the iridescent sparks danced around them. Joy surged through him. "It's the mating lock, sweetheart.

What happens when two Draicon bond sexually and emotionally."

At the confused expression on her face, he added quietly, "Two Draicon who are meant for each other. Destined mates."

Fear erased the sweet, dazed passion on her face. "No, it can't be. It can't."

"Don't fight it, sweetheart. Shhh," he crooned, trying to soothe her, but her emotions boiled into a frenzy. He felt the wondrous rapture of becoming one, of fully bonding with her, fade like a waking dream. The sparks vanished and he felt suddenly cold and empty inside.

Slowly he withdrew, confusion replacing elation.

Rolling over, Sienna stared at the ceiling, her gaze clouded. Matt collapsed beside her, thumbing a tear from her chilled cheek.

"It's nothing to be ashamed of. Among my people, this is a celebration. Finding one's mate is cause for joy. You're very special, Sienna."

"But what am I?" she whispered. "You won't accept me for who I am, Matt."

He went still, his blood running cold at her words. Gods, she was right.

Was his prejudice of the Fae coloring everything he'd felt? Forcing her into a role she wasn't ready to take? Making her into a wolf because of his needs, not hers?

"Give it a chance, Sienna. I'm willing to try, learn from my mistakes."

Never had he felt this humble, this bared, not before a woman. Or anyone.

Pulling the sheet up to her breasts, she faced him, a shaft of moonlight spilling over one shoulder. She looked like an ancient Greek goddess, regal and lovely.

He slid a warm palm over the curve of her hip. "We're no

longer wolf and Fae. We're just a man and a woman, you and me, connecting together."

Hope flared in her eyes. She touched his cheek, and his heart pounded hard. "You mean it? We can have a home together?"

"I want to try." He thought of his lifestyle and sighed. "Of course, it means I'll have to leave you a lot. I'm a SEAL."

Light faded from her eager expression. Sienna blinked fast as if to check tears rising to her eyes. "It won't stop, will it? I'd be willing to try accepting my wolf, but how can we make it together when everything seems against it? You belong more to the teams than your pack, or me. Can't you see? You thrive on adventure, danger. You're strong and courageous, but being a SEAL means more than being a Draicon. You'd leave, and leave me with your family, when I know nothing about being a wolf. And you wouldn't be there to help teach me."

Misery shone in her wet eyes. "And one day, maybe, you wouldn't come home at all. I'd be left like Adam's widow, alone again, and without even a memory of you as a SEAL."

Matt's heart sank. Damn it, he knew what was coming. What always came every time he'd hoped for more than sex. What he'd craved, and knew he couldn't have.

A real home. A relationship. The truth hit him like a bucket of ice water. Sickened, he realized she was right.

"Sienna…"

She pressed a finger to his lips, valiantly fighting the threatening tears. "No, Matt. It can't work out between us. I wish with all my heart it could, but it won't."

Matt reached out to touch her, but she rolled over. He dressed and went outside.

It made no sense…how could he bond with her? Ordinary male Draicon thrived on finding their true mates. But he was different. He was a SEAL who distanced himself from his pack.

Crushing disappointment filled him. He jammed a hand through his hair. He'd thought Sienna was the one, the mate intended for him. But she didn't want him, or the bond.

Because you *don't want it enough,* said the nasty voice inside him.

Life was so much simpler before. He felt a stab of longing for the guys in his unit and a dose of hard reality. Better than this empty coldness after feeling the delicious warmth of her emotions, the softness of her love for him, the hot wetness of her hugging him tight…

Concentrate on the mission. He had no room in his life for anything else.

Especially not a sweet, fiery half Fae whom he'd have to leave, for good.

Chapter 17

This was Sienna's last day with him. He was leaving late this afternoon. But Matt didn't return to the cabin all last night.

She'd spent a restless evening, tossing and turning, aching for his embrace. Her words had driven him away. Because she'd been terrified by what happened to her when they'd made love.

Bonding to him had thrilled her. She belonged with this Draicon.

And then cold reality had slapped her in the face.

Best to get on with life, she told herself. Enough of this emotional intensity.

Sienna finished her coffee and fetched the purse, setting it on the table, along with the decorations she'd plucked off the exterior.

It was just a purse.

Like you're just a Fae. Right.

It's inside that counts.

The thought came out of nowhere, a hummingbird darting into her mind. Sienna glanced around.

Power hummed inside her as she laid her hands on the purse. The cloth felt cold and dead beneath her fingers. It was exquisitely made, but it held no life, no warmth.

She thought of Matt's warmth, his heart beating fast as she'd rested her head against his chest.

The front door slammed as she sank back into the chair. Matt approached, his hair sticking up in places, smudges beneath his deep blue eyes. His black jeans and T-shirt looked rumpled and slept in. Never had she been more happy to see anyone. A deep ache settled in her chest. She'd missed him, his warmth, his humor and reassurance. Most of all, she missed him, the solid, steady Draicon who kept her centered.

"You slept outside all night."

Gaze steady, he regarded her. "I've had worse."

So cool, distant. Two polite strangers facing each other. She hated this, hated the chasm yawning between them. Gone was the emotional intensity. Logically, it was better this way. Yet she ached for what they'd lost.

"Any luck?" He gestured to the purse.

"I need another Fae. I've lost my powers." Sienna attempted a weak smile. "Guess there's no use calling me pixie anymore. My wings are clipped."

Matt turned a chair around and sat, arms braced on the chair's back. "No one could ever clip your wings, Sienna."

"But I can't risk bringing this to my aunt or any other Fae in the colony. My people, I don't think they're the same. I felt it, as well, last night. An air of malice. As if something dark infiltrated the colony."

Sienna thought of the gargoyle she'd stabbed. "There's a heaviness in the air, and I can't pinpoint it."

He stared out the windows. "I'm no fan of the Fae, but

they've never been hostile or belligerent. I sensed something last night. I can't pinpoint it, either."

They were on their own. No help from her colony, or anyone else. "Then we're burning daylight. We have to find the Orb."

She repositioned the purse in her lap, concentrating. But as before, nothing came to mind. Sienna heaved a frustrated sigh as she opened her eyes.

"Give it a chance." His blue gaze was scaring in its intensity. The double meaning behind his words slammed into her.

Give it a chance. Not just the handbag, but their relationship, what had blossomed between them last night.

She wanted to, oh, how she longed to try. If only she knew he'd cradle her affection, her heart, and not toss it away at the first call of duty to either the teams or his pack.

Matt looked at the purse. "All the magick, yet he concealed it on a material object. Let's look at this objectively. Not just from a magick point of view. If the Orb is light and light is heat, then its opposite is cold."

Sienna closed her eyes, a memory yanking the corner of her mind. An icy lake, dark waters, wolves howling, screams…blood.

The lake must be protected. No one must know its secret.

Her eyes flew open. "Ice water. Immerse it into cold water and the Orb will energize. Cold reacts to hot."

Matt grinned. The smile chased his tired look, making him appear almost boyish. She caught a glimpse of what he must have been like before Adam's death, before he realized no one, not even a paranorm SEAL, was invincible.

As she filled up the sink, he grabbed the ice bin and dumped it into the water, stirring it with a finger. Sienna took the purse, stripped of its pretty decorations, looking battered and sad.

She glanced at Matt. "Ready. Both of us."

He nodded. Together they began setting the beads and stones into the icy water. Nothing happened. Finally, they tried the purse.

Matt leaned over the sink. She caught his scent, pure male, spice and pine, and closed her eyes, breathing it in. He smelled so good, so tempting. So close, his firm mouth set in a determined line. A mouth that had delivered hot, wet kisses all over her body, bringing her from one height of pleasure to another.

Inching away, she craned her neck to see better.

The purse and stones all looked the same. Except one. A green and white stone, no bigger than a nickel, glowed slightly. Excitement raced through her as the stone began to grow.

It increased to the size of a quarter and then stopped.

"There's something here. But we need more water, colder water."

"There is nothing colder, except for Naide Lake." Sienna's gaze collided with his, hers wide with realization, his with sudden anticipation.

"Pixie, there must be a link between you, the Orb and the lake. It's where all your memories are buried." He began to pace, jamming a hand through his mussed hair. She longed to smooth it back from his brow, feel the silk between her fingers. The compulsion to touch him, to draw close, became a throbbing, physical ache.

"Let's go. Right now."

He hesitated. "There's something I have to take care of first. More important than that magick globe."

"Nothing's more important than the Orb."

Laser blue eyes regarded her steadily. "Yes, there is. You."

The declaration didn't scare her, not like the emotional tidal wave she'd experienced last night in his arms. Sienna felt a rush of joy. He still cared, even if it were about her safety.

"I'm leaving this afternoon, Sienna. But there's no way

I'm letting you stay with those people. Not until I find out what's going on."

"Then I'm coming with you."

As he started to protest, she pressed a finger against his lips. "No choice. It's my life, and I have a right to know. If there is evil in the colony, as you say, then I need to see it with my own eyes."

Matt's thoughts streamed through his mind, ripping like barbed wire as he steadily climbed the cliffs where the gargoyle had attacked him. The truth promised to be pretty ugly. And he was painfully aware how much the truth could hurt.

Matt grimly tried to focus on the matter at hand. Yeah, the truth hurt, but he wasn't tumbling off this cliff because of it.

At last his fingers found the grooved notch in the ledge. Taking a deep lungful of air to scent for intruders, he pulled himself up.

At the cliff's bottom, Sienna waited. He raked a hand through his matted hair. In less than two hours, a navy helo would be setting down in the clearing just outside Sienna's cabin. His ass had "better be on it," Curtis had grimly told him.

The small cave was dark and deserted. Matt hugged the walls, his keen sight sweeping the interior for gargoyles or other invaders. He sniffed the air. Dank, but fresh. The inside went back farther into the rock, but the stench became more pronounced.

Withdrawing his Sig, he crept along the walls, scanning the inside. Ten minutes later, the stench was nearly unbearable. He removed the kerchief from his head and tied it around his nose to stifle the smell.

Decaying bodies.

He removed a glow stick from his vest and broke it. The

eerie green phosphorescent glow lit up the interior, shining over a small mound of rotting corpses.

Gagging, he approached, knelt down. Sorrow punched him in the stomach.

They had died horribly, some with the limbs twisted off, some burned. Trying to separate the bodies visually, he began a count and finally gave up. He'd seen enough to realize the horrid truth.

All this time, he'd been wrong. Matt cursed his narrow-mindedness, his dislike for the Fae. They were not the enemy, after all.

Matt removed his cell, snapped a few photos. He felt sick to his stomach at the thought of showing her, but Sienna needed proof.

The air was fresh and clean against his cheeks when he emerged into the sunlight. Matt took a deep breath. When he finished descending, she came forward.

In her green cable-knit sweater and jeans, she looked lovely and ethereal, as natural as the surroundings. He breathed in her scent, drank in the sight of her. She was a cool drink of water after a long desert march, a balm to what he'd seen above.

Her anxious gaze sought his. "What is it? More gargoyles?"

"I know where Bat Boy found the bone." He gently clasped her shoulders. "Sit, honey. This isn't going to be easy."

"Just tell me. Please. I trust you, Matt."

His stomach gave another sickening lurch. She trusted him. And now he had to force her to face the truth.

"The Fae, all the ones in your colony…they're dead."

No reaction. She stared at him with wide green eyes.

"The cave contains a mass grave. The people whom you thought were the Fae, your family…no one's left. If my suspicions are right, the ones I saw are Darksider Fae, who took their place." Matt pushed on, his fingers gently squeezing her shoulders, feeling delicate bones and soft skin.

"But Aunt Chloe…she asked me to find the Orb. She was alive…. I would have known, it was her!"

"Sweetheart, they've been dead for probably six months."

She sagged to the ground, buried her face in her hands. Sobs shook her slender frame. He lowered himself beside her, gathered her against him, tucking her head beneath his chin. Wishing he could give her the luxury of grief, wishing he could chase away the piercing grief.

Her entire family was gone. The tiny, niggling suspicion flowered into horrified awareness. When she'd been called before the council, Sienna had thought they were disdainful because she wasn't one of them. Now she knew. Darksider Fae had taken their place, using her to find the Orb, while her aunt lay dead in the cold, dark cave. She'd been set up and betrayed. The enemy cloaked themselves as her people, promised acceptance and had duped her. The only person supporting her all this time was wolf, a species she'd been taught to despise.

Everything she'd wanted had vanished. Sienna pushed past the sorrow as Matt held her close. He was an anchor, solid and steady, in a turbulent sea. But now wasn't the time to cast anchor. She'd wasted enough time living for a lie.

Fiercely wiping her eyes, she glanced around. "They killed my family, the whole colony, for the Orb. All this time they've been playing with us, sending me out to find it and then planning to seize it when I returned with it."

Matt cupped her cheek. "That's my girl. You're strong, honey. You can get through this. I'll take you with me. You can stay with Jammer's sister until I return. Jammer's my teammate."

She felt sick to her stomach. "Tim was a hero. He took the

Orb to guard it. It would have stayed safe if he hadn't sold information about you to the witch. They killed him for it."

"I know," he soothed. "He was very brave. Let's go. I need to take you out of here."

But much as she wanted to run and never look back, she knew what she must do. Sienna looked deep inside herself, calling upon her dormant wolf for courage.

"We can't leave. There's a secret glen, where the Fae kept the Orb. It's a tremendous source of energy. It was warded against evil, but if the Darksider Fae broke through and tapped into this…to serve their masters, the pyro demons…" Her heart pounded hard. "We have to reinforce the warding."

Matt sprang to his feet, the move graceful and fluid. He pulled her upright. "The vortex, is it connected to the standing stones?"

"The vortex powers the stones and amplifies their power, but the power can't be unlocked except through a sacred chant. And the Orb. The Orb acts as a conduit. But even without the Orb, the stones have a natural, raw energy."

"How much energy? Enough to create an explosion and torch the entire forest, if the power were directed?"

"Yes." She drew in a deep breath, struggling to regain her composure. "It's why this colony is so protected."

"The ceremony I saw the other night, that's what they were doing. Mimicking your people…to draw out the maximum energy." His expression turned dark. "Take me there. But first, we shift into wolves. If we run into anything or anyone, less chance of detection."

For the first time in her life, she felt the wolf calling to her. Her Fae powers proved useless.

"What's wrong?"

"I need your help to shift into a wolf."

Warmth ignited his expression. Matt cupped her cheek, his caress tender and understanding. "Let it flow through you.

Your Draicon half will do the rest. Just tune yourself into the forest, into nature, and the spirit. Let go."

Sienna stripped off her clothing. She closed her eyes, feeling the wind brush against her naked body, hearing the tree limbs rustle. Smelling Matt's delicious scent. She called to the wolf inside her, long buried and dormant.

She called upon her ancestral line, long forgotten.

Help me.

The change began slowly, then sped like a light stream, shimmering crimson and white sparks spiraling around her. She opened her mouth to shout with joy.

A long, low howl came out.

Sienna blinked, saw a proud, muscled gray timber wolf, intelligence gleaming in its deep blue eyes. The wolf seemed to grin.

She nudged him with her nose, rubbing against him affectionately. This felt so right and natural.

The gray wolf pushed her hindquarters, a clear indication. *Let's roll.*

Loping through the forest, she tracked the way, Matt at her side. The thicket of trees thinned as they reached the glen with the standing stones. A heaviness sat in the air, thick and menacing.

Sienna darted past the stone circle, down a small, narrow path protected by thick brambles. After a few hundred yards, it opened to a clearing.

When she'd last been here with her aunt, the circle had been protected by a ring of stones in a cairn, a small, sacred mound. Now the cairn was gone. A blue tarp covered a small mound. Matt shifted back to human form, crouched down and tore away the tarp. Fury twisted his expression.

"More of the missing Semtex. They're not going to torch the forest. They're going to create a firestorm." He touched one orange packet, his expression sharp as a honed blade. "There's enough here to blow up half the mountain."

Sienna shifted back, the movement fluid and natural. She waved her hands, and willed clothing back on her body. "Why would they destroy the standing stones instead of drawing energy from them?"

"For the pyro demons. They need fire, explosions, energy to feed from. There's enough Semtex here to give them energy to hold a glamour lasting long enough to access a certain air force base stockpiling nuclear weapons. A base covering a bolt hole to the netherworld."

Matt glanced up, his jaw taut. "They want the Orb to gain the truth about my team and how to kill us, because we warded the base with our magick. And when we die, and our magick dies with us, there's a very small but powerful window of time in which the demons could break through, and blow the base sky-high, freeing a demon army."

She couldn't think or breathe. Sienna closed her eyes, seeing the destruction, the demons freed, roaming the world....

He reached into his pocket, but frowned at his cell. "No service. We've got to get out of here."

Taking her hand, he pulled her along the path, back to the circle of standing stones. But they were no longer alone.

Before the stone circle stood a tall, slender woman clad in a silver robe. She turned, smiling at Sienna.

Joy leaped inside her.

"Aunt Chloe!" Sienna went to embrace her, but Matt pulled her back.

"It's not your aunt, pixie. She's an imposter."

Sienna inhaled, detecting her aunt's scent of rosemary and sage. The fine wrinkles around her blue eyes were the same. And she lifted her hand and sketched a sacred Fae welcoming, just like Chloe had.

Maybe Matt was mistaken. Not all the Fae had been

slaughtered. Doubts began hammering at her. Maybe he was mistaken about many things. Then she looked at him and saw the tight slash of his mouth, the hardness on his face. He'd never lied to her. He'd risked much for her. She trusted him.

But grief collided with hope, and seeing her beloved aunt alive, Sienna wanted to cling to that hope with both hands.

"My darling Sienna. Did you find the Orb?"

Sienna said nothing, her gaze whipping back from Chloe to Matt.

"I thought it was in Tim's shop. We found out too late he'd stolen it." The Fae released a small sigh, a flutter of her right hand, exactly like Chloe. "We sent our best people to retrieve it, but a fire broke out."

"Tim died," Sienna said slowly. "He was tortured. By fire."

Bright blue eyes regarded her with sorrow. "I love you, Sienna. Come back home to us. I'll find a way to gain you entrance. Just give me the Orb, and you'll be safe."

"Liar," Matt said softly. "You're not Chloe."

Chloe turned, malice sparking her gaze. She flung out her hands and Matt gasped, recoiling. Hands over his stomach, he doubled over in a deep moan.

"He's the real enemy, my darling Sienna. You can't trust a Draicon. Remember? Draicon killed your mother. They're vicious murderers. All of them."

Blood drained from Matt's face. Sweat streamed down his face, dampening his T-shirt. He seemed in agony.

Sienna fisted her hands. "Stop it, Chloe! Whatever you're doing, please, stop it! He's not like the others."

"Oh, but he is, my darling. He only wants the Orb for his own purpose. He shared your bed. I can smell him all over you. He seduced you, only to get what he wanted. He doesn't care about you. Only his precious team, and his duty. He's going to leave you and never look back."

The truth hurt like a knife arrowing into her heart.

"I do care," Matt rasped. "And I will leave you, Sienna. I've never lied to you. Not like she's doing now."

Torn, she stared at Chloe.

Kill her, pixie. You're the only one who can. She's cast a spell on me. I'm dying, cooking from the inside out. It's how she killed Tim.

The deep, pain-laced voice inside her head was commanding. Sienna stared at Matt, startled by the telepathic communication.

I can't. She's my aunt, the only family I have left. I love her. She raised me, Matt!

She is not your aunt, pixie. Chloe is dead. Look closely at her eyes.

Sienna concentrated on her aunt, the woman who'd hugged her, fussed over her, loved her unconditionally. Remembering the times they'd shared.

Chloe blinked, her eyes flashing red. Demon-red.

Fury and grief crashed together. Had to save Matt. Had no powers…distraction.

You have powers, pixie. Open yourself up to them. Oh, gods, damn it, hot, so hot, this hurts!

A low moan wrung from his throat. Sienna's heart raced with panic, panic she knew she must quell. Chloe cackled and watched as Matt writhed on the ground. She tore herself away and went behind a tree. *Please let this work, please, it has to work.*

She thought of Matt's quiet strength and it loaned her courage to glamour into the most despicable form. A pyro demon.

As she stepped from behind the tree, Chloe gasped. "Master?"

The woman's glamour faded, showing her as a small, wizened crone.

The spell tormenting Matt snapped like a breaking stick.

As Chloe lifted her hands, pointing them at Sienna, Matt shifted.

Teeth bared, he leaped on Chloe, going for the throat. The demon screamed, wrestling with him but was no match for the muscled wolf. She tussled with him, trying to gouge his eyes.

It was over in a minute. The demon lay on the ground, staring sightlessly at the blue sky. Blood stained the wolf's thick gray coat. Matt shifted back, crouched down by the demon, examining the body.

"A lesser demon, same kind that killed Tim at the shop." Matt stood, brushing off his hands. "I have a bad feeling about this. Back in New Orleans, Stephen mentioned a convocation of demons. The pyro demons are gathering forces."

But as they turned, several figures emerged from the thick woods. Dozens of them. Dressed like Fae, they began to change, turning into hordes of Darksider Fae and demons, talons bared, lips pulled back in snarls. An army advancing toward them, armed with dark magick.

Sienna whipped her head around. Behind them came the eerie glow of red through the pine trees. Fire cut off their southern escape.

They were trapped.

Chapter 18

Matt composed himself as he set about calmly analyzing their situation. It didn't look good.

"We're not getting out of this," Sienna muttered.

He turned her chin up, facing him. "Hey, there," he said fiercely. "I've been through worse."

A tremulous smile wobbled on her soft, pink mouth. He couldn't resist. Matt bent his head, kissed her. "For luck," he added, pulling away and studying the terrain.

Weapons wouldn't cut it. Not with this crowd. He'd run out of ammo too fast. Matt's mind raced over possibilities.

He glanced upward at the treetops. There's a possibility. About twenty feet up. Not bad.

"How high can you jump, pixie?"

Sienna tracked his gaze. "Not that far."

"Figured as much. Me, either. Which is why I always travel with a backup plan."

He began unwinding the length of slim nylon rope he'd

wrapped around his waist. Matt tugged her hand, racing to the edge of the stones. He flung the rope up a pine tree, letting it double over on a thick limb.

As he knotted the rope, she looked panicked. "I can't climb that."

"Don't sweat it. I've got you." Matt gestured to his back. "Climb on."

"You're going to climb up there and carry me? What are you, Superman?"

"Super *lupus,*" he cracked. "Besides, you're a lightweight. Adam, he topped you by sixty pounds. And I carried him on my back while climbing up a lot higher."

He'd said his name, and the stabbing pain he'd felt previously had lessened to a dull ache. Matt knew he'd never forget his buddy, even when the time came for his memories to be erased when he left the teams. He could finally remember Adam's cocky grin, and feel only sadness, not the stinging grief.

Sienna climbed on his back. "Hang on. Time to go visit the penthouse. Up we go."

Flames crackled and snapped in the near distance. Heat bathed them as sweat poured down his forehead. Matt began to climb fast, his muscles pulling hard. Sienna wound her arms around his waist, her head buried against his back. As he climbed, he pulled the rope with him, preventing it from reaching the ground. He glanced down and saw the demons and Darksider Fae gather beneath the tree, their outraged roars echoing through the clearing as they tried to grab for the rope. One pointed a finger at Matt.

He paused, hanging on with one hand. Muscles strained beneath the weight. Matt reached for his blade. "Damn, always did like this knife."

The tip of the steel dagger buried itself into the demon's throat. It fell, clutching its neck.

Shimmying up the rope, he reached the limb and hooked

his hands around it. Sienna swung up onto the branch like a gymnast. Matt pulled the rope and wound it around his waist.

They made their way through the pine tree, climbing up the branches. He spotted a clearing below, far enough from the fire. Smoke curled into the air. The ominous crackle of flames was nearing the sacred glen. And the Semtex.

Minutes later, aided by the rope and a nice, Tarzan-like swing, they were on the ground once more. Together they raced to a small gathering of boulders. Cover for now. But soon those demons would catch their scent and come after them.

He pulled out his cell and checked the time. "Looks like my ride should arrive soon," he said softly.

Sienna glanced at him, dirt smudging her face. "We sure could use a team of navy SEALs about now, huh?"

"Your wish is my command." He gave a slight grin.

The chopping sound of a helo's blades echoed through the glen. Matt glanced up.

Incredulity etched her face. "Matt? What did you do?"

"Called in for a little help." He playfully tapped her nose. "I told you, we're a tight team. No man, or sweet-faced Fae, gets left behind."

The helo was opening its cargo doors. Not just any helo. One equipped with a little something-something pyro demons hated…

"Bombs away," he sang out, diving to the ground, taking Sienna with him and covering her body with his.

Thousands of gallons of water rained down on them, extinguishing the forest fire. The demons screamed in outrage.

Then came the wonderful sound of seven rough, deep voices singing out.

"Yo, Dakota. Got a bit of a sitch here, huh?"

"Always did think he was a hot dog, digging his way out of things. Taking on the world."

"Forgetting us, you'd think he'd learn not to hog all the fun."

His team. His friends.

They gathered around, faces painted green and black, clad in olive drab BDUs. Emotion clogged his throat as he slid an arm around Sienna's waist.

"Guys, this is Sienna McClare. Sienna, meet the guys."

"So glad to meet you," she said, her relief evident. "Not that Matt didn't have the situation fully under control."

"Why should he hog all the fun?" Shay's white teeth flashed in a wide grin. He tossed a rucksack to Matt, who caught it with one hand. "Extra rounds. Tough enough to take out demon hide. After your chat with Curt, we knew you needed a little special care."

J.T. gave a low howl. "Dakota always did like a little extra attention in a tight jam. But never before with such a pretty lady."

Sienna gave a faint smile. "I'm glad you came dressed for the occasion."

"Yup. And here they come. Let's do it," Matt said, his expression hardened. "Lock and load, boys. Let's kick some demon ass."

The sound of the gunfire was deafening. Crouched behind a large boulder, Sienna watched Matt and Sam take cover behind a fallen log while the other SEALs positioned themselves behind the rocks. Matt had placed her farthest away from the kill zone.

No magick. They weren't attacking with magick, she heard him tell the men. Not with the enemy so close to Sienna, he'd told her. Matt didn't want to take chances she might get hurt accidentally.

Sienna tried to calm her racing heart. A bullet slammed

into the boulder she hid behind, sending rock shards flying. She peered out, focusing on Matt.

He fired his assault weapon with deadly accuracy. Hot shell casings flew into the air from his weapon. Around him the seven other SEALs fired at the oncoming demons and Darksider Fae.

A slick, coppery scent of dark blood tinged the air. The noise was deafening. With exact precision, the SEALs took down the approaching enemy. But there were too many. And then she peered around the boulder and her blood turned to ice.

A pyro demon advanced toward Matt. The oily stench of fuel clung to its gray, stooped form. The creature spit fire from its mouth, nose and fingertips and began to glow orange-red.

The log shielding him began to burn as the demon cackled. The bullets melted as they hit the demon's superheated skin. Matt crouched down, his gaze narrowing as he set down his weapon and reached for a knife.

Hand-to-hand combat. Sienna gasped in shock as a stream of fire singed his hand. He winced.

The smell of burned flesh, the sight of blood, jolted her into recognition. Memories suddenly assaulted her. Fire. Screams. Hiding in a rotting, hollowed log, watching in terror as the orange flames came closer, the heat incredible, trying to quiet her panting breaths.

Wolves howling in…pain? Pain. Agony. They were being slaughtered one at a time, shifting into their human form as they died in agony.

Not wolves killing Fae.

Wolves…her people!

A snarl arose in her throat, born of fury. Matt was hurt. Her Matt, her mate, her love. She smelled blood and it pissed her off.

"You bastard!"

Sienna sprang up, barely feeling the heat from the approaching demon. Power flowed through her, sure and strong. The shift came as she leaped over the log and charged, feeling the wind rush against her face, feeling her body shape-shift. Magick sparked the air, good magick, her magick. Nothing but anger fueled her, anger at these demons who dared to hurt her mate, a good, solid man who fought evil, a man who loved her as surely as she loved him.

The shifting kept happening, her body twisting and contorting. Wolf to jaguar, to human and Fae, all forms happening so fast she barely knew what she was, but it felt good and right.

"Damn, look at her go," Sam cried out.

"Sienna! What the hell! Cease fire!" Matt yelled.

She ignored the shouts of the men, the cessation of assault weapons. She kept racing forward, shifting into various forms as she ran, searching for the right one like a woman trying on dresses. For the first time in her life, Sienna felt linked to the power, letting it flow through her. Floating, she was floating on air, and did belong, and this was her time, her magick.

Confusion twisted the demon's ugly face. It paused, hands raised to the sky, staring at her, and then lowered its hands, fire streaming from the tips.

Sienna released a roar and flames poured from her own mouth.

Dragon flames.

Fire against fire. Stunned, Matt watched the lovely Fae turn into a beast the size of an army tank. The demon staggered back with a squeal as she advanced, giant wings beating at the flames to fan them. The dragon's scales repelled the demon's flames, sent them hurling back into the bastard's face.

Jaws opened, revealing rows of stalactite teeth. The dragon hissed once, then snapped.

Matt blinked in stunned shock as the dragon—no, *his Sienna*—cut off the demon's head with one mighty snap of her jaws. The dragon flung the head downward. Distracted by the sight, the remaining two demons paused in their assault. The minions began to fall back, slinking into the shadows.

"Now," he yelled, pulling his fist downward.

All eight SEALs attacked. Not with ammo, but power. Magick.

Sully teleported behind the Darksider Fae, attacking from the rear and vanishing as he hit them two at a time. Jammer, the team's PSI, used telekinesis and pelted the enemy by lifting boulders and hurling them as Matt, Renegade and Dallas shifted into wolves, leaping over the log as they changed. Flanking them to the right, Shay's body crackled with power, glowing as he sent reserve electrical charges snaking into the army of demons.

The SEAL commander, Curt, pitched white energy balls one after another at the minions. And J.T., who commanded the power of water, stretched out his hands, calling the river to him. With a loud chant, he sent the stream crashing down upon the fire demons, splashing over them and flooding their flames.

Drenched and stripped of defenses, the demons turned to retreat. Matt cut them off, snarling.

This one's for Adam.

He took one down, going for the throat.

Minutes later, it was over. The pyro demons were dead, vanished into ash. The ground was littered with the bodies of lesser demons and Darksider Fae. Shay wrinkled his nose.

"Blech. Never did like the smell of rotting demon in the morning."

"Afternoon." Curt gave Matt a significant look, tapping at his watch. "Lieutenant Parker, you are officially AWOL."

Matt nodded. "Aye, sir." He didn't care. His attention focused on the dragon, still hovering above them, beating her webbed gray wings. "Sweetheart, it's okay now. Come back, time to shift your form."

Then Sienna slowly descended, and landed with a thud on all four legs. Light shimmered around her, and she shifted back into her human body.

Her naked human body.

"Whoa," Dallas said. "Nice form."

As Matt glared, all seven SEALs politely turned their heads. Matt removed his webbed vest, shrugged out of his T-shirt and settled it over her. It draped down to her thighs. She shivered, hugging herself, green eyes huge in her oval face.

"I can't believe I did that. It was all instinct. I saw you hurt…and it just happened."

He pressed a kiss onto her forehead, gathered her against him. She felt good in his arms, soft and warm. Safe.

Curt cleared his throat politely. "Lieutenant, did you get a bead on the missing Semtex?"

"All accounted for. You'll find it intact in a small glen, about two klicks north of us."

The SEALs turned to leave. Shay gave him a steady look. "You staying, Dakota?"

"Yeah," he said, settling Sienna closer to him. "Think I'll stay here awhile. Feels good."

It felt very good. And very right.

The missing Semtex had been packed and removed from the Faes' glen. With the threat of the "homegrown terrorist plot" removed, the team was taken off standby. The SEALs, with the exception of Matt, boarded the helicopter and returned to the nearby air force base.

His C.O. gave a direct order. Matt was not to return until he'd retrieved the Orb. Then Curtis had winked solemnly at Sienna. "If it takes time, say, a day or two, I'll take the heat."

She liked him and the other SEALs. But deep in her heart, she knew the truth even without the magick globe.

Matt belonged with his team. He could not leave them. He was needed.

For now, she had him solely to herself. They spent the rest of the day making love, talking, stroking each other. And then when the shadows lengthened, he accompanied her up the steep, winding path to the lake.

The green stone from the purse burned in her jeans pocket.

As before, the lake was quiet. No wildlife. Even the birds had deserted this area.

He gave her a steady look, squeezed her hand. "Ready?"

She nodded. It was time. Sienna took the small green stone. With reverence, she set it into the cold lake water.

Behind her, she felt Matt's gentle, reassuring presence.

The lake began to glow an eerie green, then light filled the water. The small green stone was no longer visible. Power sang in the air, ancient, fluid magick.

Sparks shimmered on the lake's surface. Then a round object, the size of a softball, bobbed to the surface. It floated over to the shore, directly toward her.

The Orb of Light.

Trembling, she palmed it. The Orb lit up with a brilliant light. She basked in its soft, warm glow. Peace settled over her, chasing away the confusing emotions, the terrible grief. Sienna stared into the crystalline globe, and then swept her gaze around the lake.

The scenery seemed to shift, grow wobbly, and then peel back like a strip of bark.

A tableau, like a living diorama, unfolded before her.

Wolves, dozens and dozens of wolves, roamed the lake's shore. The trees were shorter, the grass no longer yellowed and dried, but thriving with life. Birds swept over the lake's mirrored surface, skimming the water in graceful dips.

Then the wolves shifted, and assumed human form. On the fallen log sat a small girl about five years old. Seeing the people approaching, she giggled and climbed into a small hole in a hollowed tree.

"Sienna?" The man shaded his eyes and pretended to look around. "She's playing games again. Vanished. Where are you?"

Squealing with delight, the little girl climbed out. "Here I am!"

She clapped her hands as the man caught her up in his arms and bounced her, his green eyes sparking with merriment.

Green eyes like her own...

"Dad," she whispered, touching the image.

Not an evil, vile Draicon. Nothing but love shone on his face. He was joined by a woman, who snuggled against him.

Her parents. Not Fae. Draicon.

Barely had her stunned mind processed this when the scene shimmered.

It faded, shifted. Heat flooded the air, danger. She was suffocating, the smell of rotting wood surrounding her, the flare of orange flames growing closer.

She would burn alive in here.

A log. Her parents had stuffed her inside the hollowed log to hide. The images fast-forwarded like a slideshow. Two glowing demons, shooting fire from their mouths, their noses, their talons. Burning her people. Killing them.

Alone, in the hollowed log, she'd watched her parents die. Her family. Brothers, sisters, aunts, uncles. Her entire pack.

Helpless to reach out and save them, too little to try, she could only watch in horror, a terrified whisper on her lips.

Please, someone help them.

She'd heard their last gasps for breath, saw her mother reach out with one hand breaking the water's surface, a fine-boned hand that once cradled her close, soothed away hurts and touched her with pure love.

Her mother had died, calling her name. And she'd remained in the hollowed log, paralyzed by terror, silent tears tracking down her cheeks.

Then a fast, furious rain fell, extinguishing the fire. From the log crept a small girl, whose outraged wail echoed over the land. The girl's body shimmered as the demons turned to her, their faces malevolent.

The small child shifted into a dragon, rising above the earth, showering fire over the demons, clawing them to pieces. Blood. So much blood stained the ground. Then the dragon fell to the earth, weeping.

A group of Fae appeared, including a woman with waist-length silver hair. She squatted by the dragon as it shifted into a girl, who sobbed as if her heart had broken.

"The child lives," she said softly. "We must save her."

The image vanished. Words hovered in her mind, words spoken long ago by a woman determined to save a terrified Draicon child, just as she would save the vanishing species of gargoyle years later.

You are the last survivor of your kind.

The only one. I'm all alone.

Grief spiraled inside her in a violent vortex. Sienna closed her eyes against the hot tears, but they spilled free, cascading down her cheeks. She glanced at the hollowed log that had kept her safe, hidden from the demons as they'd tortured and killed her entire family.

Her pack.

Now she truly belonged nowhere.

Gently, she set down the Orb. Its light faded, leaving it cold and gray.

Matt touched her shoulder. "Sweetheart, what did you see?"

"The truth."

She stretched out her hands, their long, tapered fingers and neatly pared nails. Once she'd been proud of being Fae. Her entire life was a lie.

"They hid me. Here." She tried to keep the quaver from her voice. "In the hollowed log. My real parents. They weren't Fae, but Draicon. I come from a long line of Diablo wolves."

His eyes widened. "Diablo wolves. I've heard the legend. Draicon with the rare power to glamour, like Fae. Known for the devilish ability to mimic other life forms, and humans, so hunters would leave them alone."

"This was our valley. Our home. We, and the Fae, were the protectors of the Orb. We kept it hidden in the lake, and the Fae watched over us as we watched over the Orb. It was too powerful for any one group to have. So both species protected it."

Sienna stared at the now-dull Orb. "It was forbidden for any Fae or Diablo to use the Orb for their own purpose. But it was so pretty, I came here to play with it. And one day I picked it up and it burned its light into me."

She gently set the globe down on the earth. "It amplified my magick when I absorbed its energy and power. Instead of the ability to merely glamour, I had the ability to actually shift into whatever form I pleased."

Gathering her hands into his, he kissed her palms. "Draicon children don't manifest their powers until puberty."

"The Orb changed that. I could shift into anything. My parents eventually found out and the Fae moved the Orb to the sacred glen. But it was too late. Two pyrokinetic demons who'd escaped the netherworld saw the spectral glow of powerful magick. They traced it to the lake."

She gulped down a breath. "They tortured and killed my family. My parents hid me to keep me safe. I tried to figure out what to shift into to kill the demons…but I couldn't! All I could do was blend into the tree by becoming as small as possible."

Tenderly, he cupped her face with his big hands. "You were just a child, Sienna. A terrified child."

"But I did!" Muscles tight as springs, she shook her head. "I remembered the stories of dragons, before they became extinct. I shifted into a dragon. And I killed them. But it was too late."

He pulled her against him, holding her tight.

Sienna gathered her composure. "Chloe found me. They'd sensed the attack, sent the rain to put out the fires, but it was too late. Chloe took me in to raise as Fae to protect me. She knew if any demons or Darksider Fae found out a Diablo wolf lived, one that had the powers of the Orb of Light, they would do everything to kill me and try to absorb my magick."

"All this time you thought you were different. You were." Gently, Matt wiped away her tears with his thumb.

"Chloe wove the story about my mother and father to explain the violence I'd witnessed and so others would think I was a hybrid. She had to invent the story about my father's violence so I wouldn't search for any Draicon while I was still young and vulnerable. It was all to protect me until I got older. And I believed it myself because the memories were too terrible to bear. The glamour I projected, part of my natural abilities, could be explained if I were Fae. But she knew I didn't belong to the Fae and that's why she turned me out when I turned of age. Chloe said I would find my true destiny, but I had to find it on my own."

His embrace felt solid and sure, a steady rock of support. But she was too confused, too upset.

"I was wrong," he admitted. "I resented the Fae for what happened to Adam, for their refusal to intervene. I thought they were pacifists too cowardly to fight. And they were here, all along, keeping you safe, risking their own lives to save another."

Releasing her, he rubbed a thumb over the tracks of her drying tears. "They're the bravest of all, because they sacrificed so much."

"And now they're gone. I never had a chance to say goodbye. I'm alone now."

"You're not alone, sweetheart. Stay with me. I'll take good care of you. I promise. I don't care what you are. Draicon, Fae, even one of those blasted gargoyles… I love you, Sienna, for who you are."

Breath caught in her lungs. She loved him, too. But love sometimes wasn't enough. Life interfered.

"I love you, Matt. I think I have for a while. But your duty comes first. Doesn't it? Your duty to the SEALs and the navy. To bring this in and lock it away."

"I won't leave you alone," he said, his jaw tensing.

"And if you don't, you'll face far worse than discipline from the navy. You have no choice, Matt. They need your strength and your courage. You are meant for this job. I've seen exactly how much you're needed," she said gently.

"You're coming with me. I'll get you settled with Jammer's sister—you'll like her…she's a psi…."

Sienna gave a brittle laugh. "I've spent my entire life living a lie, thinking I'm something I'm not. I can't live with another species, not when I barely know what I am. Don't you see? I can't come with you, Matt. I need time alone."

His big hand slid up to tunnel through her hair. She closed

her eyes at his soothing caress. "Don't be alone, Sienna. Stay with me."

"For how long? Until you ship out again? Then where will I be? I have to find my own way. You want to mate with me because you think I'll fit into your lifestyle, in a nice, neat package. But I'm a misfit. I can't fit in. I'm a homeless Draicon without a pack—" she struggled with the lump in her throat "—without a people. I need to find myself first."

He started to protest. She placed the orb in his hand. "Take it. Do what you must."

His eyes were very blue. "It's too powerful, Sienna. No one group can keep it safe."

"I trust you. Promise me no evil will ever gain its power."

"I promise," he said solemnly. "I can't leave you here."

She gave a small smile, hiding the sadness spearing her. "But you must."

"I'll be back as soon as I can. Won't you come with me? I'm begging you, Sienna…we can work this out."

"You can't understand what I'm going through. You have a pack, a family. A team. You belong. You're part of a bigger picture, someone very important who's needed to fight evil." No way was she sliding into self-pity. Sienna offered a brave smile to hide the hurt. "I'm unique. Only one of me. I don't fit in and maybe it was my destiny that I never did fit in."

"I want to understand. Give it a chance. You're not alone, Sienna."

Standing on tiptoe she reached up and kissed him, a last, lingering kiss. Then she drew away, pressing her fingers to his lips.

The truth, the damn truth, shattered her. "Yes," she whispered, smiling to disguise the hot tears welling in her eyes. "I am."

Chapter 19

The cabin was empty and dark. Without Matt, it felt cold and lifeless.

He'd disregarded orders and had not taken her memories. But as she'd watched him walk away, duffel slung over one broad shoulder, she almost wished he had. Because it hurt too much to remember.

A week later, Sienna wandered around her living room, remembering Matt sprawled on her sofa, remembering how they'd made love before the roaring fire. His presence was a ghost in every room.

But that was the past. She had to make a new life for herself, now that she knew her true heritage. The Fae had set her free to find herself. To discover what she truly was.

All this time, she'd sought to belong to a group that would love and accept her for herself. She'd tried hard to fit in and please her aunt, please the others.

It was about time she finally learned to please herself.

Sienna breathed on the pane of glass and rubbed her finger over it. She traced his name.

Matt Parker.

She didn't need the Orb to discover the truth. She missed him like crazy. She loved him. His steadiness, his enormous courage and loyalty, the way dimples dented his cheeks when he gave one of his cocky grins.

She loved talking with him, arguing with him, the way he respected her individuality.

He didn't care if she were Fae, Draicon, or if her skin turned gray and she sprouted wings like a gargoyle.

Chloe's voice echoed in her mind. *Go find your destiny, my darling. Seek who you are. You've been cloistered here too long.*

Cloistered. Shut away, like the Orb itself, she'd become dull and listless. It was time to expand her horizons, seek new adventures. She was afraid before. The Fae had offered a bubble of security. It always surrounded her, even when she was apart from them. Once, she'd just wanted things to go back to the way they were. Her old life as a Fae was forever gone.

Now she had nothing to lose.

Except Matt.

Sienna realized she had everything to gain.

Sienna found her cell phone, made a call. Then she went into the bedroom to pack.

"Yo, Dakota, you're awfully quiet these days. Thinking about a little something-something?"

From across the room, Matt threw his laptop at Renegade. The Draicon ducked, sending the computer into the wall. It cracked and fell.

"Mind much, Jammer?"

The big psi shrugged his broad shoulders and flicked a

hand. The computer repaired itself and then came sailing back through the air to Matt.

"Thanks." He powered up and went back to typing his report. The "official" report of how the seven SEALs and their commander had successfully prevented a cult of homegrown terrorists from using stolen Semtex to blow up a popular Colorado tourist lake retreat.

The SEALs of the Phoenix Force were in the team's ready room in the ST21 compound in Little Creek. Bored with paperwork, they were eager and itching for action. All except for Matt.

He couldn't get a certain attractive Draicon out of his system. Every time he closed his eyes, he saw Sienna, standing forlornly at her cabin door. Alone.

He wanted her. Needed her. Wanted to grow old with her, sitting on the porch of that little cabin, watching their grandchildren play at their feet. Wanted to go to bed every night with her, and watch her sleepy green eyes open first thing in the morning. Make love with her, fight with her, seal himself to her.

"That Sienna, she provided some show, huh?"

Matt glanced up at J.T.

"A dragon. A damn dragon. She kicked ass. Saved our hides." Respect showed in the other SEAL's face. "Never seen anything like it."

"Sienna could be a SEAL herself." Shay tossed a baseball into the air, caught it and flung it up again. "She should be protected. The Orb's gone, but she's the last surviving member of a race, and the last survivor of the Orb's powers."

"And Dakota left her." Dallas snorted. The Draicon looked askew at Matt. "Surprised you didn't miss a chance to jump her. She was hot."

Fury boiled inside him. "Don't you dare talk about her that way," he said in a low voice.

"Cool it, Dallas," Shay said quietly. "Shut your muzzle."

Dallas looked up from his computer, amusement on his handsome face. "If you did jump her, maybe you absorbed some of her hot-hot-hotness. Her powers, I mean. Maybe a pretty lady like Sienna could make your ugly mug a sight more bearable."

He gave a long, low howl.

Matt stood, the chair spilling to the floor. The change came swiftly, claws erupting on his fingertips, bone and muscles changing. Wolf wanted to rip him to shreds for daring to insult his Sienna. With a snarl, he bared his teeth and leaped over the desk. Dallas shifted at the same time, a black muscled wolf ready to take him on.

Hotness. Damn it, I'll show you hotness, I'll give you heat....

He felt his body twist and lengthen, his fury building into a crescendo, his muzzle becoming elongated.... What the hell?

Dallas stood atop his desk, but instead of challenge in the other's eyes, there was stark fear. Good. Show the bastard he couldn't tangle with him...

Opening his mouth to growl, Matt pulled his teeth back in a snarl.

Flames shot out of his mouth, fanning over the wall, missing Dallas by a hair. The other SEAL's claws skittered on the desk as he jumped off and raced across the room.

Shouts of alarm, the hiss of an extinguisher playing on the flames, putting them out. Matt hovered in the air, confused and stunned. *What happened?*

"Holy shit...what did you put in your kibble, wolf?" Sully stood, hugging the wall, staring up at him.

"Hot sauce," Dallas croaked, now changed back to his human form.

"Dakota, look at yourself. It's okay. Just come down. We'll deal with it, okay?"

Shay's quiet assurance gave him pause. Matt looked down.

He hovered in midair. Papers flew off the desks, blown by something fanning the air. Matt twisted his neck.

Wings. He had wings. He looked down. Instead of a furred paw, there were long, red claws emerging from a scaled foot.

Wolf. I'm wolf. Wolf.

Forcing the thought to race through his mind, quelling the panic, he felt his body begin to shift and change once more.

He fell to the floor, stunned, shivering and naked. The other SEALs gathered around, forming a ring. Matt glanced into the faces of his teammates, those he trusted the most.

They looked at him as if a monster had dropped into their midst.

Never had he felt so alone.

A name raced through his mind, like a soothing chant.

Sienna.

He felt his body shrink, become more delicate and soft, yet within the softness was a core of steel. Strength and determination.

"Holy shit," Shay said softly.

"Maybe he's trying to get in touch with his feminine side," Dallas said, his mouth twisted in shock.

"What's happened?" His voice was a bare croak.

Shay marched him toward a wall where a small mirror hung. "Easy. Take a deep breath. Now look at yourself."

Matt looked. And screamed.

It took all of Sienna's courage to admit the truth—she needed help. For years, trained to be solely Fae, she knew nothing about being wolf.

But when Matt's sister picked her up at the airport, Sienna felt only acceptance. The Draicon female wrapped her in hugs, and took her to the family home. The males were wary at first, but in the past two days had come to accept her.

Especially when all the females ignored them in favor of Sienna.

Two days later, Matt phoned. Now he was on his way to visit "because I have something to show you."

She'd spent an anxious night, wondering what he wanted, desperate to see him again. The others had discreetly left with an excuse to shop in town. When the front door opened, all her anxiety faded like mist under a hot sun.

Sienna raced to him, jumping into his arms and showering him with kisses. He laughed, the sound utterly joyful as she buried her face into his shoulder.

"This is the kind of welcome a guy dreams of. The kind of welcome I'd always dreamed of when returning from a mission."

They sat on the comfortable sofa. Matt glanced around, gave her a long, thoughtful look. Sienna hastened to explain.

"I called Cindy and explained I needed help." Sienna swallowed hard. "She'd been friendly to me and I was hoping… I hoped…she could teach me about being a wolf. Because I know nothing about being a Draicon."

Her lower lip wobbled. "I may be the last of a species, but I'm tired of being alone."

Warmth surged through her as he cupped her face, leaned his forehead against hers. "You're not alone, Sienna. Watch."

He stepped back, stretching out his arms. Going to change into a wolf…

Shock slammed into her as Matt shifted. No longer the tall, muscled and handsome man wearing a polo shirt and gray Dockers.

She stared at a mirror image of herself. A woman with long brown hair, green eyes and a full mouth.

"Right." The other Sienna gave a shaky laugh. "I have your powers of transformation, too."

She blinked, unable to focus. Feeling like it was a dream, a crazy, wonderful dream as hope stole slowly over her.

Then her twin vanished and Matt reappeared. He gave a small smile. "All I could think about was you, so it's the shape I assumed. I did shift into a dragon at the base, when Dallas made me so angry all I could think about was frying him."

Emotion clogged her throat. "I don't understand…how did this happen?"

"It was in you." He drew close and laid a hand over her heart. "The Orb's powers. The last time we made love, I absorbed your powers. It happens to two Draicon who are destined to be together, Sienna. I am as you are. No longer Draicon. But Diablo, as well. Confession time, pixie. It scared the hell out of me. I don't know how to deal with this."

"Oh, Matt." She touched his cheek, marveling at his honesty and his courage. "I don't know how to be a Diablo, either. Or a Draicon. But I do know this. I love you, and I don't want to let you go. I don't care what you are."

His kiss was warm, assuring and filled with searing heat. When he drew away, his eyes were very blue. Matt took her hands, his touch warm and comforting. Big hands, so sure and capable.

"We'll learn, together. One day at a time. You belong with me. Not to me. You belong at my side, with me as my partner, my mate for life. I've lost the sense of being a wolf. I need you. I need you to show me the joys, the bonds, the good things again."

He paused, his jaw working. "I forgot what it was like to truly be myself. Until I met you and you forced me to see what I truly am. I was afraid of commitment. Afraid of anything that would take away my identity as a SEAL. It meant more to me than my pack. Until you came along, and you meant more to me than anything else in my world. I'm resigning my commission in the navy and bringing you into my pack as my mate, if you'll have me."

Stunned, she could only stare. He smiled gently. "I love you. You mean more to me than being a SEAL. It's time for me to return to being a wolf. Will you have me?"

"Yes." She touched his mouth, deeply moved by the enormity of his sacrifice for her. The depth of his feelings for her. "On one condition."

Matt looked puzzled.

"Don't quit. When the time comes for you to stop being a SEAL, do it for yourself. Your choice, no one else's. The world needs a brave warrior like you to protect it from evil. We'll work it out. It won't be easy, you being gone so much, but others have done it."

She gave a sad little smile. "Adam's mate did it. I bet that if you asked, she would tell you every moment was worth the gamble of losing him. Life's a risk, and I've played it safe far too long. All my life I've sought to belong somewhere. And the only place I truly want to belong is here, with you, wherever you are."

When he opened his mouth, she laid a finger over it. Then she kissed him, pouring all her emotions into the kiss. Her love for him. Her commitment to him. Sienna trailed tiny kisses over his face, his neck, and squeezed his hands, unwilling to let him go.

The truth suddenly materialized, as bright and shimmering as an Orb filled with magick. She'd finally found what she'd sought her whole life.

"Matt," she whispered, her emotions brimming. "Ever since I touched the Orb as a child, I've longed for the light. The light would show the truth of my place in the world. But the greatest truth isn't who I am or what group I belong to. It's being able to connect to someone else, and cast aside the fear to give your heart to someone. The Fae had it wrong."

He stroked her hair, his gaze tender. "The greatest power in the world isn't found in a crystal ball. It's found in our ability to love."

They had found that love, thanks to a ball of light and truth that had brought them together. It was sealed in their hearts. And there, safe in their hearts, it would remain.

* * * * *

COMING NEXT MONTH from Harlequin Nocturne®
AVAILABLE AUGUST 21, 2012

#143 SAVAGE REDEMPTION
Alexis Morgan

Conlan is a powerful half-vampire Chancellor who is forced to work alongside the one woman who betrayed him and smashed his reputation. This time they'll risk their lives—and their hearts.

#144 SHIFTER'S DESTINY
Anna Leonard

Libby is running out of time while dark forces threaten the life of her sister. Josh is racing against the clock as well—he must find a mate or stay in his cursed body forever.

HNCNM0812

REQUEST YOUR FREE BOOKS!

2 FREE NOVELS FROM THE PARANORMAL ROMANCE COLLECTION PLUS 2 FREE GIFTS!

YES! Please send me 2 FREE novels from the Paranormal Romance Collection and my 2 FREE gifts (gifts are worth about $10). After receiving them, if I don't wish to receive any more books, I can return the shipping statement marked "cancel." If I don't cancel, I will receive 4 brand-new novels every month and be billed just $21.42 in the U.S. or $23.46 in Canada. That's a saving of at least 21% off the cover price of all 4 books. It's quite a bargain! Shipping and handling is just 50¢ per book in the U.S. and 75¢ per book in Canada.* I understand that accepting the 2 free books and gifts places me under no obligation to buy anything. I can always return a shipment and cancel at any time. Even if I never buy another book, the two free books and gifts are mine to keep forever.

237/337 HDN FEL2

Name	(PLEASE PRINT)	
Address		Apt. #
City	State/Prov.	Zip/Postal Code

Signature (if under 18, a parent or guardian must sign)

Mail to the **Reader Service:**
IN U.S.A.: P.O. Box 1867, Buffalo, NY 14240-1867
IN CANADA: P.O. Box 609, Fort Erie, Ontario L2A 5X3

Not valid for current subscribers to the Paranormal Romance Collection or Harlequin® Nocturne™ books.

Want to try two free books from another line?
Call 1-800-873-8635 or visit www.ReaderService.com.

* Terms and prices subject to change without notice. Prices do not include applicable taxes. Sales tax applicable in N.Y. Canadian residents will be charged applicable taxes. Offer not valid in Quebec. This offer is limited to one order per household. All orders subject to credit approval. Credit or debit balances in a customer's account(s) may be offset by any other outstanding balance owed by or to the customer. Please allow 4 to 6 weeks for delivery. Offer available while quantities last.

Your Privacy—The Reader Service is committed to protecting your privacy. Our Privacy Policy is available online at www.ReaderService.com or upon request from the Reader Service.

We make a portion of our mailing list available to reputable third parties that offer products we believe may interest you. If you prefer that we not exchange your name with third parties, or if you wish to clarify or modify your communication preferences, please visit us at www.ReaderService.com/consumerchoice or write to us at Reader Service Preference Service, P.O. Box 9062, Buffalo, NY 14269. Include your complete name and address.

Harlequin and Mills & Boon are joining forces in a global search for new authors.

In September 2012 we're launching our biggest contest yet—with the prize of being published by the world's leader in romance fiction!

Look for more information on our website, **www.soyouthinkyoucanwrite.com**

So you think you can write? Show us!

In the newest continuity series from Harlequin®
Romantic Suspense, the worlds of the Coltons and their
Amish neighbors collide—with dramatic results.

Take a sneak peek at the first book, COLTON DESTINY
by Justine Davis, available September 2012.

"**I**'m here to try and find your sister."

"I know this. But don't assume this will automatically ensure trust from all of us."

He was antagonizing her. Purposely.

Caleb realized it with a little jolt. While it was difficult for anyone in the community to turn to outsiders for help, they had all reluctantly agreed this was beyond their scope and that they would cooperate.

Including—in fact, especially—him.

"Then I will find these girls without your help," she said, sounding fierce.

Caleb appreciated her determination. He *wanted* that kind of determination in the search for Hannah. He attempted a fresh start.

"It is difficult for us—"

"What's difficult for me is to understand why anyone wouldn't pull out all the stops to save a child whose life could be in danger."

Caleb wasn't used to being interrupted. Annie would never have dreamed of it. But this woman was clearly nothing like his sweet, retiring Annie. She was sharp, forceful and very intense.

"I grew up just a couple of miles from here," she said. "And I always had the idea the Amish loved their kids just as we did."

"Of course we do."

"And yet you'll throw roadblocks in the way of the people best equipped to find your missing children?"

Caleb studied her for a long, silent moment. "You are very angry," he said.

"Of course I am."

"Anger is an...unproductive emotion."

She stared at him in turn then. "Oh, it can be very productive. Perhaps you could use a little."

"It is not our way."

"Is it your way to stand here and argue with me when your sister is among the missing?"

Caleb gave himself an internal shake. Despite her abrasiveness—well, when compared to Annie, anyway—he could not argue with her last point. And he wasn't at all sure why he'd found himself sparring with this woman. She was an Englishwoman, and what they said or did mattered nothing to him.

Except it had to matter now. For Hannah's sake.

*Don't miss any of the books in this exciting
new miniseries from Harlequin® Romantic Suspense,
starting in September 2012 and running
through December 2012.*